TIMOTHY VICTOR RICHARDSON

CEREMONY OF INNOCENCE

a novel

Custom Books Publishing

The blood-dimmed tide is loosed, and everywhere
The ceremony of innocence is drowned;
The best lack all conviction, while the worst
Are full of passionate intensity.

William Butler Yeats

CEREMONY OF INNOCENCE

Concerto for Voice and Voices

Movement I

Introduction

So this is where you've ended up...or could end up if this is where it ends. But you don't know anymore and you hardly care. Ending, beginning? It all comes to nothing. This room, this cubicle is just another in a series, that much you can see now. First, there was the room you were born in, then a room at home, a room at school and, later, a room at work followed by a room in the hospital (that you hadn't expected, Wamblie) and, now, this one. But you've gained nothing by it or lost everything? I'm not sure.

Ah! But there you go, you've done it again. You have to be careful or you lapse into muddled thought. But pay no attention. You've been through a lot. You've become very confused by life and I know you sound depressed. But it's nothing. I mean you're all right. But this room takes some getting used to. It's not a very pleasant place, but it's all you could afford. I know it needs to be cleaned, but you've just gotten in and you have no desire to do it. You're too tired and, besides, you're not exactly going to be entertaining. Unless this, this that you're doing now, is entertaining. To some, it would be. I won't mention any names. But I suppose there's something humorous in everything. But it's really not funny. Your story is a sad one, at least that's how I think of it. Although there must be some funny parts. None comes to

6

mind, however. But now, when I think of it, it's no wonder none comes to mind. You're trying too hard because it's important to know they're there. When you try to, however, you can't. It's only when you don't that anything comes. So stop trying and see what happens....

Nothing! How frustrating. But don't get tense. Just forget about it. Just relax your mind and wait....

Do you have that absurd smirk on your face? It feels like it, but I can't tell. There's no mirror, so I can't see in, only out. But I know it happens unconsciously sometimes. What I mean is, you can't help it. I, here and there, become aware your mouth is hanging open with saliva dripping out and your eyes are bulbous like a moron's. What I don't know is how long you've looked that way. It's obnoxious I know. But it's not by choice that expression comes. It was done to you. Remember that. It was done to make you happy. But, unfortunately, it only makes you look happy to the world outside. It doesn't really make you happy. But they had no way to know that. They didn't know what was happening inside you. They never did. Maybe not themselves either, for that matter. I don't know. I couldn't see inside them any more than they could you. But then, I didn't pretend to although I tried. But they did. Tried and succeeded. Whatever! All I know is you went to them looking unhappy and they made you look happy again. Then they released you. A long awaited release I might add. In spite of the fact you find looking this way unnatural and contrived, it was worth it to be released. I mean you were no different from anyone else. Everyone there wanted to be released. Everyone! Not everyone felt they could be, was ready to be or ever would be ready for release. Some were convinced they'd never be. But that didn't mean they wouldn't want to when they were. It's the kind of place, if you're ready, you want to leave. Actually most, who weren't ready, wanted to leave too. Almost no one wanted to stay except the staff. Not that anyplace else is so different. But anyplace else would seem different because it would allow the illusion and not constantly throw in your face how unhappy you are and how powerless. That's a deep pleasure. It's been so long since you were in such a place. Yes, I'm glad you're out and on your own even though you have no idea what comes next. But I suppose that's part of the adventure, the amusement. Not knowing I mean. If we knew the future, there'd be no reason to live it, no reason to keep going. That's why knowledge is such a terrible thing in spite of what people say. And it's why they avoid it like a disease. It's not good for you, at least not knowledge about yourself. That can be devastating which explains what happened to you. Knowledge! Knowledge kept getting thrown at you until you couldn't stand it a minute more. But, fortunately, it was just when you couldn't stand it you hit bottom, you comprehended the truth of your predicament. And now, finally, you've re-covered from all that. That's positive. Or at least you appear to have recovered now that you look happy. Whether or not you've really recovered is a question that has no answer. But then, you don't want an answer. You'd rather live knowing you don't know than be burdened with the truth. That's why you leave the question alone.

As I look at the room I see it needs a cleaning. Your foot prints are visible in the dust on the floor. But you're so comfortable on this little cot, you can't move, can you? No. Not that it's a comfortable cot. It certainly isn't. It's not even as good as the one in the hospital. But it's the one you've got, so why not be happy with it? Complaining would be futile. If there's one thing you've learned, it's not to complain. So don't. Just lie here and stare at the room and don't worry about your face. It can look however it wants.

I wish there were a shade for that bulb. It's swinging from its cord. I guess that started when you first pulled the chain. All the shadows are moving and I'm feeling as if you're floating on the ocean. I suppose you should get up and stop it. But you don't really want to. Besides, why worry? It'll stop by itself eventually. I can see it's already slowed down. So just forget about it and wait....

What a room! It's filled with grime and dirt. It's smeared across the windows and ledges and it's packed in the corners and cracks. It needs to be scraped with a knife in places. The walls too. They could use a good scraping and painting. Actually, the whole interior would be better off remodeled. But you're not up to that—what's that? A drop of water hit your face? It's from that pipe. Don't tell me you have to move just when you're so comfortable! Ah! Another drop. You have to move....

That's better. I found a coffee can in the closet to catch the water, so there's no need to worry about that for a while. You just have to remember to empty it. That's simple. Otherwise, the whole purpose will be lost and it'll be all over the floor. Tomorrow, if you remember, is when you'll pour the water into the sink. Speaking of the sink, it also needs a cleaning. It's pitted badly, so badly, in fact, I'm not sure a cleaning will restore it. Another thing to do tomorrow. And the chest of drawers. Like everything else, it's full of grime and needs a coat of paint. So don't unpack your bags. Not tonight. Before putting anything in there, it'll need the drawers cleaned out and something to line the bottoms. Another task for tomorrow. You'll be busy, I can see, because the closet, too, needs to be cleaned. But don't do anything now. Just relax and rest. That way you'll be refreshed and ready to work on the place. The drip striking the tin makes a piercing sound. I suppose you'll have to put up with that. And that light! It's too bright! But what can you do except turn it off? There's no way around it. You can't reach the chain and there's no plug to pull. No, you have to get up....

How calming it is not to be able to see. Things are much

more pleasant in the dark. In the dark, the place could be a palace. Who's to tell? And now, I can see out the window although it's dirty. But don't worry about that. There's railroad tracks in a ravine in the back. That's the direction the window faces: back. I count two sets of tracks going in two directions. Beyond that are a group of old businesses—drip. One of them is a diner of some kind. I see a dog at a bin eating some garbage and there are two cats on top sniffing around—drip. Next to that, it looks like a theater, an old boarded up theater—drip! The rest I can't make out for sure, but it appears to be an alley—DRIP!

O Jesus, that drip! I've tried to ignore it, but it's too intrusive. The dripping has to stop or I'll lose my mind if I haven't already. An idle threat and of no concern to you. It just slipped out as such things do when we're pressed. And nothing's more pressing than a patter, patter, PATTER! There's no way around it, you might as well get up. I'm beginning to think you'll never rest in peace. But the drip: how can you catch it silently so you can forgo the patter reverberating in your ear? Maybe a handkerchief in the bottom would help. If nothing else, that would at least dampen it and hopefully make it a tolerable sound. Yes, that's what you'll do. But first, you must again turn on the light. But, then again (let me think now), if you put the handkerchief in the bottom of the can, the can will fill and you'll be faced with the drops splashing in the water. An equally, if not more, disturbing noise. But you could empty it at shorter intervals. But then, you won't sleep. God! Things are so confused in here. I don't know what to do. But no need to get distraught. It won't come back for a while, so don't worry. Why worry about problems that don't exist? Isn't that what they say?

Now where's that light? You want to at least get the first thing done. You want to get the handkerchief put in the can and get back to your cot and sleep. But you can never find the chain. And—ah! Here it is.

There. That's much more soothing. Much quieter. It's a good thing you had a handkerchief. I only hope you don't need it to blow your nose because I don't think you have another. But you don't have a cold, so there's no need to worry. As they say, cross that bridge when you come to it. You've had an earful of that phrase. It's what the staff used to tell you especially at the beginning. Their omniscient advice was to worry about what you can do something about and let the rest take care of itself. You fought that approach for many months, but finally succumbed when you got nowhere your way. But once adopting their method, the problem became knowing what you could do something about and what you couldn't. Further, are you doing something about something by seeing it as a problem? If everyone saw it (whatever it is) as a problem it would soon cease because it would just be a matter of arriving at a solution and then carrying it out. Consequently, just seeing a problem, provided others see it too, is a step in the right direction before anything is done. Conversely, if you alone see a problem, it may persist indefinitely since others would have to be convinced before action could be taken. And, of course, it follows that a problem is not a problem, has no hope of ever becoming a problem, if it isn't seen by somebody, anybody. In other words, if no one sees a problem there is no problem. In that sense, you create one by seeing it. And who could dis-agree, it's better not to create them although they have a way of happening in spite of our best efforts. It's like trying to remember things—actually, it's just the opposite. If you try to remember things, they never come, whereas, if you look for problems, you'll see nothing but. So the thing to do is relax and not particularly search for them. Then things tend to flow very smoothly which brings me to what you've got to learn. Relaxation! Other people do it. Other people get through relatively unscathed. You've got to do that too by simply floating through. Other people find things to smile at, almost nothing can make some unhappy. Why not you? Every day you see them always with a smile no matter what just like a commercial. Relaxed and easy without a care, that's the way to be. But I don't mean the plastered on expression they gave you. That doesn't count. I'm talking about a smile, a natural smile. That's what you'd like to have. But I'm afraid you may never smile again for two reasons: one is you may never feel like it, the other is you may not have the capacity. You certainly can't now. I'm afraid they may have damaged you too much or you may have lost whatever is inside you that brings it out. I think that may be a power they stripped you of. I think that because I find no such feeling anywhere within you.

But you're feeling much too morose tonight. It's not good to go on this way. You're being far too negative. You're worrying too much. It's a terrible problem as I've said. But you can't seem to help it. You can be sitting here daydreaming and suddenly be confronted by a terrible thought that seems not of your own making, a thought that seems injected by an outside force. Not only that, but it's often accompanied by an impulse, a supremely strong impulse, to carry it out. That's what terrifies you. I'll give an example. Just now, as I was talking about your smile, I envisioned a horrible, horrible thing. I saw you get up and get a kitchen knife (which I'm glad you don't have so you can't possibly do it), go to a corner, kneel down, plunge it into your stomach and cut out your intestines. I've seen it done in Japanese movies and I guess it made an impression on you. Of course, I pictured vividly all the blood and gore. But, surprisingly, the thought is a satisfying one in a curious way. Almost peaceful. But I won't give details. It's needless. The whole thing is needless and stupid. It's crazy! But there you are. I can see your problem. For some reason, thoughts or, rather, impulses of this kind enter your mind with a force I can hardly tolerate. Sometimes I think they're ordained by God and they should be obeyed no matter what. There are times when it seems certain, if you don't, you'll be going against the forces. Luckily, as I say, it is an impulse with a duration of only a second. If it lasted longer, who knows? You might act. But, on the other hand, it could be unlucky. I'm not sure. There's always more than one side to a question. Perhaps you're going against forces you shouldn't oppose. But that can't be either. That's a little irrational; something someone like you has to be careful of. But, as long as it leaves as fast as it comes, you don't get the chance to do it. What I fear though are two things: one is that someday, sometime, perhaps any minute, perhaps this very instant, such an impulse will come, overpoweringly, and force you to do something bizarre. The other is that to fight it off (daily, hourly for months as you've done) is to go against the forces. I mean you're suffering so much because you refuse to yield to God. But it's so hard to know. It's so hard to understand and know which way to go. But as I realize what I've said, I fear it's another question whose answer (if it has one which is another question in itself) can only be found by leaving it alone. Yes, it's wrong to hunt for an answer. You should go back to doing what you've done before. Namely, if an impulse comes, wait and see what happens instead of trying to determine anything in advance. If you manage to fight it off, assume it's because you should have. If you jump out the window or plunge a knife in your gut or put a bullet in your head, assume the same. Now that's settled, I feel much better. To hell with destiny if there is such a thing! At least, to hell with trying to understand it.

But, to be honest, I haven't addressed your real problem which perhaps explains why you can't get anything solved. I'll try again, however. Not because I really care, but because I've got nothing else to do.

Now, what you actually worry about is not so much what you might do to yourself, but what others might do to you. I'll give an example: that night, when this thing first started, you would have shot anybody in the world if they tried to hurt you. You had your shotgun loaded and ready. You would have gladly shot a person, if necessary, for protection. I don't pretend to understand it. Obviously, no one does except maybe the doctors. I don't know. Of course, I have my ideas. To me, it goes back to the forces. At the time, the forces, something (I don't know what to call them) was saying you were in some kind of unimaginable, unintelligible danger and your only recourse was to defend yourself. So you got your gun and kept a vigil. But you're not the sort to do things like that, so it had to be caused by more than your insanity. I mean a perfectly normal person just up one day and doing such a thing? Impossible! You can't have made the whole thing up as everyone seems to think. But, be that as it may, I've given a very extreme case. But it's a sample of the fears you live with and it explains why you have to be near. Because the hospital, if it can't change you, can at least contain you when you can't contain yourself. If you were a long way away, what would you do if you were suddenly overwhelmed with these thoughts and impulses? Let me remind you, I'm aware I said you felt glad to be out. That's true. I don't mean you're not glad to be out. It's just you want to be near in case you need them. After all, we never know what our minds will bring. Besides, if you did come apart, you wouldn't be responsible. You'd probably do nothing as you have in the past. Yes, it's a comfort to know they're there. I need to know you can be taken back in the event you should crumble and fold. Not that there's any reason to think you will, but, well, ditto the above. Because they can put it right. I think. I hope. I hope they're not in on the conspiracy. They could be. But it doesn't seem plausible. It seems, right now, to be your own paranoia.

Better talk about something else....Let's see....Just a minute!....

So you had to get up again. It's tiresome I know. There's always something. This time, it was a cockroach, a big black shiny one on the wall next to a calendar that was more than a few years old. So you have to put up with cockroaches too. You're not accustomed to that. You've always lived in sanitary places. Before the hospital, you couldn't have tolerated a room like this. You probably couldn't have so much as walked into it. You probably would have vomited. But your stay in the hospital taught you these things don't matter. Dirt or no dirt, what difference does it make? Six of one, half dozen of the other. I mean you're just like the others who were here before you. No better, no worse. We're all equal. We all have to eat, shit, be asleep and awake, pass time, get old. So what's a little filth? The others were content. You're not yet, but that will come in time. Your first impulse is still to clean and make things look presentable. That's why you killed the cockroaches. Or perhaps it was because one of them showed himself. That would irk you. At any rate, you saw him (or her) and automatically got to your feet (it must have been repulsion that caused it), took a shoe and went to flatten him. But, by the time you got there, he had crawled behind the calendar thinking he'd surely be safe no doubt. If he can think. I don't know. But, of course, being a superior being, you knew to smack the calendar. And when you did, an army scurried out. Some ran into cracks and some searched for them while you pulverized as many as you could. There's an example of survival of the fittest. Or smartest. Whatever. They'll think twice about coming back. That's if they have any sense. I don't know. But it gave you a start to see them flood out like that. You weren't expecting it. But you got your revenge. You got a good half dozen with the first blow alone. The only problem was disposing of the bodies. There's no waste basket here. But many were stuck to the calendar, so you threw it out the window. Just as it left your hand, however, you realized you

15

could have used it to scoop up the rest. But, no matter. You found a crumpled piece of paper that did the job. And now, you have a nice breeze coming in. You should have opened the window sooner. It's so humid tonight. Your shirt is soaked and sticking to your back. If you don't move, it's not too bad, but any activity and there's a film over your body. But you still have your coat on! No wonder you're warm. You took off your shoes, but not your sports jacket. Can you be getting senile already? At your age? Impossible!

What a stench! The wind must have shifted or perhaps you're smelling yourself now you've got your coat off. Ha, ha! The air is no good though. It's polluted no doubt, but with what? Toxins, poisons, perhaps minute electronic devices? Who knows? I certainly don't and that's what frightens me. But I suspect somebody does. Somebody knows what's in the air. But they don't do anything about it; probably because it's profitable for them not to. Why? Because, with pollution, they can control us. They implant things in us that get us to do what they want. The things, the devices are in the air. All we can do is inhale them. Fighting is futile. It can't be escaped as long as we're breathing. They're out to get us and there's nothing we can do. It's a thought so despairing I can hardly stand it. In fact, I better think about something else. I better close the window so at least I won't smell it and be reminded of the terrible, terrible things that go on in this world....

Now that's done, I feel much better though far from up to par. I don't know what's wrong, but I'm very depressed. I feel very low. Perhaps I'll look at the paper and get my mind off myself. I'm glad I remembered it or I'd have no diversion....

Ah! Here it is. What a day. I never would have foreseen it. "THE PRESIDENT RESIGNS" Now there's a good reason to be depressed. I forgot about it. It hasn't crossed my mind for hours, but I'm sure it's been affecting my mood. It's enough to bring anyone to a pretty low ebb. It was awful; the most horrible thing I've ever seen barring, of course, your time at the hospital. I saw it all on television this morning. The teary farewell, the spectators saddened not only for the President, but for the country as a whole because his resignation symbolized our downfall as a nation; something the President strenuously tried to prevent. But how much can one man do when there's so many forces against him? No one can say he didn't try anyway. The new one, Ford, was there watching him board the helicopter that took him to a plane for the final journey home. I saw last night's speech too. He spoke very movingly although I know most wouldn't agree, so infested are they by evil. But I voted for him twice as a matter of fact. But he's gone now and there's not much hope. We were on our way, but now we're lost. But what's done is done. Now we go to the next thing. Always the next thing. But what does it matter? He's gone now and we have another to look to. Maybe he won't be so bad. I don't think he's controlled by the forces. (I say forces for lack of a better word. Evil forces I mean. There are some good ones too.) But then, I know you're wrong. He's under their control. I'm talking about plots. There are people who plot. Against you, against me, against everyone. Against everything that's good. After today, there isn't anything they don't have control of. I don't know what their plans are, but I know they want control and they'll do anything to get it. They're out to get us and, if we don't realize that, we're dead! I only wish it didn't happen. I wish he weren't out. I wish it didn't mean domination. For all we know, someone unknown could be running things. And how do we know he's not controlling our minds? How do we know we're not brainwashed, that someone or something hasn't made himself God? Who knows what's going on? I've even thought they're involved with you. They could have given the order. It's conceivable, isn't it? You have to agree it's at least conceivable. Think about it. It could all be coming from him. It's happened before.

No it hasn't! Get yourself off this! What are you thinking and where is it leading you? Down the gutter. Nowhere else. Because none of that is true. It can't be. It's simply your problem, your distorted thoughts trying to get the better of you. But don't let them. If there are evil forces, you're doing what they want. But don't. You've learned their game and they know it. It's just you're weak because of all those upheavals. That's why they're preying on you. But you don't have to think of them, not if you don't want to. You can think of something pleasant. You can think about being free of the hospital. That's a good thought. It was the strangest period of your life. Some big wheels turned. Not just for you. Think who else. It's dizzying and it's got you upset. So you better get your clothes off and go to bed. Don't bother trying to brush your teeth. It's too late. Besides, to do that, you'd have to go down the hall. If you do that, you could meet someone. Some undesirable, smelly, old man (since there's such an abundance of them around) who hasn't had a bath in weeks, who has no teeth or only jagged stubs and whose eyes slither like a couple of raw eggs. No. Just go to bed....

There's no clothes hangers in the closet. What's a person supposed to do, throw them on the floor? I suppose you could. It really doesn't matter. What difference would it make? What does it matter they don't give you hangers? They don't give you anything. That's how it is everywhere I suppose. Certainly where you are. Speaking of how little is provided, you'll have to get a hot plate. Tomorrow will be a busy day.

Damn! Here you're settled only to see you've left the light on. Don't lie down without turning off the light! Only a half wit does that....

That's more like it. This place is definitely better in the dark. Sometimes we must remind ourselves sternly, otherwise we may not listen.

Well, I'm running out of things to say. That's a good sign.

Maybe you'll get some sleep although you haven't felt much like sleeping what with the excitement and anticipation of leaving. In fact, you haven't slept in days. But now I think you can.

Silence. It's so soothing. I hope a train doesn't go by tonight. That would wake you up. But the street noises, the horns blasting from time to time, the trollies clattering up the tracks and the sound of beer bottles breaking against the curb I don't think will bother you although there's a lot of all three going on out there. Your room faces the back, however, not the street, and all the noise is muffled and probably won't disturb you. Actually, you don't feel sleepy anyway. I thought you did, but you don't, not a bit. You're tired I know. But you're wide awake. Another night of insomnia? How many does that make? Three? I lose track after a while. Of that and everything else. Because something is in your mind. It's been that way for months. It might be strange, but I imagine your head to be the rock and the something to be the sword from that story where somebody sticks a sword in a rock which can only be pulled out by a hero. I don't remember for sure. But there's such a story. And that's what the something feels like. A blade in your skull you can't pull out no matter how hard you try. But it doesn't matter. What's a little pain one way or the other? It's nothing really. It just interrupts your sleep sometimes.

Oh! The drip has stopped. I just noticed. That's a good sign. It's a blessing in fact. Perhaps now you'll be able to sleep because you won't have to worry about the can overflowing. Not that you were. You had forgotten about it actually. But now, it doesn't matter if it occurs to you or not. That's one less thing on your mind.

Exposition

You can't get to sleep, but I can say you've tried. And perhaps that's why you can't: because you've tried. Like everything else (remembering, answering questions, whatever), when you pursue it, it becomes elusive. It's a curious phenomenon. You've been lying here trying everything: counting sheep, lying with your head where your feet were and your feet where your head was (that often breaks the cycle), a shot of liquor, but nothing works. You just can't relax. The more you try, the more you concentrate on not concentrating, the more wide awake you become. It's a vicious circle. If you try not concentrating, you end up concentrating on something else which has the same effect. You're wide awake. I wish there were nothing to concentrate on, nothing to worry about. But there's so much. Oh well.

How you would like to go back a year, to have that period to do over again. There's many things you'd change. You can see that in retrospect, but, at the time, you didn't know. It's regrettable. Such a waste. One thing you should have done is get out of the company. You should get out now although I have no idea where to go. But if there were a way, you would. You'd like nothing better. For many reasons, you can't, however, and it's important to bear that in mind. For one thing, you need money. You need lots more than you've got now.

After all, you have a family, responsibilities. Your only hope of getting out is by staying where you are. I mean no one else would give you a job, not in your condition. What you should have done was find something else when this all started. You should have taken the time to look when your record was clean. But then again, that would have proved futile, too, because they're probably all in on a conspiracy together. I'm sure your company is. Otherwise, you wouldn't have suffered so much. It's all at their hands. Of course, that isn't obvious at first. How could it be? If it were obvious, it wouldn't be a secret, it wouldn't be a plot. On the surface, they all appear so good and so wholesome and so intent on improving our lives. But you know the truth even if no one else does. Not that you can prove it. You're only one person against a huge conglomerate. What can you prove? But you know what's going on and they know you know. That's why they watch you. That's why they control you. That's why they ruined you. And that's what you'd prevent if you could go back a year. You've made so many mistakes; the biggest being to have trusted anyone. That you will never do again. The world isn't like that. Yes, if there's one thing you've learned, it's not to trust anyone! You never know who's in on what. It's impossible to know. These things are so insidious and originate from such secret sources, it's safer to suspect everyone. And perhaps it is everyone. It wouldn't surprise me. But who knows? Who knows? You certainly don't and you never will and you're not going to try either. Instead, you'll give them no reason to see you as an enemy. Perhaps then, they'll leave you alone. At least you have resolved that. You won't ever lose sight of the fact that, despite acting friendly and congenial, you're in an adversary relationship. To forget that would lead to your destruction. That much you've learned. You've spent a whole lifetime learning that in fact. One whole lifetime! I guess we all do. You're not alone. Children trust instinctively. But, unfortunately, growing up is a process of stripping away at our naive visions to the point where we see life as it really is. Unhappily, it's so repugnant at its core, we don't want to believe it. You're learning what the truth is, but I know most people haven't. Most people can't. They don't want to. It's too painful. They don't want to know anything. Ignorance is bliss, right? It's true. Most people don't want to find out what an ugly thing it is to be alive and have to cope with the forces. Most people pretend the ugliness isn't there, seal their eyes, clasp their lips and tell themselves they have succeeded, tell themselves they have lived when, in actuality, they have died. But what's the difference? They don't know, so have they really missed anything? Can you miss something you've never desired? Maybe their way is better. Maybe it's the only way. Why suffer if you don't have to? Why put yourself through needless worry? The world is the world is the world and it continues. But when someone like you comes along, someone who tries to pry one eye open, they pounce on you like an animal, alienate you in every conceivable way and reduce you to poverty. You're not allowed to see or try to see. To violate that puts you in opposition to the pack. That's a dangerous thing because they can deprive you of your voice and, if necessary, your mind. They'd tamper with your brain if necessary. You know. It's been done to you. I only thank God, if there is a God, you didn't lose your mind completely. You got out with at least a meager scrap. Either that or you are nuts. Most people would say that. But then again, they haven't opened their eyes or even thought to. At any rate, I think you've retained something. You'd have to to go on and that's one of the thoughts that gives me comfort. A potential for a new beginning. If you have the strength. Sometimes, I wonder; the strength to break the tie. Not to break it is to continue in the old way; you the servant, they the master. But you must continue working for a while. You have no other means of support. All you've ever done is for them. The question is, how to change? It's harder than when you're young. How do you become independent? It's all tied up in a larger whole and cannot be split apart. No man is an island, they say, including you. No, you're stuck for a while. Until you can figure out something, anything, everything I suppose. That's probably what it'll take. Until then, you remain sucking at their breast like everyone else the only difference being you know it's dry. But where else can milk be gotten? It's such a mess, such a mess. Because no one understands it, no one even begins to. So you've given up talking about it. You've tried that before. It only brought you despair, however, because people think you're nuts. People think you see things not there, hear things not said, imagine things not true. Consequently, they turned against you. They go with the pack thinking it's safer. Safety is foremost in their minds. They gather at the water fountain and stare as you go by. They laugh at you in their offices and talk about your strangeness. They think you're deranged. You don't smile enough, you're too serious. You know that's what they say. You can feel it. But, if you mention it, you're paranoid, imagining things. The negative grows and the positive recedes and their view of you becomes distorted. Then you try to reverse it with a simple explanation. But the explanation becomes gas on the fire. Then the whole thing is ashes and you're on the outs. But if you say nothing, you're accused of snobbery. If you don't find some meaningless topic for conversation, they say you're weird and unable to mix. The only thing that would satisfy them is if you acted exactly like them; smiling every morning, making conversation and jokes that make the day slip by without a thought. The weather, last week's party, who's sleeping with whom. Well, you can't do that! It isn't how you feel. But no one will listen. No one will hear something that's rooted so utterly in your being there's no denying the truth of it. So give up since you don't like being

23

there. And stop trying to talk. Why try to talk when people misconstrue everything and always look for the worst? Why go through the aggravation? Simply go there, do your job and leave. That's what you've always done, at least until last year. Then you tried to reach out. You tried to communicate because you were scared. Before that, however, you kept to yourself and did your job. And you were good at it. For twenty years you developed your skills. You didn't get involved with office politics or people's personal lives. When there was a party, you went to it and you played golf with people from the company sometimes, but the rest you left alone. You didn't want people prying into your life and you didn't pry in theirs. And so it went. You progressed in status, position and salary and life was fine. You had a wonderful wife and family and a new home in a good neighborhood until it all collapsed like playing cards. One was jarred loose and the rest fell on top. But that one you never understood. And you certainly hadn't expected it. But one day when you were working late, a man came in to see you. That was the first you knew of the problem. Then you were devoted to the company. After all, you worked for them since you were little more than a boy. You gave them your life. But I don't want to get on that. It only hardens your bitterness.

As I was saying, a man came in to see you. But you weren't happy about the interruption. It's one of the things you don't like about offices. You have no privacy. I mean people constantly barge in wanting to talk, talk about nothing. Jabber on, but say nothing because there's nothing meaningful to say. But they can find nothing to do without a superior constantly at them. But you're not like that. You'd rather be alone. There's always plenty to do. You have no time for small talk. And, if there isn't, you find something. I may sound a little put out, but you've been gritting your teeth for years and I'm a little fed up with it now. I know you don't handle it well. I mean I know you have shortcomings. And I know you have the reputation of being a cold and distant man. And, I guess, you were, are. But you don't know what to say. You're just not good socially, not good at small talk. Never were. That's why they call you a loner. You'd rather work alone than spend time talking. So you, sometimes, responded rudely when people came to see you. In this case, when you heard him outside, you made it appear you were absorbed in some work. You thought he might be tactful and leave. But no. He walked in as if it were his office, sat down without being invited, put his feet on your desk and said, "Well, Wamblie old boy, how's it going?" smiling delightedly at your irritation. He was the sort that, to your face, put on a façade of friendliness, but would stab you in the back if he got the chance. Usually, he came to try to find a way. That's what disgusted you. But it wasn't only that. It was that, no matter how much you indicated you were busy, he came in anyway without regard. In fact he'd laugh if you showed displeasure. It was as if he enjoyed putting people off. That's why no one liked him. Everyone there thought he was an ass. But he paraded around acting jolly and didn't care what anyone thought, he didn't care you knew he was a phony. You explained you were busy and asked what he wanted. He said nothing in particular, that he just dropped in to see how you were. You said fine, abruptly, and went back to your work. You thought he might leave. But no. He asked if you knew it was late. You assured him you did and told him, if there was nothing else, you'd like to get back to work. He said, "No need to get huffy!" and that he thought he was doing you a favor, that he thought you were confused and had lost track of the time. He said he just didn't want to see you overwork and there was no reason to be short because he was only trying to help. You told him you could get along without his help, but he still wouldn't leave. He just sat there looking amused. The next thing was you were working too hard. Were you aware of that, he wanted to know. He said he was worried you'd wear yourself out. That was more than you could take, so you asked him, directly, to leave. His comment was calculated to put you on the defensive, to get you to rationalize your hours and argue they weren't that long. You don't like justifying yourself, so, since he wouldn't get out, you simply began to ignore him. "Wamblie, old man," he said, "don't get frazzled. I want to discuss something with you. Something you'll agree is very important." You asked him what, but he waved his hand and sighed. "In a minute, in a minute," he said. "Don't be so anxious. And relax." You can't stand being told to relax. You asked him what in God's name you were waiting for because his presence was beginning to grate on your nerves. He said he'd get to it and then offered you a drink. "You'll need it when you find out what I've got to say," he said as he pulled a flask from his pocket. But you refused. You'd never drink at work. You knew he knew that and you knew he knew you knew the whole thing was just to prod you. So you demanded he get on with it. He snickered and said he wasn't sure he should because he was afraid it would upset you. He rubbed his lip as if seriously puzzle. But you knew it was an act and, so, went back to your papers. Eventually, he put the flask away (since you wouldn't play his game) and asked if you'd heard any rumors. "No," you said, "what rumors?" He said there were rumors of a shake up. You asked, curtly, how that concerned you. He said, "Demotion", with a playful grin. "What, mine?" you asked. He nodded with satisfaction. "Why me?" you questioned, not having believed him. "Unethical practices," he said, "and I got that from a very dependable source." You asked him who. "Wamblie, boy," he said, "I'd like to tell you, but you know I can't. I wouldn't have sources if I did." You said, "No, I suppose not," coldly and asked him why you should believe him, why you shouldn't assume it's a practical joke. He roared at that. "You don't believe me?" he said. "Why would I lie?" You said, "For the fun of it." He said you were unkind to someone there to help you, but that you would soon find out the truth. You studied his expression and sensed he wasn't lying. He stared right back without wavering a bit. So you began to believe him which flooded your mind with thoughts about what it would mean. That jarred you. Badly! To the point where you got up and began pacing. You're the nervous type, always have been. When you get upset, you become very anxious. Always have. And your face shows it. You can't help it. Never could. You were too anxious then. Understandably so. This was the worst thing that could happen. You, demoted? You had a family and a house to support, yet you were going to be demoted? Then, as you passed into middle age, the age when they say life begins, you were told you would be demoted. You were crushed. You went to the window and gazed out in bewilderment. You simply couldn't comprehend it. "Is this on the up and up?" you asked. "Absolutely," he answered flatly explaining he was sorry to be the bearer of such bad news, but he thought you'd want to know. You said, sarcastically, you could see he was concerned. Then you turned back to the window and your eyes began to moisten. In fact you were on the verge of tears. I don't know why. You hadn't cried in years, not since you were a child. And to do it then, in front of him, was the most appalling thing that could happen. You tried to hold back and finally were successful. You finally regained control. In fact you felt curiously amused all of a sudden. Your emotion turned to elation. I mean the crisis of demotion seemed comical and of no particular consequence. You just felt like laughing at the absurdity of it all. But you controlled that too and went back to him, smiling slightly, and asked if there was anything else. He looked at you with a perplexed expression for more than a few seconds. Then he said, "No, nothing else, except you shouldn't wear blue shirts. The company likes white," he warned with a confused and awkward grin. Then he turned and left. You went shortly after him.

On the way home, you began to doubt what he said. It didn't seem to be a plausible story. On the other hand, you thought it could be true. So you tried to piece things together by asking yourself some questions. For instance, does the head of the department have a relative he wants in? Or could it be a punishment for turning down the position they offered you in California? The company had been known to demote people for that. But no, that couldn't be it you told yourself. The man said a shake up, so it involved more than you. So what could it be? You just didn't know. You still don't. But you have ideas. At that time, you couldn't imagine what it was, however. That left you apprehensive about work. In fact your weekend went badly because of it. Especially the wedding. Henrietta and you had a wedding to attend and everything went wrong, remember? Your tuxedo came back from the cleaners a mess (the crease in the pants wasn't in the middle) and you couldn't find the studs for the shirt. So you began rummaging through your jewelry drawer to see if they were there when Henrietta came into the bedroom. She was still in her robe and slippers, but she was nearly ready for her dress. You were behind. You knew that because she was brisk in her manner and because she ignored you on purpose. That meant hurry up. You were stalling because you didn't want to go. There'd be people from work there you knew. You always have to watch what you say. Everything's so political. So, instead of getting dressed, you were trying to invent a reason to stay home. You'd rather be there watching TV or puttering around the yard. Unfortunately, you could think of nothing, however. Besides, not to go would have made her angry. During the years of your marriage, you always wanted to stay away from these things and she always wanted to go. She thought your preference for solitude was unhealthy and unnatural and you argued that point at length. But it got nowhere, so you began going without mentioning your druthers. It was easier and it solved the conflict since she assumed that, if the problem didn't appear, it wasn't there. I don't know when you started doing that exactly. It was sometime back. And you must admit, as Henrietta always said, it's been good for your career. It's all part of life to handle these things: social affairs I mean. And you did get better over the years. It wasn't so bad. So, all things considered, it was better to go. All the more because Henrietta loved gatherings so much. She'd never have forgiven you if you hadn't taken her. So you finally picked your jacket up and brushed it off. About that time, Henrietta returned. She sighed with displeasure (an irritating habit) and said, "You're not dressed! Why can't you ever be on time?" She was standing in the doorway all ready to go. And there you were still in your socks and underwear. She had reason to be short with you, but what could you say? You said you were coming. "Well hurry up!" she cried, "or we'll be late for the ceremony."

Needless to say, you were. By the time you got there, the parking lot was full. And it was raining. So you had to walk a distance huddled under an umbrella. There was a strong wind too. Henrietta was very displeased by all that and took it out on you. But you got there all right and found an empty pew. You looked at the woman next to you whom I'll never forget. She was old and wore thick glasses. She looked at you with rapture on her face; not your mood at the moment, but you were glad to see everyone wasn't completely discontent. You weren't interested in the proceedings at all. But...

I don't know why I'm thinking all this. They're things that don't matter. They're just details. What I intended to recall was what it was like sitting there gazing above the pulpit. That's the track I was on. You became engrossed by the gigantic crucifix mounted above the pulpit. It was watching over the congregation like a shepherd over a flock. It was very lifelike and eerie looking. The eyes were sad and full of suffering. It was the figure of someone whose spirit had been broken, utterly. But, curiously, there came a new strength from that, an invulnerability because nothing could intimidate it, not anymore. The arms and legs were sinewy with veins and muscles standing out. But, somehow, the posture was relaxed. In fact the more you looked, the more your impression changed that way, the more you saw a relaxed, peaceful body, the more the suffering disappeared and the more contentment prevailed. Even where the spikes penetrated the hands, the muscles were relaxed. I wonder what Christ looked like and how he felt being nailed to the cross. It's a terrible thing to do to a person, yet he seemed to find peace in it or so they say. Satisfaction even. Or, perhaps, relief at no longer having to cope with life. Yes, that must have been it. He probably couldn't wait to die.

Anyway, these sorts of thoughts occupied your mind to the exclusion of everything else. That, combined with the preacher's droning voice, nearly made you drop off. But it didn't matter. It was much more pleasant. The drowsiness I mean. It passed the time. So you just sat there contentedly and languishing in vague remembrances. They concerned, as I recall, Henrietta and our wedding. A picture of you kneeling at the altar came to mind, remember? You were very slight and skinny then. Some called you meek. But she was womanly and beautiful. You felt as if you had won a great prize. It seemed like a great reward because you had always dreaded getting a scrawny buck toothed woman with mousy eyes and straggly hair. You thought no one else would have you. But you were wrong and you couldn't believe it. All the more so since you hadn't really pursued her. In fact it was she who chased you. You had a big ceremony. Her father had some money and paid for a big splash. It was too much for you. You were very nervous; anxiety stricken would be more like it—or terrified. You don't like crowds especially when you're to be on display. You don't like social affairs and you don't like parties of any kind. So your wedding was a terrible experience. But, after all, it was her day, the day she had been waiting for above all others which was the only reason you did it. For her. Because it meant so much.

After that day, you got to knew each other better. You found out things you can only know by being together. Things that don't come up during courtship. I can't think of an example, but little things, little quirks. But it was good. I don't mean to imply it wasn't. You had no complaints, literally! Quite the contrary. Yours' was a good relationship because there was so much you had in common. You did many things together. All these things were enjoyable and you looked forward to them with great anticipation. Of course, everything wasn't perfect. You had your problems like any couple. You found it difficult to give up your friends for one thing. But they were the only friends you ever had. Growing up, you were a social outcast. I don't know why. I never completely understood it, but, through the years, you found a few people, people you could talk to who understood your troubles. You were in the habit of getting together for a little party here and there. What can that hurt? I don't know. But Henrietta took a dim view of it. She thought it was crass and unseemly. But that's the sort of thing her family disliked. It was beneath them, her too since she was one of them. So after you were married you stopped going out. It's been years since you've heard from any of them. It was regrettable, but, I guess, necessary for your marriage. But drinking was the only way you could relax, the only way you could drop your inhibitions and be yourself. And, I believe, Henrietta could have benefited from it too although I knew she never would, not at your behest. She had a much stronger will than you. I mean she was the dominant one. She was shy and retiring in public, but with you she could be a force. It was she who proposed marriage, she who found your first house and she who decided on children. She felt, if she didn't, you never would. Then you'd be left with nothing. Which reminds me of one of the important things she taught you. Namely, you thought so badly of yourself you would make things unpleasant and, thus, prove to yourself you're a waste. She claimed that's why you drank, that's why you did nothing to advance your courtship and that's why she took such a firm hand. I must say, you can't deny it. If it weren't for her, it never would have happened. I mean you simply couldn't have brought it about. But what you realized is she had that problem too. When it came to a little party, she would become nervous, then testy, then want to leave. Exactly the kind of gathering you could tolerate and maybe enjoy made her insecure and skitterish. And vice versa. The difference being, you thought badly of yourself. She thought badly of others. In fact, there were times when she was rude. That was such a problem, you often thought it would cause you to split, remember? But you found a way out. When it was the kind of party she didn't like, she began to bring knitting. Not a party activity, but it was something she did a lot of then. She would sit in a corner and pay no attention unless someone paid attention to her. And, usually, someone did because they found her knitting so unusual, unusual at a party that is. But she didn't care. She would begin expounding aggressively on the joys of using the hands. But none of this really solved the problem. Not for you at any rate. She just didn't like your friends. After a while, she got so she'd rather not go out to knit. Then she called your friends some names. "Purposeless nothings," was one. I can't remember the rest. But that began a war which ended in your giving them up. You had to because you didn't want to lose her. She was the best thing you had. After all, she can be credited with bringing about much of your success. She took a deep interest in your career and did everything she could to help. How many men can say that? You could never have gotten where you did without her.

Without her, you probably would have remained in some lowly position forever, but, with her, you rose through the company ranks. That's why you thought you had such a good relationship; because you had done this together. What it comes down to is you needed her support. You just weren't sure you could handle responsibility; work, support a family, be a father. Lots of times, I thought you would crack. But you didn't. The money came rolling in, so you settled down as the years went by. Of course, there was a price to pay. All your childhood dreams were lost. But they were unrealistic dreams all children have. And you had so much else. A career you were good at for one thing. That's something to be proud you—I just got an awful thought! I thought maybe this whole thing, this whole career was wrong for you. Maybe it was wrong and, now, you're being punished. But you were afraid then. What would you have done for money, how would you have lived and what woman would have married you? It could have been a lonely existence and I'm not sure that would have been good. You were always afraid of it, afraid you'd get strange. Fortunately, you've never had to live...what am I saying! You're alone now! You're living as you would have had you chosen differently. It makes me think you're right, you did choose wrong and you are being punished. But no. That can't be true. That's just your paranoia. You've got to be careful or you'll let it go too far. After all, that was a long time ago. It's got nothing to do with now. Now, you're a professional. You've always been a professional. You couldn't have done anything else, not and marry Henrietta which was all part of growing up. To pursue something dreamy would have been to remain a child. No, the course you chose was right. Although I can confide your sex life was bad. In the beginning, you were clumsy and inexperienced. Neither one of you knew a thing. I don't mean you didn't know how it was done (you weren't that naive), only that you had never done it. It was like groping in the dark. It was stiff, contrived and mechanical. Not that you didn't feel affection. But the sex act is embarrassing and you were just too ill at ease. Consequently, you avoided it; the result of a tacit understanding. You only had it once a month or once every other month. You found other ways to gratify yourself. I assume she did too. Although they say women have less drive. But who knows? But what I'm trying to say is you couldn't satisfy each other. It was never good, not until five years later. Then there was a time when everything went right. I remember it perfectly. It was an afternoon and you had just gotten back to the house, the old place you lived in then. You were in terrific moods. Things had been getting better for some time. You were working at your relationship and had made some progress. This was the culmination of it. You were in the kitchen when you noticed the afternoon light shimmering in her hair. I don't know why, but you were overwhelmed with desire. It was the same with her. The next thing you knew, you lost all inhibitions. She, too, felt no reluctance. You had a terrific time. But it was not just that, not just physical. Something changed mentally, spiritually almost. You had conquered a problem. It was a triumph that brought you closer and led to a talk that was just as incredible, remember that? You spoke about how you had changed, about how you had grown, about how she was no longer a girl and how you had become a man. You talked about how much you each brought to the marriage and about how much you appreciated the other's contribution. I can't remember what else you said, but you went on for hours and ended by embracing with a genuine affection that's not often found. In fact that was the time you felt best, the very best you ever felt. But it was all. I don't know why. Things changed, we grow old, we get settled and life falls into a routine. It happens to everybody and it happened to you.

But, to get back to what I was saying, that was the day she

first became pregnant. A boy was born nine months later. Your excitement continued from then on and lasted for months. Or something like that. I don't remember when it faded. She was occupied with him as you were with work. The years slipped by. But there were good times. You took trips and vacations and spent holidays with family. Her parents, your parents. You alternated a lot. You kept pictures which you enjoyed very much. But, somehow, nothing has ever been the same. You were never so happy again.

But what does it matter? I've been going on so long I don't know what I'm saying. I'm talking foolishness and I'm beginning to bore myself with these silly reminiscences. Besides, recalling the past makes me melancholy and depressed, very depressed. And it's all water over the dam. It's all fixed, it's all happened for good or bad and cannot be altered no matter how much we wish it. That's the thing about the past: it's set in stone and it's all we have since the present is so short it's barely perceptible let alone comprehensible. It's only afterwards we make sense of the present which, by then, is the past which leaves us the future; an unknown. So the past is all there is. That sounds muddled, I'm aware. I can hardly make sense of it myself. How I ramble! I only wish I would stop. I wish I could turn off like a light.

But what was I saying, before, about Henrietta?.... Marriage! I was talking about the wedding. I was explaining about the ceremony. About how you were sitting in the pew daydreaming. You were barely awake, on the verge of dropping off. Your mind began swimming in and out of consciousness. You sunk suddenly and hit your head on the pew. Quite hard. It made a crack which attracted attention. The preacher looked up to see about the disturbance. You smiled and indicated you were all right though very embarrassed. You've never been so embarrassed! You put your hand to your head to find a big lump forming. You smiled nervously at the crowd again. Then everyone faced forward and the preacher went on. You glanced at Henrietta who appeared annoyed. She turned from you as much as to say, I don't know you! But what could you do? It wasn't your fault. Besides, what's done is done. But she had a tendency to harp on these things. Her bad mood continued as you fed into the stream and slowly moved toward the lobby. So you left her. You didn't want to see anyone or talk to anyone. All you wanted was to get out, so you went directly for the coats. When you returned, however, you found her in a conversation with a woman. They had cigarettes going and were laughing about something. I don't know what. When she saw you she glared, came and took you by the arm and brought you to the woman clamoring, "Why, you don't want to leave already, Darling!" It was very embarrassing. But you made some excuse: not feeling well and wanting fresh air, something like that. Then you said, hello, to her friend and managed a smile. Henrietta apologized and introduced you. You said, hello, again. So did she. Then you offered to leave and let them gab. Nicely, of course. Henrietta asked where you'd be. You said around the lobby. The three of you smiled and you walked away still carrying the coats.

You found a corner where you thought you'd be unnoticed to smoke a cigarette when a man from the office saw you and came over to say, hello. "Well, if it isn't Mr. Wamblie, the best department head around! How ya' do'n buddy?" he asked shaking hands and patting you on the back. You said fine and attempted a smile although you didn't understand his comment. It seemed a bit sarcastic. But you weren't sure if that was intended or not. Besides, you had no choice but to talk to him, so you disregarded that and tried to be nice. You had just begun a conversation when three others joined you. They greeted you with friendliness, ostensibly, but, somehow, you felt uneasy with some of the comments they made. In fact you had the impression they were laughing at you, that you were the brunt of some joke. You didn't know if they knew about the rumor, but the chances were good it had gotten around. And, if they knew, it was something they'd kid you about. To give an example, one asked you with a chuckle if anything interesting had happened lately. You said no uncertainly, unsure of what he meant. He stared at you intently, then asked why you seemed so serious. You weren't aware of how you looked and it made you nervous to have him focus on it that way. But you brushed it off and tried to change the subject by bringing up the wedding. You commented that you found it long and tedious. Another remarked he had seen you hit your squash. That was the word he used, remember? Yes, and it drew some snickers which embarrassed you mostly because you weren't sure if they were laughing with you or at you. A third said he had spent the time looking at some pretty nice stuff. "And I don't mean faces," he added with a grin. "Ah! The delights of youth," the first said as he elbowed your side obnoxiously. "But you're too tired for that. Isn't that right, Wamblie?" "Well...I wouldn't say that," you retorted uncertainly because you were unsure how to take all that. I mean you didn't want to offend them if it wasn't necessary. But you also didn't want to be the target of their quips. It's so hard to draw these lines. It's hard to know when you'll appear priggish if you can't take a joke and when you'll appear the fool if you do. But it all came clear when the fourth started in wanting to know if you had seen the knockers on the new secretary at work. You told him no, but, attempting to banter back, said you would and soon. That started them chortling. But when he said, "Good! Because no one else will since she's sixty years old," they all broke out into hysterical laughter. All but you. You just stared. Finally, he asked you what was wrong. You said, "Nothing." "Nothing!" the third bellowed mockingly, "it doesn't look like nothing." "Com'on. We're only kidd'n ya'," the fourth said, "Can't ya' take a joke?" "Is that what it is?" "Of course. What else could it be?" "You tell me." "Hey, we're only ribb'n ya'," the second said, "Relax." You can't stand being told to relax and you were at the end of your patience, so, without saying goodbye, you went to find Henrietta. You just walked off in the middle of it all. There's nothing else to do with people like that—*He's really uptight*—"Okay, we'll see ya'!"—*More than usual*—"Bye, bye!"—*Does he know?*—"So long!"—*I don't know*—They were boorish people with no brains in their heads. They said goodbye as if you had done something wrong! They're the types who go thoughtlessly along with no regard for anyone. Anyone who's different, they think is peculiar. Well I think they're peculiar. They talk about how strange you are, how nervous and upset you get and how you don't smile and enjoy yourself enough. But the only strange thing about you is you bothered to talk to them!

Ah! It was just a bad day. A bad day all around between the company and the wedding, not to mention the rain. It was depressing. But you finally got through it and got back to the house. You immediately went to the bedroom where you could be alone. You needed that sometimes. It's the only place conducive to thought. And that's what you were doing, thinking! You were sitting on the bed thinking about the rumor and whether or not you should tell Henrietta. And, if you should, how you should do it. You wanted to lessen the blow. You knew it would be a devastating one; perhaps worse for her than for you. But, since you hadn't been told formally, you contented yourself that perhaps it wasn't true. That gave you room for hope anyway. And you decided to spare Henrietta until you knew for certain one way or the other. But you weren't sure how long that would be and that made you anxious. So you rehearsed telling her to see how it felt. It felt hard. It would be hard to say, "I got demoted, we'll have to live on less money, our life style will have to change." It would be hard to admit failure. But had you failed? That's the question that bothered you most. You couldn't stop mulling over the words "unethical practices". Which of your practices that referred to you had no idea. You had done nothing different in how you administered your department. You had your procedures, but unethical? There's nothing unethical about you. You've been using the same techniques for years. They were in the company manual. So you concluded you were being singled out. You were to be reprimanded and punished unjustly. Why, you didn't know. Perhaps you were used as a scapegoat. The company was undergoing a suit for monopoly. The timing was curious to say the least. It was (is) a big suit. Maybe they thought it would help to clean house. I don't know. But I have my suspicions. It's a pretty good guess if you think about it enough. But, you told yourself not to worry. You were getting overwrought. You had resolved not to tell Henrietta and for the rest? Nothing to do but wait.

You yawned and stretched. You felt exhausted. You hadn't realized how tired you were. You got up and noticed yourself in the mirror. For some reason you were intrigued and went to stand in front of it. You seemed more old than young. You were struck by that immediately. There was nothing young about you. You had aged. For some years previous, sleep had been a problem. I don't know why. At that point, you hadn't slept for days. Your impression of yourself had changed completely. Your chest and shoulders seemed sunken and your skin was milky white. Your face was drawn with circles under the eyes. You pulled at the skin beneath them and looked at the tissue; not that that told you anything. You don't know what to look for. But it made your face grotesque. You never were what I'd call attractive. You're too short, for one thing, and you've always been slight. Your face is round and you don't have a chin. Your ears stick out and your beard is sparse. You've always worn glasses, something you were ridiculed for as a child. But you don't want to pity yourself. I was thinking about the years you had put on. Then you felt silly gazing at yourself. So you turned away and a chill ran down your spine. You began rubbing your arms and went to the window. The backyard light was on. There were leaves floating in the pool as a result of the wind. You looked at the lawn, at the chain link fence and at the neighbor's back yard and house. Then you noticed the trees swaying in the breeze and the moon, faint, behind a mass of grey clouds. It was still drizzling and pattering against the glass. Then there was a flash of lightning, the silence followed by a distant rumbling. The storm was moving out. You returned to the bed and yawned again. You were very tired and you hoped, as you hope now, you'd sleep. It was getting harder. You didn't bother saying good night to Henrietta. You just switched off the light and laid down.

Development

Time went by. You heard nothing. Everything was as usual although it wasn't usual with you. You couldn't relax and forget about the demotion. It plagued you interminably. Living in constant fear wore you out. By the middle of the following week, you were exhausted as well as a lot of other things I don't want to describe. I mean I don't want to be a bore. But a few days later, you woke up early. The week had been a struggle and you found it difficult to go to work, almost impossible. You just couldn't do it. Every day there was like a day in hell waiting and waiting for the demotion. You constantly wondered what form it would take or, to put it another way, demoted how far. Nothing was said, however. So you waited. You thought something would happen. When it didn't, you were relieved, momentarily, until you realized that didn't mean it wouldn't. But nothing was said. Everything seemed normal. Everything but you. You were tense. Too much so. You couldn't smile and say good morning—*He looks down*—You were nervous and shaking—*He's got the jitters. Something's going on*—Enough so it was noticeable—*Have you seen him lately? He's acting funny*—People would look at you as if you were some strange creature they had never seen. The secretaries were distant and apprehensive and people talked as if you had some gross deformity they were trying not to notice—*Does he know what's going on?*—Every time your boss appeared you ground your teeth—*I Hope no one's told him*—You chipped an incisor and lost a filling—*He shouldn't know until the time is right*—People noticed you were acting strangely—*Should we say something to him?*—They began to talk—*Would that calm him down?*—You could tell by their expressions they were talking about you—*Somebody better do something! He shouldn't be working in that condition*—Probably about your demotion—*Do you think he knows?*—If they knew—*I don't see how he could*—They may not have—*Word gets around*—I don't know—*Somebody probably told him*—But you knew they noticed how morose you were. You gave them something to talk about—*He's a funny man*—And they did.

After a long period of this torture, you had had enough. That's all. Enough! You woke up that morning feeling afraid. You can admit that now. You were more scared than you've ever been. But why? You don't know. You didn't then. Perhaps you do now. I'm not sure. Either that or you are crazy which could very well be true. But whatever the case, you couldn't go, not to work. It was too much. You couldn't stand another day. It was too tense. So, when you opened your eyes, you just laid there next to Henrietta. There was a cool breeze drying off your back. That felt good after a sticky night. It was very humid. It was sunny too. You could see a rectangle of light on the floor. Henrietta got up finally. You were facing the other way and she couldn't see you. But you felt her standing there staring at you after she got her slippers on. Why, I don't know. For an instant, it was like being at work. But that was your imagination. At least that's what you told yourself. Eventually, she left and went to the bathroom. You sat there thinking about what to do. You weighed the consequences of going and not going, of telling Henrietta and not telling her, of where your life was leading and where it wasn't. But you could decide nothing. None of it made sense. It seemed like a bad joke. You felt curiously distant. You tried to decide (while at the same time nothing mattered) one way or the other. You felt as if you could laugh hysterically or cry your heart out. It was a strange feeling. You never had it before, but have many times since. Almost perpetually in fact. The feeling that nothing matters, nothing makes any difference and anyone who thinks it does is a fool. A stupid fool! But I'm rambling again.

As I was saying, Henrietta walked back into the room just as the alarm went off. The same alarm. Everything else was the same too. Everything but you. You were different. I can't help but emphasize that. It was so striking. It was like waking up and finding you didn't know who your were, that you were a vastly different person from what you imagined. But it felt good too. It felt good not to take anything seriously and to see the futility of life. But it was, at the same time, so strange you could respond to nothing Henrietta said. In fact when the alarm went off, you did nothing. You didn't move or blink. You just laid there paralyzed. She asked if you were awake. You said nothing. She nudged you and told you to turn off the alarm. You heard her, but you didn't answer. You couldn't. You were watching events transpire without being able to participate. She stomped over and shut off the clock. Then she noticed your eyes were open. She asked if you were awake with an edge to her voice. You said nothing. You didn't want to argue and you couldn't muster a reply. She asked you why you hadn't shut it off. You didn't move a muscle, but you finally announced you weren't going to work. "What do you mean you're not going?" she demanded. You answered by saying, again, you weren't going to work, that's all. She was confused and stunned. She said you had to go unless you were sick. You told her you weren't sick, not physically. "Then get up!" she cried. You told her you couldn't. She asked you to explain since she understood nothing. You told her, again, you weren't going.

But she still couldn't comprehend it. "Why?" she cried. "I don't feel like it," you whispered. She couldn't accept that. She reminded you you never missed a day without good reason. You interrupted, however, to tell her to leave. And you informed her, again, you weren't going to work. She thought a moment and then asked if you weren't at least going to call. You said you had no idea. "What do you mean you have no idea?" You said or, rather, screamed you didn't know and that's what you meant. She bristled with fury and said she didn't know what had gotten into you, but you were not yourself. "Do you know that?" she asked. You told her you knew. "Well, what's the matter then?" You asked if she couldn't see you didn't want to talk about it. But she disregarded that and said, "So you know what it is then?" You told her you knew. "But, Darling," she began suddenly full of compassion, "how can you take care of it in bed?" You told her you needed to rest and think. She made a face and offered to call work and to make some coffee and then she said you should talk. You told her there was nothing to talk about, but she seemed not to hear that when she left the room. It was only then your anguish diminished. It began a slow tapering off while your own personality returned. I know that sounds strange. But the way you acted with Henrietta began to seem silly and childish. You began to think you acted badly and stupidly and foolishly. You felt you were responsible for a ridiculous scene and you couldn't understand why you caused it. Henrietta returned with the coffee. She handed you a cup which you sat up to take. Then she took a sip of her's and eyed you. She was studying your face, your mood, your thoughts. I think she knew you changed while she was out. She asked you to tell her what was wrong. Although you were better, you didn't want to speak about it since you couldn't understand it. So, instead, you asked if the kids had gotten up. She said they had gone to play and went back to her question. You tried to go on about the boys, but she made a face of disgust. After that, you didn't talk. You could feel her disappointment as you silently sipped your coffee. Disappointment in you I mean. Finally, she asked if you were feeling any better. "All right," you said. She asked if you wanted to talk. You said you didn't know what to say. "Tell me what's happened," she urged. You couldn't see the good of that and that's what you told her. She said, at least you'd get it off your chest. But there was nothing she could do, so you said, "Why bother?" She could share the burden, she said. "Can you get me another job?" you blurted out. "Another job?" she gasped. "That's what I need," you said. She said she didn't understand and asked if you were joking. "No," you said. She stared into space blankly, then said, "So that's why you don't want to go." But then, you said you'd get up and go with quiet determination. Then you asked her if she called in sick for you. She hadn't. She inquired about your pay which was exactly what you didn't want. You didn't want her to worry. Not that you could stop her. But you tried to ease her anxiety by explaining how the company takes care of its own. You said it was just a matter of reorganization, that you'd temporarily be reassigned. She seemed hesitant to accept that. She commented that, before, you were acting like disaster had struck whereas, now, you thought nothing of it. She added tearfully she had the feeling something terrible was going to happen and then she began to cry. You asked with a chortle if that was her woman's intuition. She scolded you for making fun of her. You apologized, but added she should guard against becoming too melodramatic. "I'm not being melodramatic," she shouted. "I'm just saying something's wrong." You tried to calm her down. You said everything would be fine because you were going to work. You went to her, put your hands on her face and looked into her eyes. Then you drew her head to your chest and patted it reassuringly. You...

What's that? Do you hear that?....That voice? No?....You

don't—there! Right there! You don't hear that? That's funny. Listen now...listen....It's stopped. I can't hear it. But I could have sworn I did. Someone yelling. It sounded like somebody in pain. And I thought I heard your name. It sounded like somebody calling you for help. But, of course, that's ridiculous. You just got here. You don't know anyone. No one knows you. So how could it have been calling for you? If there was a voice at all. It could have been my imagination; especially since you heard nothing. It could be my condition. But, no matter. Let's leave that. I don't want to talk about it anymore. It's very unpleasant.

As I was saying, you continued going to work after that. I don't know for how long exactly. A few weeks maybe. I'm not sure. Then, the day came. You had expected it right away. But then, you forgot about it. Well, I can't say you forgot about it because your nervousness increased. But you hoped it was untrue. Every day you couldn't wait to get home, to get away. That's all you wanted. All you did was watch the clock. No, I can't say you forgot about it, but I can say you stopped thinking about it. All you thought of was your anxiety. You wondered when it would stop. There were times when it seemed it never would. You couldn't accept that, however, and continued hoping. But it got worse and worse and worse. Then, BANG! Demoted! You were called in by the boss and told. From there, your anxiety got worse. Intolerable in fact. You had to leave. Just get out. So you went home early. You didn't tell anyone. You just couldn't face it. You just left. Had you done otherwise, people would have seen you were troubled. You couldn't hide it and you couldn't explain it. They were already suspicions. You had seen them, seen people talking. You didn't want to fuel their gossip, so you left.

It was quiet at home when you arrived. But when you went into the house, you heard shots in the den. Then you panicked. You saw blood. Someone shot...

But why go into it? Needless to say, you were frightened. You rushed in to see about it. And that's when you knew your nerves were frayed. It wasn't shots, but a T.V. movie the boys were watching. Your oldest was fourteen, then, and the youngest was eight. The youngest was a good boy. He did everything you asked with no complaints. The oldest was that way too once. But he got into a defiant stage. Adults do everything wrong, he thought. Anyone over thirty was wrong, automatically. And, I'm afraid, the trouble was only beginning. He started smoking, drinking and taking drugs. Last summer, he grew his hair long. It's that way now; like a girl's. Shoulder length in fact. But then, it was a little shorter. That led to problems at school. He was kicked out. You must admit, you couldn't handle him. He did nothing you said, showed no respect and seemed not to fear any form of punishment. So you couldn't help him. You could only sit and watch him ruin his life like so many of the young. I only hope he doesn't run away. It's so sad, sad because he doesn't know what he's doing. He mouths phrases, but doesn't know what they mean. It's rebellion for the sake of rebellion. There's no other purpose. He got everything he wanted, so there was nothing to rebel against. When you were a boy, you couldn't have gotten away with it. You were afraid of your father. If he said go swimming in winter, you went swimming in winter. Not to would have been unthinkable. But, today, it's different. Today, age doesn't matter. Wisdom doesn't mean a thing. If you live past thirty, you've done something wrong, outlived your usefulness or some such thing. Put them out to pasture as soon as they reach their prime.

But none of this is important. I was explaining that you rushed into the room. But neither of them noticed. They were too engrossed. When they were younger they would have been watching to see your car pull in. They would have jumped in your arms and given you a hug all full of giggles and laughter.

It made you glad to be home. But now? It's gone. Except from the youngest. He, at least, smiled when he noticed you were there. But the oldest told you to keep quiet. "I'm trying to watch," he said indignantly. You felt like hitting him. The youngest asked you why you were home. You told him it was because you wanted to be. He found that a strange answer. He screwed up his face and went back to the program. It was too much out of kilter for him. Fathers are supposed to come home at night. To arrive in the middle of the afternoon is out of place.

You left and went to your chair. It was hot that day. You were frying. It had been that way for a while. There was pollution in the city; enough so there were warnings to the old not to go out. So you switched on the air conditioner. You took off your shoes and loosened your tie. Then you settled down with the paper. Things weren't good in the world. Not that they're any better now. But then, the news was very depressing. So much so, in fact, you couldn't get involved with it. You just couldn't concentrate. You were becoming less and less coherent with each passing moment.

But I've forgotten what I was saying....Oh yes, I was talking about the boys. Then, about the news. Then, about?....Oh yes...oh...that's it! Yes, you were sitting there when Henrietta pulled in the driveway. She was returning from the supermarket. You got up and went to ask the boys to carry in the bags. The oldest protested that his show was being interrupted. That really galled you, so you told him to get off his fanny and help. At that point, the youngest ran out. As I say, he was a good boy. He required no discipline. But the oldest was another story. He didn't obey. He said he'd help when the show was over. That made you furious. That kind of defiance from a child! Unheard of! You went toward him with your hand raised. He stood up as if to defend himself. You couldn't believe it! He was ready to fight his father. There was a time when an old man could beat his son without fear of reprisal. You just didn't raise a hand to your father. Now, it's different. "Well," you told him, "if television is so important, I feel sorry for you," and left. You went back to your chair. You felt like thrashing him. Maybe you should have. Maybe he should have felt the back of a hand. You did and at an early age too. And you learned. The only reason you refrained was because of Henrietta. She was against it. Always was. She must have read too much when they were little. She said hitting teaches hitting, nothing else. You thought hitting taught respect. Her and her methods! It's her fault he turned out that way. You never would have let it happen. But no, she wouldn't listen to you! Well, I hope she's satisfied! She's made her bed and, now, she can lie in it without you. She's probably home right now enjoying herself—*It's better without Daddy*—They probably all are—*Your father isn't well*—They're probably talking about you right this minute—*Daddy's strange*—So maybe it's a better life with you gone—*I'm glad he's gone*—I hope they appreciate that at least! Damn it, she makes you mad! Just thinking of her gets you boiling. I don't know what comes over you. You're bitter I guess. But you're bitter with reason. But let me get back. I can't go into this....

I remember where I was. In my chair to be exact. The oldest continued watching while the youngest brought in the bags. When that was done, Henrietta appeared. She stomped in as much as to say, I'm angry and, if you ask me what's wrong, I'll scream! So you didn't. She said, "There's a job you could help me with if you would, please." You asked her what it was. She invited you outside. She said she wanted to show you something as if it were you who had caused it, whatever 'it' was. You informed her, rather sharply, you were in no mood to be pushed. "Don't you dare raise your voice to me!" she said. You apologized and told her you hadn't meant to shout. But you explained you had had a rough day and you just wanted to talk a minute. She said, "Alright!" harshly and explained she was upset. It was just one of those days for her too. She listed all the inconveniences and finished with a little story: it seemed, on the way home, somebody threw garbage on the windshield of her car as she went under a bridge. It blocked her vision and almost caused her to crash, she said. It also made her angry. You wanted to know who did it. She wasn't sure, but assumed it was kids. But you had other ideas, ideas that frightened you. You thought it was something more serious, something to do with your job. It was designed to help drive you, well, over the edge you thought. You didn't suggest that to Henrietta, however. She wouldn't have believed it. She would have said you were imagining things. She asked if you would clean the windshield while she went in to make dinner. You agreed. It was a mess, so you took it to a car wash to save some time.

Imagining things! You were imagining things. You did nothing but imagine things. Because of that, you couldn't sleep that night, just couldn't drop off. You tossed and turned and tried every trick (counting sheep, a shot of liquor, putting your head where your feet were and your feet where your head was), but nothing worked. So you got up and went downstairs. You sat on the couch and thought. But the more you thought, the worse you felt. The worse you felt, the angrier it made you. Then the anger turned to fear, indescribable fear. I guess it was because you didn't understand it. But it was, put simply, your predicament, your situation. I don't know how else to describe its cause. Everything was going like a car without brakes and you were the driver who had to sit by helplessly until the crash. That's what made you angry. I mean because it happened to you. But you hadn't done anything. Far from it. Yet there you were. And it terrified you. I can't convey how much. It's like having an expansion in your stomach get bigger and bigger and bigger. And the bigger it gets, the more you try to make it smaller. It gets so you'll do anything to decrease it, anything that will make you feel safer, that will make you feel some control even if it appears irrational. That's the point you reached. It got so bad you couldn't sit still. You had to be walking. By walking you could ward off the fear the same way you ward off peeing. As soon as you stopped, however, it threatened to overwhelm you. But as long as you kept going, you could hold together. That's how Henrietta found you; walking around in the dark. Pacing, pacing, pacing. You couldn't stop. As soon as she saw you, she gasped with surprise and asked what was wrong. She said your face was grotesque and frightening. But you couldn't answer—Don't speak—You couldn't begin to explain—You don't know, do you, Wamblie?—Why you were pacing—Keep going!—Or when you'd be able to stop. So you said nothing. She pleaded with you to answer—Don't answer!—It scared her that you didn't— Don't dare to!—But you couldn't—Don't dare to!—Your speech was paralyzed—Say nothing—You could find nothing to say and no way to say it. But, suddenly, you were seized by an impulse—Lock them!—To go to the windows and secure them— You'll be safer—You went to one and twisted the latch—That's right—You went to the next and did the same—Keep going—And to the next and the next and so on—They'll get you if you don't!— Henrietta followed—*Stop! Stop it!*—Continuously screaming, "What are you doing? What's the matter? What are you doing? What's the matter? Have you gone crazy?" She was nearly hysterical. After you locked all the windows including the basement, you were able to tell her you were protecting your family—That's right, Wamblie—"Against what?"—Don't answer!—You couldn't answer—You don't know—You didn't know the answer. "What are you protecting us against?" she repeated—Tell her now!—"Them!" is all you could say—Tell her, Wamblie—That confused her. "Them? Who's them?" she asked—Tell her!—Again, you couldn't answer—TELL HER!—

You could think of nothing to say—You're defying me!—So you said nothing—Wamblie!—And went back upstairs—Wamblie!—Followed by her—WAMBLIE!—She continued her questioning —Don't stop!—Once back upstairs, you went back to pacing—Keep going—It was urgent that you do—Keep going—You walked from the living room to the dining room to the kitchen six times when you were, again, approaching the hall. She was standing there with an amazed expression—*A gun!*—She was looking at the shot gun standing against the door. You put it there earlier, but had forgotten all about it—You're better off with it—Seeing it made you feel safe, however—Better off!—She shrieked, "What's that doing there?" and darted toward it—Don't let her!—"Stop!" you yelled—Don't let her get it!—"Leave it alone!"—You'll need it—The thought of not having it terrified you. She halted and threw her hands over her mouth—*He's nuts!*—Then she whispered you were crazy—*Nuts!*—"That should be put away," she said—Don't!—But you warned her to leave it alone and resumed your pacing. "But what's it for?"—You know!—You repeated that it was for protection. "Against what?"—You know, Wamblie!—"Against them!" "Who's them?" "You know," you said. "No, I don't," she insisted—Tell her!—So you explained there were people out to get you. "What people?"—Tell her!—"People! People! You know what people!" "No I don't"—You should tell her, Wamblie—"Yes you do." She looked at you with apprehension. She didn't know what was happening. You didn't either. Neither of you could comprehend it. So you just stopped talking and remained silent; you pacing and she staring at nothing, apparently thinking. Then she suddenly blurted out, "Will you stop pacing for God's sake! PLEASE!" You told her you felt better pacing —*He's nuts!*—"Something's terribly wrong," she muttered—*He's crazy*—You asked her what it was—*Crazy*—She said she was afraid to say it—*Crazy!*—You didn't ask what she wanted to say or why she was afraid. You simply continued pacing—

Crazy!—It was then she blurted out you were strange—
Nuts!—"I am?" you said acting mildly surprised—*NUTS!*—
"Yes, you are. Can't you see that?" she cried. And then, you
could. The irrationality became sharper than the fear. "I mean,"
she went on, " standing a gun by the door! Something's wrong
and I think we should do something." You asked her what.
"Call the doctor," she said. "Why call him?" "Because you're
not yourself," she said. "So?" "So, he advised I call if things
got worse." "You've spoken to him before?" "Yes." "About
this?" "Yes." "About me?" "Yes." "Okay, okay! Call him,"
you urged on the verge of panic. She seemed vastly relieved
and hurried to the phone. A second later, she called out to ask
you what his number was. She said she couldn't find it in the
book—She wants him badly—You could hear her swearing under
her breath although she tried to sound casual when she
addressed herself to you. That made you reluctant to give
it—You don't need help—The idea of her and the doctor caring
for you filled you with dread—You're fine—You didn't feel it
was needed—You're fine, Wamblie—You might have had a bad
moment, but you could take care of yourself—Fine!—But she
called again, so you told her where it was. You didn't want to
fight with her. Not then. She was on the phone a while—*It's
my husband!*—You could hear her whispering—*I don't want
him to hear*—Purposely—*He's acting strange like I told you*—
To prevent your hearing—*Except, now, he's much worse*—
You wondered what she wanted to hide—*He's acting insane!*
—But reflecting on that, you knew she was scared, confused
and disillusioned herself—Because of you, Wamblie—Your
behavior had done that. Understandably—What are you doing?—
It was beyond her comprehension—What, Wamblie?—As it was
yours. But what could a doctor do?—Nothing!—What could
anyone do?—You're alone.

Finally, she came back and said, although she had
awakened him, he'd come. You asked her what she told him—

Going crazy—Suddenly, it seemed of the utmost importance —That you're crazy—"I told him you weren't well," she said —She told him you're crazy!—You accused her of telling him you were nuts—*He's in trouble!*—She claimed she did no such thing—*Bad trouble!*—"But that's what you think," you said —*He's doing strange things*—She disclaimed that too, saying she thought you were unhappy and in need of help. "What kind of help? What do I need? Tell me!" you demanded—Easy, Wamblie!—You were bordering on hysteria—Easy—Everything was happening so fast—Slow down—"I don't know," she said. "That's why I called the doctor"—Easy—Your anger evaporated and you suddenly felt sad. You turned away and began to snivel. You asked her, finally, if things were all right. "Is what all right?" You asked her if she was on your side. She reassured you by saying, "Of course I am! I've been married to you since we were kids." "Yes," you said. "Well then!" she exclaimed. Again, you couldn't look at her and say what you wanted to say. You were too close to bawling. But you finally got it out. "It's just, after a while, you don't know who to trust." "You can trust me," she assured. And the way she said it made you feel you could. But the next thing was the doctor. "What about him?" you asked. "Honey," she said, "what's all this talk about trust?" You couldn't explain. It was a mess in your head. "I don't know," you said. "Well, just settle down and wait," she advised. "Okay," you said although you kept on pacing anyway. I mean you wished you could have gone to bed. You wished you could have slept. But you couldn't. The only way you could relax was by moving. And so you did for twenty minutes. It took that long for him to arrive.

Of course, he came with his little black bag—*What's he doing now?*—Why you didn't know although you soon found out—*Still pacing*—He looked like he had gotten up, thrown on some clothes and gotten there quick—*Is he any better?*—There were bags under his eyes and he seemed somewhat pensive—*I don't think so*—Henrietta showed him into the kitchen after they had talked. He put his bag on the table, sat down and beckoned to you to do the same. But you were reluctant for reasons I've explained. He insisted, however, saying he couldn't easily talk with you in constant motion. So you finally agreed. You were a little less tense and able, you thought, to do it. So Henrietta made some coffee while you sat and talked. The first thing he asked was what you had been feeling. You asked him what he meant by that. He said he wondered what was happening inside you. He wanted to know what you felt. You told him, "Nothing," perhaps a bit abruptly. I mean he raised a brow and glared and asked if you felt frightened. You said, "No." He said, "Why do you have the gun out then?" That threw you. You had forgotten all about it. You stammered some. You were conscious of that and how it looked to him. But you couldn't help it. You got confused trying to explain. He could see you were struggling and losing your train of thought, so he asked if he could put it away. You agreed to that. It seemed like the best thing to do. In fact, by then, you had no idea what possessed you to get it out. It seemed silly and childish. But you had done it. I can't explain why except to say it made you feel better. The instant you agreed, the doctor was on his feet. He rose so quickly, in fact, his knees hit the table and spilt the coffee. That embarrassed him. He knew he betrayed his anxiety and he knew his expression was one of distress. Nevertheless, he went quickly for the gun while Henrietta sponged up the mess. He took the two shells out of their chambers. You could hear that. Then he put the gun in its case. He came back in looking very relieved. You were tapping your fingers because you had tremors in your hands. You spilled your coffee when you lifted the cup. He commented on that and said you seemed nervous. He asked if you were scared. You told him you were. He inquired if your mood had anything to do with work. You asked him why he asked. But then, Henrietta broke in. She said she told him about your troubles on the phone. "Well," you said, "it could." "You're unsure?" You said, "Yes." He rocked back meditatively. Then he asked if you knew yours wasn't an unusual condition. He said, "Lots of people feel like you do." You asked him what it was you felt, perhaps a bit provocatively because you resented his assumption that he knew. He faltered, at first, but said, finally, he knew from what he heard and he was quick to add it was a treatable condition. You said, "What condition?" He said the feelings you had could be treated. You asked if he meant he could make them go away. He said, "For a time." You asked how. "With a little medication," he said. And he went on to explain he had some with him and, then, he reached for his bag. But you replied you didn't want any, you didn't want him coming into your home and giving you any drugs. He asked if you knew how worried Henrietta was. You said, "Yes," you knew and, then, looked at her as she stood by the stove. She had a pleading expression as much as to say, I wish you would take something. That made you consider it, to make her feel better. You felt so responsible. You asked the doctor what it was. He said it was just a little shot. "Something to calm me down?" you asked. "That's right," he said. So you said you'd take it if it would make them happy. "Good!" he said and told you to let down your pants while he prepared the syringe. You stood up and hooked your thumbs in the elastic of your pajamas, but you couldn't pull them down. It seemed too degrading and unnecessary. I mean it wasn't what you needed. You felt better by then and you didn't need a shot. You told them that trying not to sound too adamant so they'd see you were calm and concur. But Henrietta sighed and reminded you you agreed. You didn't want to argue. The easiest thing was to go along. So you said okay and pulled down your pajamas. There was a swipe of cotton against your cheek. You could feel the alcohol evaporate. Then came the prick which caused you to flinch. Then he pulled it out and dabbed you again. You pulled up your pants. The others looked relieved. Henrietta asked if you'd have more coffee. You both said yes. She poured it and sat down.

Several minutes of silence followed. It was quite uncomfortable. But you could think of nothing to say. They couldn't either I assume. They were staring at you though. Studying your face and your every expression in an attempt to decipher your mood I guess. For several minutes, that went on. You pretended not to notice. But you couldn't help it. It was horrible to be watched like that. Any slight twitch and they might misconstrue it. Yes, they might think, He's coming apart! That made you determined to appear in control. But the more you tried, the more anxious you became until you could feel your face quake with the strain. That caused them to exchange glances. Then Henrietta said there was something else. You asked what. "See another doctor," she said. You shuddered and blurted out you were fine. "Are you?" she asked. "Yes!" you insisted. "Then why are you being so defensive?" the doctor asked. You said you weren't being defensive. But he ignored that and said if you didn't need a doctor, the doctor would say so. "Besides, you've put your wife through a lot," he said. You thought for a while and finally decided to go. As I say, the more you resisted, the more they thought you needed help. Also, if you went and acted normal, you could all go your way and forget about it. That settled, the next question was when. You assumed they were talking about the morning. But no. "Right now," they said. "This minute?" "Yes." "Can't it wait until tomorrow?" "You need to go now," the doctor said. So you agreed. What else could you do? It was futile to fight them. The only way to get it over was to put their suspicions to rest. Otherwise, they'd never leave you alone. So you prepared to leave and then got into the car. He drove with Henrietta next to him and you in the back.

You wanted it that way. You didn't want anyone next to you acting like you were sick. You felt, already, they had blown the whole thing up. And you resented the way they were treating you. Yes, you got nervous and temporarily lost your head, but dangerous? You wouldn't hurt a fly. It's not in your nature. They should have known that. But perhaps they were scared. I don't know. I suppose you could have appeared changed in some way.

Anyway, there you were, driving. You didn't know where. They hadn't told you. So you asked. But the doctor sighed and waved his hand as much as to say, Your question is inappropriate. You asked again with an insistent tone. He told you to calm down and leave things to him. You were calm, however, and you resented his accusation. Every time you asked a question, they acted like you were nuts. That was getting on your nerves. I mean you weren't behaving badly by then, so you couldn't see why they were so rude. Unless you were doing things you didn't know about. It's possible and it would explain it. Or perhaps they were reacting to your state of mind before. Perhaps they couldn't see it had changed. You just didn't know. You couldn't read their minds. But you were still curious about where you were going, so you politely tried again. Tactfully, you asked if you were going to a doctor's office. "Hospital," the doctor said. "Oh!" you said a little surprised, "I thought we were going to a doctor's." "Yes. A doctor in the hospital. Where else would you find a doctor at this hour?" he asked. "But don't worry," he added, "just relax and leave it to me." Leave it to him? That was an idea you could barely adhere to. But you did. You suppressed your anger and said nothing in spite of his coarse and condescending tone.

So they were taking you to a hospital. Your first reaction was one of relief. That was unexpected. But, momentarily, you felt a weight lift off your shoulders. You pictured mothering nurses and you felt whatever was wrong would soon go away. But you thought further and got other ideas. You tried to imagine what it would be like and how you'd be treated. A million questions shot through your brain. But you were reluctant to ask them because the doctor was so testy. He wouldn't talk unless you insisted. And, if you insisted, all he did was try to calm you down. That made you wonder why he wouldn't answer, why he was so reluctant. Was he afraid you would ask more and more questions, that you would find out what kind of a place you were going to? You kept thinking that way and started to believe it. They didn't want you to know because you might just refuse. Then what would they do? You were more than they could handle, so it was important you go to the hospital. Reaching that conclusion made you feel you were in the presence of enemies. But you weren't convinced. It was only a possibility. It could have been your imagination. That's why you launched no protest. But you kept wondering about the hospital. You had never been to such a place.

At the entrance, you expected a gate with a guard checking passes. You thought the grounds would be enclosed by a high brick wall. The inside would be flat and open with bleak buildings which housed the patients. Inside them, everything would be white: the uniforms, the floor and ceiling, the walls, everything! It would all be white and immaculate with an odor of ammonia. There would be rows of metal doors with small windows and iron bars that kept the desperate and deranged. Arms would be stretching and grabbing for anything, anything in reach. Hair, an arm or an ear perhaps. Hands would be contorted in attempts to seize and tear. There would be a lot of howling and screaming. They would be tearing their hair and smashing their heads. The only thing to quiet them would be food which they would devour like animals. And that's where you'd be: locked in a little room where you'd be reduced to an animal. Henrietta would come and find you mad! A terrifying vision. Then, it was unbearable. You were on the verge of leaping from the car. You felt certain it was coming. But no, you thought, it can't be like that. That's absurd. They wouldn't take you there. It's just your paranoia talking. Then you slowed down your breathing and wiped away the sweat. You reminded yourself nothing had been decided, this was just a meeting to discuss your problems. If you appeared coherent and in control, he would probably prescribe some medication and that would be that. On the other hand, if you jumped from the car, you would have to come back sooner or later. Where else could you go? Start a new life somewhere else? That would he crazy! No, you'd have to return. When you did, it would be the same or worse. So the best thing to do was relax. After all, there was nothing seriously wrong with you. You had gotten a little upset, that's all. Everybody does. You were no different. It was impossible you could be hospitalized. Preposterous! You certainly didn't need that you were convinced. The idea anybody was against you seemed ludicrous. You felt completely safe and secure. You even began to feel happy and euphoric. In fact, interspersed in your thoughts was an awareness you were smiling, remember? Yes, you kept catching yourself doing it. Then, suddenly, I guess because you felt so much better, you had a craving for ice cream. I don't know why. It just came. It was overwhelming. Nothing would have given you greater pleasure. So you suggested it to the others. They both looked over their shoulders wearily. You could see they hadn't thought much of the idea and they were confused by your sudden bliss. You were too.

But you were just at the entrance, so that was that. You turned off the road and started up a hill. There was a sign at the corner which you couldn't see well enough to read. But there was nothing else. No fence and no guard. It was much different from what you expected. That was a relief. The road led to a building that looked like a mansion. There was a sign in the courtyard which was the only indication it wasn't. It read: ADMINISTRATION BUILDING. You parked the car there and went inside.

The lobby was full of paintings. You immediately went to look at them because you wanted to appear interested in such things, cultured, a man of the world to the psychiatrist. That would demoralize the others and make them look like fools you hoped. So you stepped toward the first for a better look. Then to another. They went back many years. So you got some history. That would look good you thought. But the doctor called you before you got far. "What are you doing?" he demanded. It seemed obvious. "Looking at paintings," you said. "Why don't you come and sit down?" he beckoned as if your behavior were odd. He was quite adamant that you obey him. You could read that from his tone. So you did as he asked. You didn't want to get into an altercation. Not then. Not there. It was crucial not to. From your chair, however, you continued looking. While you were doing that, Henrietta sat on a couch which faced your chair. She stared at you when she thought you didn't notice. You kept avoiding her gaze hoping she'd stop. She didn't, however. The doctor went to the switchboard operator who was sitting in a booth. He introduced himself and explained why he had come. She said he'd have to wait and invited him to sit down. He did so next to Henrietta.

You sat silently for several minutes before the psychiatrist finally came in. He was surprisingly young. You expected an older man with a calm and cultivated manner. But he seemed youthful although the wrinkles were there if you looked close enough. His suit was rumpled and he appeared very tired. He went straight to the doctor, introduced himself and said when he heard his name, "Yes, yes. You've been here before. I'm sure I've met you." "Yes," was the answer, "sometime ago." "Oh yes, I do remember your patient. How's he doing these days?" "Fine," was the reply, "as far as I know." "Good,

good," the psychiatrist said and motioned you to follow as he turned and started out. As you walked, however, it occurred to him he neglected to speak to you (Henrietta and you) because he excused himself and told you his name. You responded in kind. That gave you an opening to make the desired impression. With that in mind, you commented on the building saying it reminded you of a mansion. That seemed to make him leery. One brow went up inquisitively as he scrutinized your expression closely. You smiled politely. He answered distantly that there were eight buildings on the grounds one of which was the original structure. That was the one you were in. It had been a private home. The other seven were services that had been built over the years, he said. Then he turned away. You couldn't judge what impression you made. He answered perfunctorily and seemed anxious not to talk. That could have been because you caught him off guard. He probably wasn't expecting as lucid a person as you. But you weren't sure. And you weren't going to persist. The best thing to do was keep to yourself. You didn't want to taint the proceedings by appearing too eager. So you walked on and not another word was said.

You passed large doors with brass name plates attached. They bore the names of psychiatrists. Looking at them caused a morose feeling to come. You felt somber suddenly, remember? I'm not sure why. Perhaps it reminded you of your father's grave. You often thought of it during the weeks before going there. You wanted to take the boys and tend the site; water it, rake the leaves and plant some flowers. But Henrietta wouldn't hear of it. She thought it was bad to do something so morbid. You thought it would do no harm. Maybe you're wrong. I don't know. You went yourself, anyway, in spite of her. It must have been the summer that put it in your mind. You wanted your father comfortable and cool. His grave was very dusty and dry. Then, as you walked, you were reminded of that. It gave you the same melancholy feeling.

You continued on, but, still, no one spoke. You wished they would have. It would have been easier. The silence was tense. You stared at the floor for lack of a better place. You could see yourself in the linoleum with the others surrounding you, remember? You looked like a prisoner.

You finally came to his office. It was unremarkable. Just a desk and chairs, some books and a plant. That was all. You sat down where he indicated. By then, you felt tired. You could hardly stay awake. Your body was like lead. All you wanted was rest. I suppose it was the medication. Be that as it may, you couldn't. You had to see it through. It would look bad to refuse. So you tried as best you could. You settled down and got comfortable, then waited to see what the psychiatrist would do. He was fumbling with some forms. Then he said he'd like to ask some questions and get your signature on some things. That wasn't a short period. In fact you went through your entire history year by year. Everything from where you were born, to what insurance you had, to your allergies. It was exhausting, but you finally got through it. That's when they started in. It began with the psychiatrist. He said, "I'd like to make an observation if I could"—You're crazy!—"What's that?" you asked. "Well," he said, "after going over some of these forms and hearing your responses, I'd say you present a picture of an apprehensive man"—Crazy!—"So?" you said, "wouldn't you be in my place?" "We're not talking about me," he replied, "we're talking about you." "What about me?" "The question is what can be done?" "About what?" you asked—Crazy, Wamblie!— "About your fears." "What makes you think I've got fears?" you asked. He chuckled and said he said fears from what you told him, particularly, about work. You didn't answer, but shrugged slightly. "Mr. Wamblie?" he called. "What?" "I was asking what can be done?" "You tell me," you said. "I don't know," he said. "Well," you said, "I don't either. Maybe I just need a rest." He quickly agreed and smiled. "I think it would do you good to rest," he said adding it seemed you were under more pressure than you could bear. That's when you grasped what he was driving at and you, to make your position clear, said, "I don't want to be admitted"—You won't!—"You sound scared," the psychiatrist said—Won't let them force you!—You explained you weren't afraid, but you didn't want to stay there—Don't let them, Wamblie!—He asked Henrietta how she felt obviously looking for support. She said she didn't want you to stay either (anything but), but she thought you should, then, come home and go back to work secure in the knowledge you could handle it. "It's better than coming home now when the chances are you'd fail," she said. That disgusted you. They were ganging up. Plotting! I'll give an example. It was obvious they agreed you should stay. And if they agreed you should stay, your vote being the only dissent, the reason for that would be obvious: because you were sick. The psychiatrist assured you you could leave when you wanted and said he imagined you would like it perhaps more than you thought. Then he went into a long explanation of the attributes of the place. You thought it over with them looking on, waiting and watching, watching and waiting. You didn't want to stay, but you could see no alternative given how things had progressed. You felt Henrietta would be so leery and suspicious, living with her would be hell. Besides, as long as you could leave with the hospital's consent, those around you would soon relax in the knowledge you were sound, mentally. So you said yes, reluctantly, thinking you'd be home in less than a week. It was the stupidest thing you've ever done, but you had no way to know that then.

The psychiatrist pulled another form from the drawer and handed it to you. At the top it read: APPLICATION FOR CARE ON A CONDITIONAL VOLUNTARY BASIS. He drew an X where you were to sign and handed you his pen. Then the doctor signed in the space marked witness. "Good," he said when you finished. "Now," he went on, "I want to get a few things clear so, later, when I make out a report, it'll be completely accurate." You shook your head in vague compliance. You wanted it over. You were feeling extremely tense. But what could you do? The psychiatrist asked what brought you there and indicated you should answer—*You're crazy!*—"What brings me here?" you repeated not having understood exactly what he was after. "Yes," he said, "could you tell me why you've come, please?"—*Crazy, Wamblie!*—You told him it was the doctor's idea. You didn't know what else to say. "I beg your pardon?" he said leaning forward to hear. "The doctor, the doctor here," you repeated as you indicated him. "You see," the doctor started in, "he's been"— But the psychiatrist cut him off. "That's all right," he said, "I'd like to hear what Mr. Wamblie has to say if you don't mind. So, why are you here?" he asked again—*He's crazy!*—The doctor was embarrassed, but didn't say a word—*It's them!*—You tried to answer the question—*They're after you!*—"Well," you began, "I woke up last night...tonight, I mean, in the middle of the night"—*After you!*—"Actually, I had never been to sleep," you told him—*Their fault!*—"So I went downstairs and tried to relax"—*They brought you*—"What happened then?" he asked— *So don't trust them*—"Well," you said, "then my wife came down and found me"—*It's my husband*—"Yes, and then what?"—*They've conspired!*—"Then she got upset," you said— *He's worse than the other day!*—"And why was that?" he asked—*He's pacing*—"Why don't you ask her?" you said— *And talking strangely*—"Because I'm asking you," he answered—*And he's got a gun!*—"Well, I don't know," you said—*Yes, a gun!*—"The gun, Darling," Henrietta cut in, "tell him about the gun"—*Careful!*—"What's this about a gun?" the psychiatrist asked—*Look out!*—"Well," you said, "I don't exactly know"—*Careful, Wamblie!*—You were tense—*Careful!* —I guess you were having an anxiety attack—*Look out!*—You were shaky, sweaty and breathing a little hard. "That's all?"—*Don't say too much*—"Were your thoughts racy?" the psychiatrist asked—*Out of control!*—"And was it then you got the gun?"—*His wife found him pacing*—"No," you said, "not then"—*And he had a gun by the door*—"When?" he asked—*A shotgun*—"Before that," you said—*What's your advice?*—"When before that?"—*Get him medicated*—"Before I started pacing"—*Then bring him in*—"And what did you do with it?"—*He's extremely paranoid*—"I walked around with it." "Carried it in your arms?" "Yes"—He knows—"Why was that?"—Knows everything—"Because it made me feel better"—They told him on the phone—"And what happened then?"—He knows you're nuts—"I put it near the door"—Knows you're crazy—"Is that when your wife came down?"—*What are you doing?*—"Yes," you said—Knows!—"And she called your doctor who suggested you come here?"—Who called him—"Is that right?"—Who knows—"What?"—Knows!—"She called the doctor who suggested you come here?"—Knows!—"Why are you hammering!"—Knows!—"You know the answer!"—*Bring him in*—"What makes you say that?"—*Soon!*—"You told him!"—*Right away!*—"I don't follow you, Mr. Wamblie"—*And medicate him*—"You talked on the phone!"—*Is he dangerous?*—"Darling, calm down"—*Threatening to use a gun*—"You're all against me!"—*On himself?*—"Sweetheart, that's ridiculous"—*On who then?*—"You want to lock me up!"—Them—"We're not against you, Darling"—*Forces, he said*—"Yes you are"—*Out to get him*—"You seem very worried about what others might do"—They told him—"You know the answer to that"—Told him!—"No I don't"—Told him!—"Well, it's YES!" you screamed. "Okay, okay. Let's get back on the track," he said. "Now, what happened when the doctor came?" "Nothing." "Nothing?" he repeated. "By the time he got there, my attack was over." "I see," the psychiatrist said before asking why you had gotten the gun—Say nothing—

You told him you didn't know, you really couldn't explain it. He asked why you couldn't explain. "I can't," you told him, "I don't know why"—Can't, Wamblie—"Well you must have some reason"—Can't!—You told him you didn't—Can't!—He asked if you thought you had a problem—You're crazy—You said, "I do probably, yes"—Crazy!—"Everybody's got some"—Crazy, Wamblie!—"But don't you think it's strange," he said, "to walk around with a shotgun for no apparent reason?"—Shotgun!— You said there was a reason, but you couldn't explain it—He knows—He asked what it was—You never said that—You told him again you couldn't convey it—But he knows—He asked you if you knew Henrietta was worried—It's a plot—"Yes," you said—They're against you—"Why should she be worried?" —Plotting!—"Because I've been upset!" you snapped—Against you—"No need to get that way," he said. "Yes there is!" you insisted and began to shake with rage. "Calm down, Mr. Wamblie! It's all right." "I'm leaving!" you yelled, "I'm leaving!" Then you got up to go. But you were disoriented by then. So when they stopped you, you didn't resist because you couldn't. "Stay here, sweetheart," Henrietta urged. "Should I?" you asked in confusion. "Yes," she said. But you had another impulse to run. That time, the psychiatrist caught you by the arm saying, "You've already signed in, so, if you try to leave, you'll be stopped." You looked at him apprehensively. All you could say is, "Really?" before you fell back in your chair exhausted. The psychiatrist then made a call explaining he had admitted a patient who was not in the best condition.

Within a few minutes, two men appeared to take you to a unit. They were young, dressed not in whites, but in regular clothes. Resigned to going with them, you said good night to Henrietta and grabbed hold of her hand. In fact you couldn't let go. I don't know why. Your hand just wouldn't do what you wanted. She said you were hurting her, panicked and tried to break away, but she couldn't. They had to pry your hand off her. Then they brought you to another building and showed you a room you could sleep in. Which you did for the first time in days, like a rock, because of the medication.

Coda

What a picture! It's not a very pretty one. You couldn't imagine it if you hadn't been through it. That would be too difficult. Perhaps, someday, you will, however; again go through it I mean. You may scoff at that, but it is a possibility and, therefore, something to consider. After all, it happened once. Why not again? No, you're not immune. But I'm talking as if it's going to happen. That could be wrong. But let's, for the sake of argument, assume it does happen again. Then, when becomes the question. It could happen right this instant or tomorrow. The day before it happened to you, it was the furthest thing from your mind. So it's not inconceivable that, tomorrow, you'll be put away again. It's something to think about. It's hard to imagine, but be wary. It could happen and not necessarily because you're sick. Not that I say everyone in hospitals is a victim of conspiracy and no one's condition warrants it. I certainly wouldn't imply that. There are so many people who need it, who are dangerous, who could hurt someone, but you're not one of them. Neither are many of the people there since there's two ways to go: because you're sick and need it or because it is convenient for someone else, someone who has the power. It's that you were a victim of as well as many other people. Like Nixon, for example. I wouldn't be surprised to see him in an institution as crazy as that may sound. It could happen. Believe me! Crazier things have occurred. Who knows what powers forced him out? And, if they ruined him, they could ruin anyone. Including you, so don't think you're above it, not yet. But I don't want to upset you. That wasn't my intent. I only want to warn you. That's why I've said all this. To tell you to always be on guard. Keep a vigil, never let it stop because, tomorrow, it could be you, again. But enough of that.

You're feeling tired. I think it's time you slept. But I'm glad your first attempt failed. Had it been otherwise, you would be cleaning the filth, but you wouldn't have explained the situation and warned yourself as you've done. That's important. Besides, you enjoyed it; primarily because it was coherent from the beginning, notwithstanding a few small lapses. You're not always able to control your thoughts and it's easy for your explanations to get muddled. It's a sign things are better with you. Ha, ha, ha!

One last thing. I don't comment on this out of anger, but I think you should know I know what you think. I could tell when you laughed. Is it because of that silly smirk you feel such repugnance for yourself? Well, after all, you can't help it if it's there. I already told you and...

But...but, enough, really. I didn't mean to be hostile. I apologize. It's just you're tired and getting cranky. Let's leave it at that. I've been rambling on all night and, now, it's almost dawn. That'll make it harder to sleep, at least for you. And you have to clean this place tomorrow. But there's time for that. You'll sleep until noon, make a trip to the store and stop for breakfast (or dinner since it'll be dinner time by then) and come back and get to work. And, if you don't finish, you'll have the next day to complete it. Well, good night—morning, I should say. Sleep well.

Movement II

Introduction

Who's there?....Who's that?....I can't tell!....Are you dreaming?....I can't tell!....And it's been like this all night. Or is it day? Yes, it's day. I didn't know because the shades were down. You pulled them down this morning. But what time is it now? Late afternoon? You've lost all track. You've had no sleep. You couldn't pass off into sleep. So you paced instead. I couldn't stop you. You heard voices. That's what they were, not real. I thought they were real, but they weren't. Only your imagination. I can see that now. You've been pacing since last night. I couldn't stop you. I thought it would be awful to stop you. I thought you'd die if I stopped you. And the voices were plaguing you. They were telling you what to do. Nothing pleasant. Only bizarre things, violent things to yourself. I can't go into it. It's too insane. But for a while, you were listening. I thought they weren't coming from you. I thought they were from outside you. I thought it was the forces. That's why you fought them off by pacing and concentrating on other things, as well as you could. And, perhaps, it was the forces. I believe they exist although that's why they call me paranoid. But I don't care. I know you heard something, at least I think you did. It's sometimes hard to distinguish. It's easy to confuse the thought of a voice and a voice. That's been your problem. But whether they created a voice or caused you to think it is

72

unimportant. What matters is they did it, they're plaguing you and they won't stop. But, then again, they have stopped. For an instant they've stopped. I hear nothing now....Oh well.

You're in such a sorry state. But it's been a bad night—day I mean. Well, night too, for that matter, and day too as well. If I wanted to keep going I could. I could go back a long way because the whole thing's been sorry from the start. Everything about you is sorry, everything about your life. How could it be worse? But, then again, it could be. It always could be worse. Not that you see how. But take comfort in knowing it could be because I'm sure it could.

Ah! What are you saying? It's all probably nothing. You're making a mountain out of a molehill again. You've been accused of doing that on many an occasion. And perhaps you do. There's probably nothing so bad as you make out. On the other hand, you don't want to get caught unaware, not ever again. You don't want to be expecting the best and get the worst. That's already happened as I've explained. But it won't happen again. You won't let it. And how will you avoid it? By simply expecting the worst. I suppose that's what you do and why you do it. If you expect the worst, you'll never be disappointed. Things can only be better than you thought. Unless you miscalculate and something worse happens than you ever anticipated. That could take place. And that's why I worry so much. It's because much worse things than you expected have happened. You can't win. What I've just said is proof. I've spent the last few minutes convincing you you're too pessimistic, but all I've done is convince you you're not pessimistic enough. You must learn to be more pessimistic and see the deepest potential for things to be rotten. Only then will you avoid disappointment, only then will you find things better than you thought. So you were right in the first place. I think. But there's your problem. You can't think. You don't know what to think or how to think it. You can't tell what's good from what's bad, what's harmful from what's not. Consequently, you run around in circles, probably always have unwittingly. But that's being far too negative. You're prone to self pity tonight—day I mean. It's the result of going too long without sleep. I guess you can attribute it to that as well as anything. It's the best explanation I can think of anyway. A few days without sleep is enough to boggle anyone's brain. And yours is certainly boggled. The thoughts are flying. They go where they go despite your wishes. But after you rest, that'll change. I know it will. Your whole outlook will improve. But how can you sleep? You're mind won't relax. Every time you rest, your thoughts race and you have to pace to slow them down. It's the only way. And you get tireder and tireder. You can feel it in your bones. Your limbs ache for rest. They're tired of being tense. But what can you do? You're mind won't give in. It won't let go. It's a rebel. And here it is Saturday afternoon and you've done nothing, made no progress toward getting the place clean. You're not going to be in any condition for work. And what will you do then? Kill yourself perhaps!

But you didn't mean that. You're just spiting yourself. You're trying to get even because you're so obviously pessimistic. And punishing yourself is a good feeling because you deserve it. It's just. But you don't mean what you say. At least I hope you don't. I hope you don't want to take your life, my life. But one is never sure. It could be your strongest desire. You've often been close to it. Sometimes it seems the loveliest thing that could happen. And what would they say if you did? Who would miss you? Your wife? Your children? Your friends? Would they feel bad, guilty, or responsible? Probably not. They probably wouldn't care. After all, what difference do you make? It wouldn't change their lives a bit. Except they'd have to ask themselves why you'd rather die than live. And as much as they asked, they'd never get an answer. They'd never know the answer because you couldn't tell them. So they'd have to live with that, that abyss of understanding. It would be a cruel thing to do, a cruel thing. You wouldn't want to be cruel. But, then again, who knows? Death could rear it's ugly head and drive you to end it, if that's possible. And it is possible because you have a gun. You bought it on the way with just that thought in mind, in case you wanted to obey the forces, in case you wanted to do what's right or be able to at any rate. Should you check to see it's there in your case? Perhaps not. That could influence you to use it. Who knows when the impulse could arise? But, on the other hand, what if it did? If you carried it through, you wouldn't be bothered even if it were wrong. You wouldn't know. You'd he gone. Destroyed! That would be the point: to end consciousness and cease this misery. But there's no guarantee that would be the outcome. No way to know what lies ahead. If you knew it were nothing, nothing but the end, nothing but death, you would pull the trigger in an instant. It's not knowing that keeps you from doing it. But how long can you cower in the face of destiny? Someday you will die. Does it really matter when? Dying is where life leads, so why not go there? Because it might be too soon? You must not forget to consider that. Besides, you're not ready to do it. You're too unsure. You're just as content in this room as you would be dead. At least I think that's true. But there's no way to know without trying both states. So you won't find out, not now. Maybe today, maybe tomorrow, but not at this instant. You haven't got the will. A few moments ago you did. All evening you've felt you could. You could have gotten up, stuck the gun in your mouth and shot it. It was an overwhelming desire or so you thought back there. You didn't let on that it was, but it was. I know it was. You were acting as if it had gone, but it hadn't. But you got through it by means of a stronger impulse. I guess that means you should go on living. But we'll see what the future brings. As long as we're alive that is.

Now, since we've decided to spare you, what must we do now? I guess prepare for work? What else matters? You must get the place clean and be ready for work. That means sleep. But why are you being tormented with insomnia? There must be a reason because there always is. But I can't see any. I mean what is there to be gained from such an experience?....Ah! The answer just struck me! (Or one plausible answer. I mean nothing is for sure.) You haven't been taking medication. Perhaps that's why you're so run down. Let's see, how long has it been? I believe the last dose was yesterday noon. It was just before you left. There. You're not so disoriented. And now, it's late Saturday, so you've missed three doses. Three doses a day, morning, noon and night is your quota. So maybe you've missed enough to throw you off. I don't know. But it could be the reason you're in such bad shape. But, to correct it, all you have to do is swallow some pills. They're right there in your valise. It's a miracle that's all there is to it. It simplifies things considerably. That's the beauty of it. But why are you allowing me to go on? Why are you not up? Why are you not taking them? Perhaps for some unconscious reason? That's what a psychiatrist would say. You're going on as a means of avoiding the act. That's simple enough and perhaps true. But it doesn't answer the question: why do you want to avoid it? So the question is what is the answer? That's always the question and, since there is no answer, the question will persist. It always has and always will. So it's insanity to try to answer it. Yet, we continue. Unless we happened to find one. In that case, we would stop. There would be no reason to go on. But, this way, there is. So go on you shall even though it's futile. Ironically, knowing it's futile is exactly why you will though, isn't it? I mean knowing you won't find answers is a comfort. You can proceed knowing the outcome and be completely secure. Isn't that a comfort? But here you are at it again. Going on I mean. You must stop. It only leads to doing it more, but answers nothing. So start again. You're not taking your medication because (it can't be escaped. Questions must be asked), because of time. You don't know the time, not for sure. You know it approximately. You always know if it's dark or light, morning or evening, afternoon or night. But you don't know the hour, not unless there's a clock. That's been going on for a while. I'm not sure when, but I know it was while you were there. Around that time, you stopped your watch, you stopped it as a reaction to convention. The doctors thought it was crazy. Not because you did it, but because of your reasons. They thought they were insane. They never told you that of course. They wouldn't tell patients what they really thought. That would be considered unethical. No, they never told a patient they were crazy. They just thought it. They had it written all over their faces under a veneer of honesty. And if a patient inquired, they implied they're imagining things. But I could see what was in their eyes. And I knew that psychiatric smirk of their's. And I knew they wrote it in your chart, that you're crazy I mean. Not in those terms of course. They used more scientific jargon. But you're letting your bitterness show. Get off this now. They really weren't so bad. I mean it was you, not them. But that's enough.

Now, where was I? The question I was addressing was time. At least I remember that much. Why you stopped keeping track of it, that was it. It was because you got sick of ticking off the seconds in tiny little blocks. An appointment here at this time, an appointment there at that time. Everything ran on the clock; a mechanical way to conceive of time. For you, it got to be the only way. But in the hospital, you found yourself longing to pass it without being so aware. I mean when you were a child spending afternoons in a field or the woods you could feel the afternoon grow into evening; the approach of dusk as the planet revolved marking the passage of time. It was such a soothing memory you wanted to bring it back, you

77

wanted to feel its passage again, the same way. It goes slower like that and it has more meaning, at least for you. But in their infinite wisdom, they wanted it to be measured and they called that understanding. That was understanding time to them, but not to you. To you, it was absurd! You rejected that flatly. So they called you crazy! But it was sane. So all you can do is never, never, never, never, NEVER start your watch again. End of it!

Now, what caused you to go through all that? I can't remember....Let's see now, what was it?....Was it medication? That's right it was, wasn't it? You don't know when to take your medication because you don't know the precise time. But do you need to know it precisely? The dosage is three times a day: morning, noon and night. It's late afternoon now, probably evening. And it must be Saturday because yesterday was Friday, the day of your release. It's not possible you've missed a day. That much time you can't have missed. So you've skipped three doses. You should take one now and stick to your schedule. But why did I think it was time that stopped you? I guess it was another stall rather than an answer to the question: why are you not taking medication? Things can be illusive if you study them enough. Here you've tricked yourself again. You pursued an answer which led to the question. But what, then, is the answer? There must be one although it's not our fate to find it. But what can it be? (You pursue this knowing you'll fail, knowing you'll be led to the beginning and not to the end. After all, you'll always end with a question, not an answer. Accept that. If it were otherwise, you'd be hallucinating. It wouldn't be real. And so it is with all of them. It's our nature to pursue and our fate never to find. So again: why are you not taking it?) I wonder. I'll get bored if I don't. Besides, there's nothing else to do....I've got it! You don't because you don't want to. You don't believe in it. Now you're on the right track. Either that or you're fooling yourself into thinking so. You don't believe in it! You don't believe in it! You don't believe in it! You established that long ago, didn't you, back at the hospital in the beginning? You took it because you were forced to, but it was always against your will. And you were stupid enough to say so, to protest. And why was that stupid? Because, to them, it proved your insanity, your resistance to getting better. To them, it indicated you were trying to stay insane. Absurdity of absurdities! It was the exact opposite. It was precisely because you wanted to improve you protested taking their pills or shots when you refused the pills. Isn't that clear? No. Doesn't that make sense? No. Or can't you at least believe it does? No. Well then, let me go over how it happened. In the beginning, you met another patient. Yes, and he was a young man. You got along with him well. Not at first, actually, but let's leave that for now. He was a professional patient of sorts having been in and out all his life and was grounded not at all in reality. In fact he was crazy and, therefore, sane. (That logic is learned through a stay in the place.) And he brought you some enlightening realizations, realizations that turned you away from their treatment. And what did he say to sway you? That medication is a way to change behavior. It's a method to exert control, make you conform, make you into what they want instead of what you are. And who, in their right mind, would submit to that? No one, of course, unless they're crazy. Or forced. So doctors are the enemy. Next, he said, they'll be putting it in the water. Then we'll all walk around without our souls. It might sound crazy, but there's more truth in it than you'd like to think. After all, they do it to hospital patients, so why not the public? Why not avoid these problems in the beginning? That's preventive medicine. I know that sounds strange. In fact that's what you said when he first explained it. But the more you considered it, the more sense it made. You began to see it's part of a larger conspiracy. Then you realized he was right. So you protested and were labeled crazy, resistant and belligerent and were forced, with a needle, to take the stuff. That taught you to obey. Or appear to. But now? Now, it's different, there's no one to force you. Now, you can do as you please. And what do you please? Not to take it! I mean you don't believe it's anything more than a form of control. In fact you know it. I can't say how. I can't prove it. But I know you know it, just know it, that's all. And you will not budge! So much for that.

Now, the question becomes how will you get the rest you need? There's probably no clear answer, probably no answer at all. So don't trick yourself into looking. You're too tired and you've suffered too much. Yet, you can't get away. You can't sleep. So what else could occupy your mind? Perhaps your feet. That could be a diversion especially since they're soaked. Your slippers are sopping because of the puddle. You should clean it up. You would if you had a mop in fact. I mean you've been traipsing through it all night without knowing—afternoon I mean. But that's not all that's wrong. This place needs to be sprayed. It needs fumigation to kill the roaches that are becoming bolder and bolder and bolder. One just ran across your foot in fact. I just saw it. And they think nothing of crawling in the sink. And the pipe is leaking more and more and more. It's becoming a constant drip. So mopping up will do no good, not unless the leak is stopped. But you know nothing about plumbing. Nothing about blood in the veins or water in the pipes. If only you could leave this room. But you can't. You've tried and found it's futile like everything else in life. There's no escape and no point in trying. These walls are your walls. Everything, for you, exists here. It's where your life happens. What happens here, happens to you, at least for a while. I'm sorry to keep adding that, but I have no choice. I have to to convince you it could change. But, then again, it won't because it never does. You're destined to be here forever. Or until you die. Here with all this chaos. You won't be ready for work. Work will come and you'll be looking for excuses, reasons to explain why you haven't changed, haven't progressed, have found nothing new but the same old thing....Ha, ha!

I've lost all track of what I'm saying. I'm becoming more and more delirious. I can't develop any forward movement. It's all sinking in the mud with the twine breaking thread by thread....

What's that scattered all over your robe? Dead skin? It's flaking again. It's a condition, like so many you have, that developed while you were away. The skin around your nose and eyes cracks and breaks profusely. They prescribed some salve to stick it together, but you don't use it since it came from them. But the flaking makes you look like a freak. That, combined with the smile, causes people to stare at you. That's why you don't enjoy going out. But there's nothing to be done. These things must be faced. It's your fate for some unknown reason.

God, but I'm morose tonight! I mean why try to pretend? I don't want to admit my level perhaps, but just because I'm in terrible straits is no reason to plague you with my despair. But then, what about honesty? I'm low. There. That wasn't so bad. No. The question is how much do you need to be protected? I feel as bad as anyone could. Does that bother you? My life is more than you can handle. Can you accept that? That is, if I include all the things that have happened. If I view it as my existence here, perhaps it isn't so bad. It's a vacuum here. Except for you, who knows what goes on? If you're the only one, it can't be bad because it makes no difference, not to anyone but you and me. And I'm of no consequence except as I affect others. I mean if I affect no one, I don't matter. I could kill myself and it wouldn't make a difference. The universe would go on. See how low I am? Things couldn't be worse late on a...Saturday is it? Afternoon? Whatever. Things couldn't be worse except physically. And no physical pain could match what I've suffered. I can take satisfaction in that. At least I know what pain is. I'm almost used to it. It may be to the point where I'd be lost without it. I mean there'd be nothing to fill the emptiness. Now that's a revelation! I can say freely now I'm as low as anyone can be. And why? Because I like things as they are, otherwise I'd change them (which I've done without success). But I must play a part in it somehow. So I'm responsible to some degree. Burdening myself, consequently, gives me great satisfaction. It's a welcome change if it lasts. But nothing ever does. That we can count on...or, rather, we can count on what we count on being a myth. Actually, it can work either way. If you count on something lasting, it'll probably die. And if you count on something dying, it'll probably last. And so it goes. We tell ourselves we're masters of the planet when, in fact, we're nothing more than slaves. How stupid we are when you...you...

Now why has everything gone black? Have you died or fallen asleep? Or blown a fuse? A fuse! That must be it! You have to replace a fuse. But how do you do that? You don't know where the box is. And it could be circuit breakers, in which case you're in luck since you have no fuses. But again the question: where is the box? I don't remember seeing it. Up near the ceiling maybe?....Nothing! You've probably blown a fuse in your head. Except I have no circuit breakers in my—whoops! The lights are on. On again, off again isn't that what they say? Well, that's good. That solves that. It was a power failure. I never thought of that. But, then again, maybe it wasn't. I mean they've gone off again. But what can this be? You're going crazy like this. You must stop all this wondering. You should get onto something solid and forget about the lights. That's why they told you to think in concrete terms and, I suppose, that's right. Otherwise, they wouldn't have said it. So, since you can't sleep and can't stop thinking, perhaps you should go on. At least there's something to hold on to in that. Some foundation to pile block upon block upon block into a structure. I already told you how you got there. Now, I'll tell you what the place was like before you get the gun and do it.

Exposition

The first day you were slow to wake up. But they provided help. Nobody you had seen before because the shift changed, so you knew no one. Nevertheless, the help came in the form of an attendant, a big man, who was calling your name. But you didn't answer. You were too tired although you heard him vaguely through your drowsiness. But you had gotten to bed only an hour before after a heavy dose of medication. Besides, it was a hot day and the sun was pouring in. You weren't in the mood to bask in it as if you had no problems. No, you wanted to bury your head under the sheets when the attendant threw open the curtains especially since the room was so awful. It smelled of the last patient and that was made worse by the humidity. And it was cramped like a box with four small walls. The front had a door which led to a hall full of other doors opening on other boxes. Two sides had a cot, a desk and chair and a chest of drawers in that order. There were also two closets. The fourth had a window and a screen which was locked so there'd be no escape; as if you'd try by going out the window. Consequently, fresh air was not available without asking and often waiting; something you did a lot of. But that was the room. Your new quarters. Your office, home and club. It wasn't very pleasant; especially your side. Your roommate's was very clean and neat, but yours was empty and dirty. The night before, you had put nothing away since you had nothing but your clothes. You hadn't known you'd be staying. A nurse said the rooms were usually cleaned, but they hadn't gotten around to it in your case. "But," she said, "you'll be cleaning it yourself from here on out, so you might as well get used to it." You didn't appreciate that very much because the place was filthy. There was dust under the cot and on the closet shelf (which had only one bent hanger) and the drawers of the chest were lined with faded newsprint. I guess the previous patient didn't care much about his quarters. Your roommate's side was nicer by comparison. There were pictures of his family on a dust mat on his desk, remember? And sitting on his chest was a glass of something containing a comb and brush, an electric shaver sitting square with the corner and a half empty bottle of hair cream. He was always so precise.

Anyway, that's where you woke up and what you woke up to. And, as much as you acted asleep by pulling the covers over your head, the attendant persisted. "Wake up! Come on! Wake up! It's time for medication!" He wouldn't give up, but you still didn't move. After all, you could determine what time to wake up. But he was growing impatient. You could feel that. "Come on, I said, get up. Medication time is 7 a.m. The nurse is waiting. So get up!" This began to wear on you. You certainly wouldn't succumb to coercion, not if you could help it. You, therefore, didn't move. But he took your arm and yanked it. "Come on! Come on!" he said. But you wrenched free and told him to leave. "So you are awake," he said. Then he patted you on the back more gently. "Come on now," he said again, "you've got to take your medication." You flatly said you didn't. "You and every other patient," he said, "but you've all got to take it." "I don't," you told him and again buried your head. "Look," he said, "I might as well tell you, if you don't take medication, I've got to go get the nurse and she'll give you a shot. So, unless you'd rather have a shot, get up." "Well I might as well tell you," you said, "I'm dead tired and I'm NOT getting up!" "I know you are and I sympathize with that, but all I'm asking is you take your medication. Then you can sleep all you want." "No!" you yelled. "All right," he said, "I'm going for the nurse." And, when you didn't move, he walked out in a huff. Then, I don't know why, you thought the better of your actions and sat up to call him back. But nothing came out. Your voice just cracked. So you listened to his footsteps fade and thought about what had happened—*He won't get up*—It was a silly battle over nothing and you knew you'd be the one to suffer—*Why?*—Yet, you couldn't give in —*Because he doesn't want to*—Even when he returned—*We'll see about that!*—Something wouldn't let you—*You'll come down then?*—While he was gone, you thought you would, but you couldn't—*Yes*—"The nurse is on her way, so this is it," he said as he sauntered back in the room. "Will you get up?" You didn't speak or move. You no longer felt belligerent. You felt little of anything in fact. It was like being a child who wants nothing but to suck his thumb and stare blankly at the wall. "Okay," he said, "we'll wait." Then he got the chair and sat down—*You and you come with me*—That period, though it seemed long, was short because the nurse came promptly as billed. She wasn't what you imagined, however, not a middle aged woman, stiff and rigged with a tightly pinned bonnet. No, she was young and very attractive wearing blue jeans and a purple blouse with the tails tied at the midriff. She had brunette hair pulled back by a scarf and she carried a tray with a cup, a pitcher and a syringe laying on it. Though beautiful, she was brisk and had a look of violent impatience. You remember that well like so many things from that period. Yes. "What's the problem here?" she asked—What's the problem?—You spoke up and said, "I don't want any drugs"—You won't take them—You saw, over her shoulder, another attendant leaning against the door—So don't give in—So there were two men, now, ready to persuade you—Don't!—The nurse replied, "You have to take your medication"—Don't let them—"No!" you said—Don't!—I don't know why—Because they'll hurt you—Probably out of anger—So don't give in—You don't like to be told—Don't let them force you—"I realize you got in late last night," she said and sat on the edge of your cot, "and I know this was your first night here and I hate to see it start this way. We're here to help you, but we need your cooperation. Now, will you please take your pills?"—No!—But you didn't want to—Refuse!—And you reiterated that politely—Now!—"You'll just have to trust us," she said—Refuse!—"Now, if you won't take your medication" —Now!—"I'll just have to give you a shot"—Refuse!—"I can't spend any more time"—Now!—"I have other patients to worry about"—Before it's too late—Then another attendant appeared making it clear the choice wasn't yours—*Be ready to restrain him*—So you gave in and said you would take them—*That'll get him to do it*—Then you snatched up the cup and gulped down the pills. "Need water?" she asked. "No!" you replied. A moment passed and a grin formed on her lips. "Thank you for cooperating," she said. You said nothing, but you turned away and waited for them to leave. But no one moved. Finally, the nurse asked you to open your mouth and let her check it. "I swallowed them," you said. "Well then, let me look." This was an insult as far as you could see, but, since you had no other choice, you threw back the sheets, sat up, gripped the cot and opened your mouth wide enough to make your jaw ache. After she looked, you snapped it shut and asked if she were satisfied. "Yes, I'm satisfied. And thank you," she said as she left. The others followed and closed the door—*What's the matter with him?*—Then you tried to sleep, but couldn't—*I don't know*—Your adrenalin had come up because you were so upset—*He's paranoid*—I mean sorting things out was impossible—*He thinks we're out to get him*—The more you thought, the more confused you became—*So maybe he knows*—You couldn't understand your behavior—*About the plot*—But, somehow, you were estranged from your wife, your doctor treated you like a madman and everyone in the hospital was bearing down hard—*But we'll fix that*—But you weren't sure what you did to deserve it and you couldn't decide if people were helping or hurting you—*He'll do what we say*—You even wondered if there weren't somebody else, somebody hired to do this—*They'll tell us how*—There were reasons to think so, but you couldn't judge if they were a product of your insanity or because you could see the truth—*How to make him*—You laid there on the cot shaking and sweating and thinking that way—So don't trust them—You were frightened and alone, but feeling it was best to stay that way—Or anyone else—You could let no one in on your thoughts, not until you knew where things stood because, after that, you weren't at all sure—Remember that—But it seemed you were being mistreated—Always remember that—You might have misread it, but what were you supposed to think when strangers barged in and ordered you around? You thought it was wrong and that everything you were told was just a façade to lure you there—*We have to get him in*—In view of what happened, what else could you conclude?—*I mean he might be dangerous*—They wanted you there so they could practice their brutality—*We'll get him to sign*—I don't think your wife or doctor were part of it although the thought crossed my mind many times—*Don't worry*—But what I really believed was the hospital's policy was to attract new patients by not making the treatment fully clear—*We'll think of something*—That's because they assumed any candidate for hospitalization was crazy necessitating, therefore, that extraordinary means be used—*Don't worry*—And you had, it dawned on you, fallen victim to that trap. So what was to be done? That was the question. You laid there on your cot contemplating it, but you thought of nothing new. What you felt all along still held. The only way out was to convince them you were sane, healthy and in complete control of your life. Then there'd be no justification for keeping you. You resolved, as you had in the car, to do this from then on. You knew you hadn't started off very well, but, you told yourself, given the lateness of your arrival and the medication, not to mention all you had been through, your reactions weren't so unreasonable and it wouldn't take much to redeem yourself in their eyes. So, from that moment on, there'd be no outbursts from you. You'd give them no reason to suspect you in any way. You felt better having decided that. If nothing else, it gave you something to work toward. God knows we all need that.

You rolled over then thinking about rest, but you still couldn't fade. There was something pressing you. You tried to resist for reasons that need not be gone into now. But relations with your wife had been strained for a period, remember? She had cut you off saying it meant nothing anymore—*I don't love him*—It was just a matter of going through the motions—*Not anymore*—She complained of a lack of feeling, a stiffness, a mechanical quality. As far as you could see, it was as always; nice, enjoyable. But she had begun refusing no matter how much you asked her—*He's repulsive*—It was a temporary thing you thought, just one of those things women go through. Nothing to worry about since, with a little patience, it would change. But I admit there was a question in your mind—What's wrong?—I mean when a wife stops desiring her husband, he has to wonder about what's wrong—Not a man—It was something you wondered about growing up—You're not a man— Not a lot, but it's well known all boys wonder about themselves and you were no exception. But this with your wife called all that into question. Not that it was serious, but you did wonder about it, didn't you? Yes, and you didn't want to encourage it. That wasn't you, you would never let it be you. So the question was what to do. You're normal. You were normal then. You have your desires, but you're not the sort to get it someplace else and you didn't want to encourage the practice, not with your future at stake. You had indulged growing up (all boys do), but not enough to damage yourself. It was just normal experimentation, not an obsession. But...

But what are you going on about? Stop this now and get back on the track. What happened next? That's what you were thinking about....What was it?....The nurse's station? Right! You went to the nurse's station. In fact you spent the rest of the day there. That's where they kept the medication safely away from the patients; as if any of you would want it. It also had a door which led to a room where patients weren't allowed. That's where the records were. It was a place the staff liked to be since it was away from us; the patients I mean. Consequently, getting them out was often a chore, so it wasn't by choice you were there so much, it was because of the privileges they handed out. Because of them, because new patients were allowed nothing, you had to tap at the glass to get their attention. If you wanted a cigarette, silverware or a breath of fresh air you had to have them supervise you to do it. You couldn't eat, walk, take a shower, receive a letter or have a visit in private. This, they said, could change if and when you proved you could handle it. And, when you asked how long that would be, they said, "It's up to you, Mr. Wamblie." An ambiguous answer, but they were many. Needless to say, it was hard to put up with especially for someone like you who's used to responsibility. But you had no choice, so you went along. Besides, they were busy. After all, there were twenty four patients and only four staff, so, as I said, there was a lot of waiting. But you continued with your requests until late that afternoon. By then, the delays were grating on your nerves especially because of Henrietta. When it came to her, you were nearly in a panic. She hadn't called all day; a fact you couldn't reconcile. You were without clothing and all of your possessions. You expected, her knowing this, she would come, yet she hadn't, not all day. So you were convinced something was wrong: an accident or some sort of mishap. You didn't know what. But you desperately wanted to talk to her. That meant calling. Fine, except you needed supervision because a conversation with your wife could be upsetting you were told. To remedy that, there were, like everything else, supervised calls. That meant you could only call with a staff member listening in so the conversation could be terminated in the event you became distressed. It was late afternoon before you got that supervision. They apologized and explained it was a very busy day. You were simply expected to understand. By then, you were scared, however. You were scared for Henrietta and suspicious of their motives. What information were they after and how would it be used you wondered. Why was talking to your wife suddenly so hazardous? "It's all in the interests of getting to know you," they said. An explanation you could hardly believe. But by the time you called, you cared less about that. You just longed to hear her voice and know she was all right. Of course, you didn't suggest any of this to the staff knowing they'd probably consider it a product of your paranoia; something, at that stage, you weren't completely sure wasn't true.

At any rate, you called collect. When the operator clicked out, you said, "It's so good to hear your voice!" "The last time was only yesterday," she said. "You sound as if it's been months." "That's how it feels," you said. Then you asked her why she hadn't come and you told her you were worried. She said she was sorry, but sounded disgruntled. Then the attendant interrupted because you hadn't explained the call was supervised. "A staff member has to listen in," you said. "It's a rule they have so you won't upset me. Can you imagine that?" You didn't think that was a provocative statement, but, apparently, Henrietta did—She did—"Honey," she said, "I hope you're cooperating"—Since she's against you—"They're there to

help you"—Against you!—Her comment didn't please you—
Against you, Wamblie!—But you tried to ignore it—Because
you're crazy—"Yes, yes! I'm doing everything I'm told," you
said hoping she would drop it. But, of course, she didn't. "Are
you, Darling?"—Aren't you?—"Yes!" you said and went back to
your question—Aren't you, Wamblie?—"Will you come this
evening?" you asked—Aren't you sick?—"I can't make it then",
she said—Aren't you crazy?—That astounded you—Crazy,
Wamblie?—After all, it was of great importance to you—
Crazy?—But she seemed not to realize that—Do you matter?—
"Why can't you come?"—Do you?—"Because I'm exhausted"
—Do you, Wamblie?—"But I have no clothes, no watch and no
glasses!" "Well," she said, "none of this is so easy for me
either. Did you ever think of that?" She had strain in her voice
and you could hear her sniffling—Because of you—You hadn't
thought of her even once—You and your problems—"When I got
home last night, the children were worried"—You haven't
thought of the boys—"You can't keep things from them"—Not
one thought for your children—"They just know somehow"—
Because you're selfish—"It was dawn when I got home and
morning before I got to bed"—And a fool!—"What did you tell
them?"—For not noticing—"That you're tired and need to get
away"—Wamblie!—That wasn't completely untrue—Are you
listening?—"How did they take that?"—Listening to the
voices?—"They're terrified!"—Are you?—"That's why I
shouldn't come"—Are you?—That was fine, but you still
wondered why she hadn't called. "Look," she explained, "I
only got up an hour ago. I mean, with the children and the
house, not to mention the meals, I haven't even put on my
makeup yet"—Wamblie!—"I see....Well, will you come
tomorrow?" "I can't promise, but I'll certainly try," she
said—Wamblie!—That, at least, was comforting. "Well, come
when you can and don't worry about when," you said. "I will.
And Darling," she said, "I know how unhappy you are, but it's

a hard thing on all of us." "Yes it is," you agreed. "But we can weather it like we always have"—Wamblie!—"Yes, that's the truth"—Listen!—"Okay sweetheart, take care of yourself and I'll see you soon," she said and hung up.

After that, there were three days of nothing. You got a calendar from a patient who had an extra. Each morning you rose, put on your clothes, washed, went to the calendar and crossed off the day with a thick, black X. That was comforting because it marked the passage of time. Other than that, there wasn't much to do. Waiting and wondering, guessing, but not knowing. There was no treatment you could see, no demands except you be out of bed and take your medication. When you asked about the lack of anything to do, you were told a treatment plan would soon be devised. You had no contact with the staff, however, except for supervision or when they had a form to fill out and, of course, for medication. For that, you saw them three times a day. For the rest, however, they had no time especially since you caused no trouble. You were left to wander the halls which was fine with you I guess. At least it gave you time to think which you did a lot of, remember? You thought about the hospital and what would happen to you there, if you'd be changed and often of when you'd leave. It was obviously being prolonged—*He'll be here for a while*— Originally, your estimate was a week at the most, but it was clear it would be longer than that—*He's very sick*— Disappointing to realize, but what could you do? You had to go along. You also dwelled on a certain question a lot; the question of what had gone wrong. I mean why were you in a hospital being treated like an incompetent? After all, you came from a good home with a normal upbringing, you went to good schools, you married well, had plenty of money, plenty of friends, all the comforts and you got promotion after promotion and had risen quite high. So how did you come to a hospital? It was a question you couldn't answer. It was, you see now, unanswerable. But you spent those days trying and perhaps being allowed that was good therapy in itself. It didn't seem so at the time, however. But perhaps that's why they bothered with you so little. Perhaps they got knowledge of new patients by seeing how they reacted to having nothing to react to. I don't know. What I do know, however, is you were horribly embarrassed and you couldn't face anyone. I mean what would people say?—*He went crazy*—Friends, acquaintances, people who knew you as a good husband and father, what would they say if they saw you there?—*Did you see him?*—You couldn't imagine, but you knew the only way to face them was to return to your normal routine—*He looked terrible*—You wouldn't have them visit you there, no. You needed to be at work and back with your family, existing normally instead of locked up, stripped of your dignity, being treated as if you couldn't cope with your life which wasn't true at all. You could have coped. And the desire to do it was very strong within you especially after finding out what hospitalization meant. That was a fate to be escaped at all costs. But how could it be? That's what you wondered. You came back to it again and again. And the answer? By convincing them you were normal. But, to do that, you had to act normal; something that's easier said than done. But, somehow, you thought you could. You felt you must put things back on track before they deteriorated any further. The only hitch was that meant treating the staff as an adversary or, at least, thinking of them that way. You found it paradoxical they were the barrier, not the savior as everyone pretended. But that's how it looked to you although you couldn't completely convince yourself which left you unsure as to what your approach should be. It was evident that many, many patients felt like you because there were only a few that weren't unhappy. In fact a good handful were downright hostile. But they had mental problems or they wouldn't have been there, right? So it was quite possible your attitude only confirmed you were sick, as sick as the rest. In spite of that, however, you decided to stick to it for the simple reason it was right or so you thought. You had always done what was expected of you, always, all your life. Now you were doing what was right, what felt as if it would lead to your goal. Forget logic, you told yourself, forget questions and answers. They only led to circles and questions, but never out to firmer ground.

So that was it until Henrietta came. That shook your confidence and led you to question whether or not you could see your plan through since they could induce you to act in ways that weren't you. I mean your method to gain release failed, increasingly, starting with that visit. That afternoon, the third afternoon you were there, Henrietta called and said she'd be coming. You were thankful for that because you needed the things you knew she'd bring. But you were surprised and demoralized by how long it took. I mean three days was a life time! But, be that as it may, shortly after dinner an attendant came in and said she had just signed in at the administration building. So you got up and went straight to the foyer. It was quiet there. There were sometimes upheavals, but that night was quiet. You were glad of that because you didn't want Henrietta exposed to any unpleasantness. There was nothing she could do and it would only make her worry. So you sat with two others, two women; one knitting and one reading—*Look at him*—You said nothing—*He's nervous*—There was nothing to say—*Very nervous!*—You simply smiled and nodded—*Does he know?*—Then you gazed at the wall until Henrietta appeared at the door, whereupon you got her attention and told her to wait. Then you went for the attendant. He was in the back room, so you had to knock. It seemed like forever before he appeared. Then, as you walked across the foyer, he asked where you wanted to have it. But you didn't know what he meant. You weren't paying attention because a wave of apprehension came over you, suddenly, for reasons I can't explain. "The visit," he said, "where do you want it?" "In my room," you said. It seemed like the most private place. He unlocked the door and introduced himself. She did the same, then said, hello, to you in a warm but, somehow, selfconscious way—*I hate seeing him*—But she was probably a little nervous —*It's depressing*—She said she brought your things and indicated your suitcase. You went to take it, but, before you could, the attendant grabbed it and said it would have to be gone through by a staff member for contraband and, then, be brought down to your room. What could you say? You said okay and asked if Henrietta and you could go ahead down while he put the case in the nurse's station. It wasn't strictly legal since your visits were supervised, but you didn't think he'd say no. After all, it would leave you alone for only a minute. And he didn't. So you pointed the way and started, but, when you walked, Henrietta took on a startled expression. She said it was because you moved so stiffly. She also wanted to know why your mouth hung open. "It must be the medication," you said explaining how it slowed you down. Then you asked her for a cigarette. It was nice to smoke one you hadn't borrowed. You must have owed a canton by then. Then you sat down; she on your chair and you on the cot. She glanced around the room with a repugnant expression—*It's awful*— You thought that was because of the crampness and because your side was so empty compared to your roomate's—*So depressing*—But, when she became aware you had noticed, she smiled selfconsciously as much as to say, I'm pleased with the place. She probably thought it was better to emphasize the positive and downplay the negative. A lot of relatives did that. Then she asked how things were in a tone that indicated she wanted the truth, but was afraid to hear it—*I can't wait to leave* —"All right I guess," you said halfheartedly. Then the attendant came in. At first, he smiled, but then he looked solemn. You were solemn too never having met in a hospital before. It wasn't the most comfortable situation. He asked Henrietta for her pass. She got it out, but, accidentally, dropped it. He picked it up and tore off a sheet which he put in his pocket. The other half he handed to her explaining she should keep it in order to prove she signed in. That bothered you. The regulation of it I mean. They knew where every person was at every minute. That's why that business with the pass. Ostensibly, it was for security, at least that's what they said. But you believed there were other reasons, you thought there was more to it than that. After all, why did this have to extend to your wife? Why was that so essential? You saw no reason. You weren't dangerous and, even if you were, you would never harm your wife. And she certainly wasn't there to scheme with you. So there was no sense to it. None! It made you wonder if the staff wasn't paranoid. Why else did they have to know everything that went on? Why was that a constant preoccupation? The more you thought about it, the more the answer came clear. It was...was...

But what was I saying? Oh yes! I was talking about the visit, about the pass system, about the reasons for it and...now wait...oh yes! The next thing was the attendant explained why the visit was supervised. Yes. "We feel," he said, "it's important for the staff to be aware of what's going on in your husband's life in order to get to know him better and, ultimately, to help him. I know this poses an inconvenience on you both, but, I hope, not too much so." He paused, then said, "It's got to be limited to half an hour, that's the regulation visit." Henrietta said that would be fine since she had to meet with the social worker to finish filling out some forms. You thought that was short and you were surprised she didn't. I mean not only had you been apart for three days, but the reasons for your separation created a strain on you both. So you had plenty to talk about. But you didn't show your displeasure because you didn't want to seem distraught. And no one else was speaking by then. The three of you were just sitting in silence. You began gazing at your hand which was resting on your knee holding the cigarette which had a long, grey ash, remember? It was bending more and more as it grew in length. You wondered when it would drop. You tried to pick the precise moment, but you never could. It fell when you weren't expecting it and, then, the smoke rose up and clouded your face. You glanced at the others. The attendant seemed to be studying you, you and Henrietta who seemed suddenly full of movement. She pulled down her skirt and crossed her legs, pulled down her skirt and uncrossed her legs, checked her stockings for runs, patted her hair, etcetera, etcetera, etcetera. She seemed to be building toward something. You didn't know what, but, finally, she blurted out something about a letter. She rummaged through her purse and pulled out a letter. It was from your mother. She said she had nearly forgotten it. When she handed it to you, you tossed it on your dresser with barely a glance because it didn't interest you in the slightest then. Correspondence with your mother was a chore you fulfilled faithfully like a good son should, but it wasn't something you enjoyed. Henrietta seemed disturbed by that—*What's he doing?*—She thought she found something to fill up the space, but you put everything right back where it was with a mere flick of your wrist—*He's not even going to read it?*—She looked at the attendant as if he should say something. I can't imagine what. He didn't see her, however, because his eyes were on you. I must admit, you took some pleasure in that, in seeing her discomfort. You felt like saying, How does it feel, huh? How does it feel? That was an unfair attitude, I realize, but you were bitter toward her because she was out and you were in. Not that that was her fault. Not entirely anyway. But you were bitter...toward the hospital primarily. But you couldn't show that, so you took it out on her. After all, you had to get back at somebody, didn't you? And she would get over it. She always did. In fact she found something to go on about right away. She wasn't one to let things lag. Dead silence was very uncomfortable for her. So she started talking about the latest gossip. She said she found out, just the day before, the new bride was pregnant. She said someone at the club had given her the news and that the baby was due in February. Last February it is now. "How nice," you said with little emotion since you couldn't have cared less about any of that. But she paid no attention to you. She went on, instead, about the new bride's parents and how they had just gotten back from a trip (the Caribbean I think it was) and how they had brought you and she a serving tray as a gift. "Great!" you said sarcastically. "Well, it is" she exclaimed. You didn't respond. There was nothing to say. Then you noticed the attendant eyeing you like a bug. You despised him for that. He said he got the impression you weren't interested in the visit and he asked you to explain the reason—Upset!—"I'm interested," you said—You're upset—"But I don't know what to say"—Upset about everything—"Tell your wife how you feel"—Your wife—"About what?"—Your life—"Right now"—Everything!—"Right now! Right now what?"—And that's your punishment—"Maybe you could tell her how you feel right now," he said—For disobeying the voices—"There's a lot I want to tell her, but, to tell you the truth, it's all quite private." You said this, perhaps, with a degree of hostility, but you wanted him to realize the only thing in your way was him; something he apparently missed because he assured you everything that went on was strictly confidential. "You mean you won't tell another soul what I say?" "Well," he said, "of course, I have to tell the staff"—Don't tell him—"They're involved in your treatment too"—Tell only her—"I only meant that no information of any kind will go outside this hospital." "That's comforting," you said sarcastically—Because he's in on it—You just couldn't resist—All that's hurting you—But it was a mistake—See how he's hurting you?—It got Henrietta started—See how he's made you look?—"Darling," she said, "don't be so belligerent"—It's his fault!—"It's not his fault you need help"—Wamblie!—That made you mad—Do you hear?— Imagine her siding with him—Hear what they're saying?—What for?—You have to win her confidence—"I don't need help!"— Wamblie!—"All I need is to get out of here"—Are you listening? —Then you had another episode of tears. That was the second time in only a few days—*Look at him!*—This in you who hadn't cried since childhood—*He's weeping*—But that's what they reduced you to—*Like a child*—"I suppose the way you're acting now is normal?" she asked—*It's disgusting!*—You wiped your face with the cuff of your shirt—*Disgusting!* —"It's normal under the circumstances," you said—*I hate him now*—She shook her head as if you missed something. What, I don't know. You were silent after that. None of you could think of anything to say. Then a warm breeze swept the room, remember? You watched the curtains flare and die and flare again causing the shadows to wave softly on the walls. After a moment, you reached for the cigarettes which were still laying next to you on the cot. Henrietta asked if she could have one too. You told her she could help herself. She did have to stretch to reach them I admit. It would have been easier if you handed them to her, but you couldn't. Doing something for her seemed like giving in somehow. Yet, you could feel her contempt as she sat there with a cigarette in one hand, a dead match in the other, waiting for you to hand her the ash tray. But you didn't, didn't out of spite. "Darling," she said, "can't you see I'm waiting?" "Nothing will come if you wait," you said. Then the attendant asked to make an observation; something you were sure you could do without, but something Henrietta welcomed because she thought he would say things favorable to her, she thought he would detail your many faults. That's what she thought, I'm sure. "Well," he said, "one thing I've noticed is neither of you have really talked about yourselves. Neither of you has talked about your feelings." "How are we supposed to do that? We're not alone," you reminded him. "Why should that make any difference?" he said, "if you're really interested." You just shrugged. Then Henrietta said, "Sweetheart, the young man may have a point. Why don't you listen and try to learn for a change?"—Don't!—"I'm sure he's had a lot of experience"—Don't listen!—And, to him, she said, "Could you explain further? I'm not sure I understand." But she didn't care about understanding. She just wanted to look good in his eyes. But he, in his wisdom, missed that completely and went on to explain seriously...whatever it was. I don't remember now. But you, at that moment, puffed on your cigarette which triggered a violent cough. You had been having a bout with it for months by then, remember? From smoking. You smoked a lot. Your spasms were often uncontrollable, but, that time, you were doubled over with your head between your knees. Your face was red and tears streamed down your cheeks. The attendant slapped your back several times. You tried to tell him it hurt more than helped, but you couldn't get a word out. But, in spite of that, you were glad it happened since it saved you from his speech. "You must be catching cold," Henrietta said. That was interesting coming from her since she heard you repeat the cause many times. But you explained it again and told her not to worry. "Don't worry?" the attendant exclaimed, "if I were you, I'd quit!" You said, "Maybe I will," (you thought of it often) and that caused another spasm to break out. Then another attend came in. It was the one who checked your suitcase. The other one went and took it at the door, then you got up and took it from him. You laid it on the cot and looked inside. You went through the contents anxious to see what she brought you. There were clothes, a clock, chewing gum, a few decks of cards as well as three murder mysteries for some unknown reason (I mean you weren't in the habit of reading them, but that was Henrietta) and, also, a carton of cigarettes. You had forgotten to tell her to bring one. You were glad she remembered and you told her that. "Of course, I remembered," she said, "you didn't think I'd forget a thing like that?" Frankly, you did. It would he just like her to forget them. Or your lighter. It wasn't there, so you mentioned that too. Henrietta looked puzzled and claimed she packed it. But the attendant said it had been taken out, that you'd have to come to them to use it. "Oh yes, I forgot," you said sarcastically. "But you'll do what you're told won't you, Dear?" "Why, of course," you said with a big, fluffy smile. She said, "Good!" then sighed and said, "If there's nothing more, I'll be on my way"—*I've got to leave!*—And, without waiting for a reply, she got up—*I've got to get out of here!*—You didn't move, however. The pleasure of receiving a few of your possessions was erased completely by the confiscation of your lighter. If you had thought, you would have known why they'd taken it. But you didn't think, you didn't expect it and it's occurrence left you in a very bad mood. Henrietta asked if you would walk her to the door—*Get up*—She wants to leave—*Will you!*—"Sure," you said and even managed a smile—Leave you—Then she extended her hand—Because of him—You took it unsure as to how much affection was intended—Because of them—You started out and down the hall; her with her little swagger and you with your robot like stride followed by the attendant—So warn her!—As you walked, you remembered something you had been thinking about telling her—Warn her of the evil!—Something that couldn't be spoken of with others—Of the danger!—You had contemplated it earlier—She needs to know—You hoped she'd understand—Before it's too late—So you seized the opportunity—Tell her—Put your lips to her ear—Tell her now!—And whispered, "I think our affairs are being checked on." A moment passed—*He's really sick!*—Then she looked at you and began to laugh—*I can't believe it!*—"What's so funny?" you asked. "Why, you're not serious are you,

Darling?" "Of course I am!" you said, "so you better be on guard"—Make her understand—"Against what?"—Make her believe you—"The investigation"—Make her see the truth!—"Who's conducting it?"—Before it's too late!—"The company, perhaps the hospital and maybe even the government"—Too late!—"I don't know everything, but you can't be too careful"—Too late!—She laughed again, unnaturally, because she wasn't sure if you were joking or not—*I can't believe him*—That's when you realized you never should have told her—*He's crazy!*—If you had a chance, you could have convinced her it was true. But, as it was, you started something you couldn't finish since you were already at the door. Henrietta turned and glanced at the attendant, then she looked at you—*He's sick and he doesn't even know it!*—A smile showed faintly at the corners of her lips, but her eyes were full of apprehension—Because of you—You felt responsible—Because of how you act—You would have done anything to see them relaxed and happy—Because you look like a fool!—But there's a lot over which we have no control—A stupid fool!—"Well, Darling," she said, "I guess I'll see you in a few days." "Okay," you said with a cracking voice. "Should I kiss you?" you asked. "Why of course!" she answered as if there never should have been doubt. So you leaned toward her a bit. She pecked hesitantly at your lips, patted the back of your head as if to apologize for her reluctance, tried to sustain a gaze at your face, but found, for whatever reason, she couldn't, then turned away to open the door and leave—She thinks you're sick—But it was locked—Crazy!—Something she apparently forgot—You stupid, crazy fool!—She was flustered by that and looked toward the attendant—You insane fool!—He reached for his keys suddenly, but couldn't get them out—Do you hear?—His hand was stuck in his pocket—You're a fool!—Finally, however, he pulled them loose—Are you listening?—Henrietta thanked him, stepped out and quickly descended the stairs—Wamblie!—The attendant

103

closed the door and checked to see it was locked—Wamblie!—Then he patted your shoulder as much as to say, Don't worry—Do you hear?—Everything will turn out right, and quickly rushed to the nurse's station, probably, to record the visit.

You went back to your room and laid down full of selfreproach. You stared at the ceiling and tried to relex, but you couldn't defuse your anger not so much toward the hospital or even Henrietta, but toward yourself. Already, you had broken your vow and made it appear you weren't ready to leave. Not only did you regret having acted like a child, but what grieved you the most was the huge distance you created between you and all the rest of humanity it seemed. And, no matter how much you tried, it widened with your every attempt to close it. All you wanted was to return to your life; something that became increasingly obscured in a mass of peripheral objectives. You couldn't help but think, if you had remained composed, it all might have been different, you might have been going home. But, for some reason, maybe because you were in and she was out, just the sight of her provoked in you a hostile quiet you hadn't made enough effort to hide.

You just rolled over and tried to sleep. You couldn't do anything else. Even though you finally had a toothbrush, you didn't bother brushing your teeth. You were too disgusted. You just told yourself, I'll do it all tomorrow, that and try to change my image. That was your chief priority, so you got up early to do just that because it was, finally, hall meeting day (your first) and another chance to get things on course and because you had nothing better to do. In preparation for that, what you thought was your grand appearance, you ate your usual breakfast: eggs, bacon, toast, orange juice and coffee, you showered and shaved with supervision so you'd have no opportunity to slit your throat, then you put on clean clothes, took your medication and went into the meeting to sip your coffee and wait. But not another patient had stirred by then which surprised you. I mean the meeting was due to start in five minutes, but you were completely alone in the room. So you checked your watch. The time was right according to it. Then an attendant wandered in and said good morning. He looked tired. "It's pretty early for this, ain't it?" he said as he pulled a key from his pocket. "I'm used to it," you said. "Well," he said, "I guess I better open up the place and get some air in here. It's gonna be a hot one!" "Yes, it is and very humid," you answered. He began the chore one by one. First, he unlocked and swung open the screen, then he raised the window, then he swung the screen closed, then he locked it and checked it. You remember that well, don't you? You must have seen it done a thousand times. As he went around, the yelling began. But it wasn't until later you found out what it was, you found out the meetings were mandatory and the staff was going to all the patients still in bed and telling them they had to get up. And if they didn't, quickly, they were told again. And if they still didn't, and this was almost everyone, they were told they'd lose their privileges. That worked, for the most part, but there were still some holdouts; usually patients with little or no privileges to lose. They were told they were being put on hall restriction and they would be locked out of their rooms if they refused any longer. That's when the yelling began. There were always a handful who wouldn't obey and you were among them at one point. They would then be dragged into the hall and their doors would be locked. They usually just slept on the floor outside. All of this was done quickly because, on the dot of starting time, most everyone was there although unfed, unwashed and still in their pajamas. Because of that, they often began with a lecture on the importance of attending. They'd say, "It's valuable for you to relate to those you have the most in common with: your fellow patients," They'd say, "You can help each other with your problems," in meeting after meeting,

105

and that we had to learn to use each other for help. "If you could do that, you wouldn't be sick," they'd say.

Anyway, it was a testy group as you soon found out. Some were curled up in their chairs, some sat straight and erect with suspicious eyes darting around as if to let them rest would result in catastrophe and some appeared perfectly normal and relaxed, a category you likened yourself to. You greeted everyone with a cheerful good morning, no matter what motivated them to come, so as to make a good impression. Some responded in kind, some didn't at all and some glared at you as if you were a freak. The attendants and nurses wandered in after them having done a last check to make sure the hall was clear. There were some patients (adolescents) who were hiding under their chairs. The staff prompted them to, if they couldn't act like adults, at least sit up straight with their feet flat on the floor. Then the professionals, who were always late, came. I mean they did nothing but preach the virtues of taking responsibility and getting to appointments on time. But, again, that's the difference between being out and in.

Anyway, the first to arrive was the unit social worker. She was young and attractive. Her auburn hair was in a bun, probably so it would stay off her neck and help keep her cool. A bulky leather bag hung from her shoulder which caused her to lean the opposite way to compensate. It was stuffed with files and papers, that kind of thing. I can't imagine for what. I never saw a person carry so much. She found a chair, sat down and scanned the group as she settled herself. At one point, she caught your eye and smiled—*There he is*—You returned the gesture—*He's meek looking*—Then a nurse opened the meeting. She said she had an announcement to make which was the doctor would be late due to car trouble. You thought, "That's reasonable. It could happen to anyone," until you were there for a while and found it happened as often as not. And car trouble was the standard excuse. But how could they expect you to believe it? With what he made you were supposed to think he couldn't afford a decant car? Ridiculous! It's the most galling thing I've ever heard. You had to be there, that was so important. But he could wander in whenever he liked. Well, what can you do? These things you got used to since there wasn't much choice. Everyone groaned and one patient mumbled, "He's never here on time, so why the hell should we be?" The nurse pursed her lips, but didn't answer. She just waited impatiently for silence. When it finally came, she asked that the minutes of the last meeting be read. A squeaky voice started in and all heads immediately turned toward a girl, a young girl (couldn't have been more than twelve or thirteen) who was tugging at the neck of her gown as if that would help her to speak, remember? She read with a self consciousness that was so painful, most of you were embarrassed beyond description. She struggled through it, however, and finally finished. Then the social worker said, "Well, I see we have a new patient today." She waited for a reply, but no one spoke. Everyone just ignored her. "Well," she said irritably, "I'm the hall social worker," and she gave you her name. You, in turn, introduced yourself which wasn't easy because you were nervous with the focus being put immediately on you. She repeated your name and asked if she had mispronounced it. She had, so you corrected her. She apologized. You said, "That's quite all right," with as much charm as you could. Then there was a silence of excruciating proportions. You didn't know why. Everyone just sat there like bumps on a log, so you considered asking what exactly the meetings were for. But, before you did, the social worker asked if anyone else planned to introduce themselves. But no one answered, so she looked toward the staff. A nurse, who seemed suddenly shaken out of a daydream, spoke up. You acknowledged her with a nod. Then everyone else took a turn, all the staff I mean. You nodded to each of them, then you went back to silence. There was an occasional leg swinging or finger tapping, but that was all. Everyone was still, staring at the floor or ceiling and apparently lost in thought, so the silence went unbroken for a time. In fact it never would have changed if the doctor hadn't come in. People began to move in their seats the moment the door lock clicked. The doctor was much younger than you expected, probably in his thirties. He was a strange man too. He wore mismatched clothes that were wrinkled and drab and his hair appeared to have been hacked with a razor. You found out later he cut it himself for some unknown reason. He trotted across the room, found a chair, then gazed from face to face speculatively, the way psychiatrists do. Then, in a very deliberate way, he sat back and crossed his legs. He followed that with a, "Good morning," and went on to apologize for being late. No one looked at him, but several groaned. Then he asked if everyone had greeted you; something you were glad to have dropped and didn't want to get back to. But no one so much as acknowledged he was there. "Well," he said, "if no one will answer, perhaps I'll, at the risk of being repetitious, introduce myself." Then he said his name, as you did yours, and went on to explain he was the hall psychiatrist. Then he asked you if others had introduced themselves. You said the staff had and that you already knew most of the patients. It was a diplomatic answer you thought at the time. He nodded knowingly as if that were the answer he expected. Then a patient who you later learned was crazy (a schizophrenic) said something about a picnic. He wanted to know if anyone had anything to say about it. No one spoke, however, so he finally asked if anyone wanted to go besides him. Another patient, an emaciated middle aged woman simply told him to shut up with a great deal of anger. "We're sick and tired of your lousy picnics!" she said. "I think it would be good," he said. "I think patients need more to do and should enjoy themselves more. I think that's therapeutic because, if we enjoy ourselves, we don't think about our problems. Not thinking about our problems is good because, then, we have passed time without them and the more we do that, the less we have them and the better we get. We'd have a good"—But the woman broke in and cried, "Shut up!" Her hands were clasped over her ears and her eyes were ablaze with hysteria. The psychiatrist made an acute observation. He said the woman seemed angry. But she began sitting with her eyes shut, her hands folded in her lap and her feet flat on the floor which rendered her sightless and deaf and, therefore, senseless; the effect she apparently wanted. The doctor tried again by inviting her to discuss it, but she remained stiff and rigid and didn't acknowledge he had spoken. So he looked around and asked if anyone else wanted to make a comment. Then a young blonde haired man you were thinking about before spoke up. He was naked except for a pair of shorts which exposed many sores on his arms and legs. You later learned he burned himself with a cigarette, at least that's what he claimed. Imagine burning your flesh that way! But it takes all kinds. He constantly picked at the scabs, apparently getting pleasure from that. Strange! Anyway, his voice was very deliberate and had an edge to it. He said, "I think he ought to talk if he wants to," for which the first guy thanked him. "Just because she's got a poker up her ass," he said, "doesn't mean we all have to bow down to her." Then a negro boy, couldn't have been more than fourteen, said, "She'll be running the place if the rest of us let her." Then another patient, an older man, piped up and defended the woman. But the boy insolently shunned him off saying the woman was nothing but a jerk. But the man insisted she wasn't and slapped the arm of his chair. Then he accused them of being up past the curfew and the staff of doing nothing about it. He said, "They were sitting in their back room while she was telling you she couldn't sleep because of all the noise you were making." That caused the blonde man to blow up. He shouted, "We didn't bother anybody, you old fart!" The negro kid giggled and said, "With your snoring, you couldn't have heard it anyway!" That drew snickers from several of the younger ones. The younger ones were often a problem. Yes, but most of the adults looked stern and solemn. You were among them, the adults that is. They were a lot of misbehaving young toughs, as far as you were concerned, and you were dismayed to see them allowed to go on that way. They needed to be taught some manners, you thought. But, since this wasn't your job, you, of course, said nothing. What you couldn't understand, however, is why the staff didn't stop them although the doctor did say something eventually. It was something about control....Let me see....Oh yes! About how control was an issue for both the blonde man and the negro kid, if I remember correctly. Yes, and the boy screamed, "I got control! I always got control!" Then the psychiatrist said, "Apparently you don't," which prompted the blonde man to say the doctor was unfair. But, under the attack, he remained cool and calm. He simply said slowly there were times when patients weren't in control. "That's why you're patients," he said. And he also assured them that, for anyone who couldn't control themselves, the staff would do it for them. You thought that made sense at the time, notwithstanding the medication incident. That was unfair because you were anything but violent. But you thought for someone who was, there'd have to be controls. Later, however, you changed your mind because they drove them to it, drove them to it constantly until the patients wanted to kill them. It's an insidious feeling, but strong. They could greatly disturb a patient.

But don't go into that. I don't want to get off the track. It was just that you didn't see yourself as one of them; the patients that is. They all looked like misfits. The behavior of these people was as abhorrent to you as it was to the staff and, since you were sure you'd be leaving shortly thinking it would be clear, after the meeting, you were not one of them (the patients), but a normal human being, the staff would understand you. After all, you were all professionals. But no. All that changed in a matter of minutes.

But, to get back to the meeting before I forget: the patients, especially the two boys, began saying the doctor was too quick to use force. They said in the face of the smallest complaint he would call the attendants and have them thrown in seclusion; that hot, stuffy room at the end of the hall with nothing in it but a mattress. Remember it? Yes, very well. The doctor, of course, refuted that by saying he did such things only when forced; something entirely in the hands of the patient or patients involved. He said it helped anyone unable to control themselves to feel some sense of security. But it only helped him to feel secure, the staff to feel secure, but it did the patients no good at all and that's exactly what they told him. But, to divert attention away from that since tempers were flaring, the social worker asked you how it felt to be ignored. That's where it started, where they started in on you. You were flustered, naturally. You couldn't gather your thoughts and you couldn't control your voice at all. That's how unnerved you were. But then, that's what she wanted; to unnerve you. You finally managed to say, however, you didn't mind if there were something to talk out. Then you glanced around the room and found that every eye was on you—*Look at him*—That made you even more uncomfortable—*I guess he's new*—The social worker put her hands on her hips and said, "Well, I, for one, would like to hear something about you"—About you?—For a moment, you tried to think of something to say—That's what she wants—Nothing came, however, because you wanted to get the focus off you—Nothing!—That's all you could think of—Because she's against you—Finally, you were so confused you just blurted out, "About me? I'm not sure I understand" —*What's wrong with him?*—"I'd be interested in hearing what brought you here"—*Can't he understand a simple question?*— That wasn't something you wanted to go into, not there in front of everyone—*I guess he's sick*—You were astounded she could ask such a thing—*Crazy!*—You didn't know they did it to all new patients. "That's something I'll discuss with the doctor," you said. "I mean I don't think anyone really wants to hear it." "I do"—Don't explain—You didn't know what to say— Don't tell her—She wouldn't let up—Don't tell her anything!—And it made you angry—Just stop her!—"This isn't the place to discuss it," you said—Stop her now!—There, the doctor made a sign to quiet her. Then he looked at you. "Is there some question you'd like to put to us?" he asked. "I can't think of anything in particular," you said, "except how long will it be before I can leave?" "Why is that a concern?" he asked—*He's suspicious*—"Because I want to be home with my family," you said, "and because I want to go back to work"—*But does he know?*—"When do you envision leaving?" he asked—*Know we're against him?*—Careful!—"I feel ready to leave right now," you said. "In fact I feel fine"—Be careful—Then a girl called out that you should simply submit a 3-day. I guess, to her, that was funny, but it wasn't funny to you....A 3-day; the notice you could submit which meant you could leave against medical advice three days after they received it unless they could prove you incompetent in court, remember? Yes, you do. It was a good idea, too, and most everyone would have done it only, if you left against advice, you couldn't get a job since no one would hire you and your family would do anything to get you to go back in the interests of your full recovery. At least that was true in your case.

But, as for the question, you weren't sure whether to answer or not—Don't!—You didn't know what to say—Don't answer—You didn't even know what a 3-day was, but you didn't want anyone to know that—Don't answer!—You were afraid it would make you look stupid—Don't say anything—So you said nothing, but you tried to act like you were thinking—Because they're against you—"Why don't you answer?" the social worker asked—*He's very strange*—Then you realized everyone was waiting—*Very strange*—"It's because I want your approval," you said—*Our approval!*—That drew no reaction—*He wants our approval!*—"Do you feel you've profited from being here?" the doctor asked—Careful!—"There's nothing I can think of," you said—Because they're after you—"But you've been unable to hold a job"—Against you—"But that's a temporary thing. I'm sure I can cope with it now"—Wamblie!—"In fact I'm sure I'd be better off at work"—Are you listening?—"Why?"—Do you hear?—"Well, I just...because I can talk to people there...easily. You don't find many people you can do that with"—Wamblie!—You thought your answer was a reasonable one—Are you listening?—But you were wrong—Don't tell them—They weren't people looking for the best in you—Don't trust them—Not people you could trust—Keep it in here—No, they were determined to bring out the worst—In here!—They wanted to make you appear in bad condition so they'd have an excuse to keep you—Because they're against you—And they wanted to keep you because it was their job—Because they'll hurt you—They were hired to do it—So be careful....

But you're straying again. What was I thinking?....Oh yes, about the meeting. You thought you had given a good answer, but the doctor said, "You don't?" as if your statement were crazy, what you said about work I mean—Get out!—You hesitated because you were a little confused—Out of here—Then (I don't know why, it was stupid) you said, "No," sheepishly and sunk in your chair—Out of this place!—That was exactly the reaction he wanted—Wamblie!—To make you look sick—Are you listening?—But you didn't know what was going on—Listening to the voices?—You just wanted to get out—You should listen to the voices—Then he made a general statement about how hard it is to leave people—*He's confused*—You barely understood what he meant—*We've got him*—It seemed a little scattered—*Got him upset!*—In fact you were becoming increasingly angered by his meaningless questions and his misconstruing everything you said—*So he'll think he's crazy*— And you acted too hastily and forgot where you were— Rebel!—You let your anger flare up again—Rebel now!—"You don't understand!" you said, "I only said that about work because I thought it was what you wanted to hear"—Do it!—"I don't have any problems and I couldn't care less about anyone at work!"—Do it now!—"Well," the social worker said, "you sound very defensive"—Wamblie!—"I'm not defensive, but you have entirely the wrong idea about me"—Run out!—"Mr. Wamblie," she said after taking a breath, "why don't you tell us what you're feeling right now." "I feel you've gotten the wrong idea," you said—Run now!—"I don't care about work!"— Before they have you—"It's got nothing to do with anything and if you'll give me a chance I'll..." But that was as far as you got—Don't you see it's a plot?—She cut you off and said, "That's not what you're feeling, Mr. Wamblie"—To make you look sick —"You're describing your thoughts"—To make you look crazy—"Tell us what you feel"—To make you look insane!—"I'm trying," you told her, "but you'll have to listen"—So rebel!— Then you proceeded with your explanation only to find they paid no attention—Before it's too late—The two of them were sitting back with self satisfied smirks. They looked around as much as to say, See how sick he is? See how sick our new patient is? See how he yells and screams like a madman?—Too late!—Then you realized you were, so you finally trailed off and stopped. You wouldn't go on with them acting that way. After all, there you were honestly trying to explain while they just looked at you as if you were crazy! The hell with that! You just glared at them because they disgusted you. You couldn't believe what they had done. You were so worked up, you could

114

feel sweat run down your sides and your pulse banging away hysterically, but what could you do? Not a thing. Nothing! So you edged back in your chair and tried to calm down. You wanted to look as calm as possible to ease the effects of your outburst although you knew full well they were convinced they saw madness and there wasn't anything you could do to change it. Nothing! Because they didn't want it to change—*We've got him!*....

But there you go getting worked up again. I know it's hard not to. When you've suffered such abuses, it's hard to hold your temper. But try to go on without going off on a tangent.

Now, where was I? I went through the meeting and then...oh yes, remember? You had an appointment for that afternoon. But after the meeting you had some time to kill. You spent it sitting in the foyer. Yes, and after a while an attendant called you to come and line up for medication. That's when you had that talk with the blonde man, remember? Yes, the one with the cigarette burns. He and you were near the end, so you talked for a while although you were revolted by him when he first addressed you. But when he commented he had only two more doses to take, you got interested. He explained he had submitted a 3-day that was up that night and, since they couldn't prove him incompetent, he was leaving that evening. And he added something interesting. He said, "Then they can't control me." You found that curious since it was a subject that occupied your thoughts a lot, so you asked him what he meant. He explained by launching into a diatribe about Hitler. He said Hitler was similar to a mental hospital because, like Hitler, psychiatrists wanted complete control. They wanted everybody doing what they wanted, when they wanted them to and that's why he was happy to be leaving. It was a weird thing to say. Imagine equating Hitler and psychiatry! Very grotesque and bizarre you thought although the more you mulled it over, the more sense it made. It may sound odd, but you were interested in hearing more. He said he was going to stop taking medication, so you asked if he'd have any problems with that. He said confidently, "Absolutely not!" and asked if you ever heard of diet as a cure for mental illness. You said no. He said it was and that he paid more attention to that than to anything and that all medication did is dope you up so you can't feel what's inside you. You said, "Maybe it's too terrible to feel." "Not for me," he said, "I want it all and that's my right." You pondered that for quite a while. It was something you had never given a thought to (about the diet I mean) and you went over yours in your mind. You had always eaten well and were always healthy. Meat was (is) the center of your diet, so how could you go wrong? And you wondered why, if food is an answer, it wasn't more widely accepted as such. It made you think he was young and didn't know what he was talking about. But, when you thought about it further, you were led, as usual, in two diametrically opposed directions simultaneously. On the one hand, it was obvious it wasn't widely accepted because it wasn't true. It was just another fad of the sort young people are attracted to. After all, if there were a way, doctors would certainly use it. However, on the other hand, it could be a conspiracy on the part of drug companies and the medical profession to sustain the money making capacity of certain products, certain medications. They could want people ill so they'd continue on drugs. When you think of it, there's a case to be made for that too. But you couldn't decide which argument was true. One made as much sense as the other. However, you leaned toward the latter because you had been overwhelmed, several times, by what seemed like absolute insight. This came in the form of a vision of yourself as a robot, remember? In fact there were times when you were actually convinced you were a robot. This was something you mentioned to no one, but something you felt strongly at times. At other times, however, the idea seemed ridiculous and you couldn't believe you had ever taken it seriously. You considered asking the doctor about it in your meeting that afternoon (you were anxious to talk to someone in authority), but realized in time it wasn't a good idea because he would have thought you were crazy. And maybe you were. I don't know.

Anyway, that's it. A crazy guy got you suspicious, more suspicious than you already were, of the drugs they were giving you. But you didn't know whether to believe him or not. I mean how can you tell, how can you know, who should you believe? It's tiring trying to figure it out. So don't try, not right now, anyway, because you'll get no further than you did before which is nowhere....Just go back to the meeting.

It was something all new patients had soon after their admission. On occasion, it took longer because he was, quote, "A very busy man" (that's what the nursing staff constantly said) and because he only worked on the hall part time. He also saw patients privately as a psychotherapist, had several books he was researching and writing (as well as giving lectures on) on borderline personalities. That was his specialty. There were other things he specialized in, too, but I'll get to that in a minute. Yes, that was it...whatever that is. Anyway, you knew nothing about him then, but learned a little during your stay. He was new there. He came only a few weeks before you. And acting as administrator was his first job after finishing his residency. But not only was he new, the unit itself was new too. It had been used for storing hospital equipment, but they remodeled it and opened it shortly before you came. Consequently, they were going through a period of adjustment. And, to top it off, they had a new psychiatrist who didn't know much as far as you could tell. He might have been a figurehead. I don't know. Maybe he was controlled by someone else. It's possible. I'm not sure. But the unit was touted as a forward looking experiment. They were going to use new techniques that would be a model for the nation of modern patient care. And to lead the operation was a new, young doctor who wanted to revolutionize the profession. At least that was the theory from what you could tell. But it didn't turn out that way, not in your opinion, at least, although a patient's vantage point is probably the most obscured. But it seemed to backfire beginning with the door policy. That was the doctor's first innovation. It was an attempt, you were told, to create more freedom. It didn't do away with the privilege system and allow patients to come and go as they pleased, however. Not at all. What they did was put some tape over the latch of the door from 10 a.m. to 7 p.m. and plant an attendant in a nearby chair to regulate the traffic. In other words, it gave no new freedoms, but meant, instead of dealing with a door, you dealt with a person. Infinitely more therapeutic he probably said. At least, that way, it was a human blocking your way. That's personalized service for you, right? But the effect for the patients was that, whereas before, there were four staff people on duty (usually two nurses and two attendants) to supervise visits, do escorting and so forth, now there were only three because, during those hours, the business hours, the hours when they were in most demand, one was always guarding the door. And that couldn't always be done alone because some of the more angry patients would challenge anything they could whenever they could. The door was no exception. So not a day went by when at least one patient didn't dive bomb the entrance. That usually resulted in the door getting locked while two or three attendants went racing down the stairs after the one who escaped. Then they dragged the body, usually kicking and screaming, back to the hall and, if they didn't calm down, into seclusion. That's if the patient didn't get away. Sometimes they did especially the younger ones. There was one incident like that you remember well. Yes, it was a fifteen year old girl who, at times, was hard to deal with. One day, when she was in a particularly highcharged mood, she rushed the door and made it out. It was probably more for attention than anything. At least she had been in a giddy mood and threatening to do it all day. Of course, the staff chased her, but they came back in fifteen minutes and notified security she had gotten away. Shortly after that, security called back and said she was on the roof of the building. She was threatening to jump, too, although giggling mischievously which made you wonder how serious she was. Within seconds, there must have been twenty or thirty people out there. There was the doctor, her therapist, several attendants and nurses, the head of the hospital who looked extremely discouraged, the security police, the local police and fire department, an ambulance, anyone who was passing by and several members of the news media. She kept all of them sweaty for an hour and a half. The megaphone was going constantly. They kept telling her she should come right down. Finally, she did, probably because she was tired and hungry. Needless to say, this did nothing for the unit. Since attendants were always chasing patients out the door, the policy was being called into question. Now they had an incident written up in the newspapers which caused people in the community to demand the door be locked like any other unit because it posed a threat to the town. A violent patient could hurt or kill someone (maybe a child), or themselves, they said. After all, you can't let crazy people run around loose, right? People on the outside always picture mental patients as...well, like you did; raving loonies who are dirty and filthy and ready to tear you apart if they get the chance. But that's not true. If they get that way, it's because of the way they're treated. You could take the sanest person in the world and put him in a hospital and end up with someone that's ready to kill.

But that's not what I wanted to go into. What I wanted to say was, as a result of this incident, a great deal of pressure was brought on the doctor to lock the door and keep it locked. But he wouldn't do it. Instead, he went to his superiors to justify his policy. He laid his reputation on the line. At least that's what the staff said. You didn't know for sure. There's doubt. That's probably just what they told you. But it could have been true. I mean there were times when he did extraordinary things. There was one young woman, about twenty, very attractive, jet black hair, a college student, who came in in extremely bad condition. Apparently, she was bananas. She stuffed peanut butter up her nose and claimed it brought her visions of God. Within a week or so she seemed to be herself, however. Then she insisted on leaving. The staff attributed her recovery to medication and said it was only a first step and it would be premature for her to go. But she came from money and didn't like being told, so she called her grandparents (her parents were dead) to fill them with horror stories about the hospital. Although they were on a trip to Europe, they showed up within a week very determined to get the girl out. No one, but no one was going to take a relative of theirs and lock her up against her will. They weren't frail people, but rather hearty, old world types. They entered the hall with a force and demanded to see the doctor. He showed them into his office. They were already haranguing with a heavy Italian accent and the yelling continued for some time inside the only difference being the doctor had joined them. He screamed over their hollering which seemed impossible at the rate they were going. He said to take the girl out would result in her complete mental breakdown; something he would allow if they thought they could handle it. From there, the yelling continued until, at one point, the doctor screeched at them and batted all the books on his desk crashing to the floor. Then the noise stopped. And, shortly after that, the three of them came out surprisingly smiling and friendly. They had agreed to leave their granddaughter there and thanked the doctor for all he had done. The girl wasn't happy, but they left her there anyway.

So that was the doctor, remember? Yes, and going to see him put you very much on edge. I mean the hall meeting had gone so badly you had no idea what he thought or where you stood. You just didn't know what to expect. The first thing he did was sit you in a chair directly across from him. His desk was between you. Then he leaned back looking very relaxed. You remember that because the springs on his swivel chair creaked so much. Then he had another idea, got up suddenly, pulled his chair around and placed himself in front of you. Then he sat down and smiled or smirked. I'm not sure which. He said it would be easier to talk with the desk out of the way. You would have been more comfortable with a little space instead of having his face glaring in yours, but that didn't seem to enter his mind. So you said nothing. You didn't want to seem fussy. He grinned at you for some time without speaking —*Well here he is*—It was a silly expression he had on his face —*Our new patient*—It was as if he were about to burst out laughing, as if you were hilariously funny—*Who doesn't know what's going on*—"Well?" he said finally. You said, "Well...well what?" He said, "What do you want?" You told him you didn't want anything and reminded him it was he who arranged the meeting. He said he arranged it because he was sure there'd be something you'd want to ask. His voice exaggerated every word. He said, "If not, you can go," and then he got up and motioned toward the door. The grin was still there. It was difficult to tell if he was serious or not. You didn't know what to do. There were things you wanted to discuss, but you assumed there were things he'd want to tell you. "Well?" he said again and laughed. "Well," you said indignantly, "there is something if you're not too busy"—*So he wants to talk*—He came back to his chair and said he was sure there would be—*He wants to know if he's crazy*—"I'm rarely wrong about these things you know"—*He'll find out he is*—You ignored all that and started in about your privileges because you had way more restrictions than you needed. So you asked him if it was necessary for your every minute to be supervised. You explained you were not like the others and you wouldn't hurt people or try to escape. He answered by saying you'd have to work it out through the system. You said, "What system?" He explained, under the system, you'd be assigned a coordinator (one of the nurses or attendants) who would, with you, work up an entire treatment plan. "So anything in the way of your program goes through them," he said; "privileges, activities, all those kinds of things." All of that seemed a little strange. After all, the nurses were just nurses and the attendants had no professional training at all and, in some cases, no experience either. You said, "Isn't that too much responsibility for them?"—*This guy's too much!*—For that, the doctor mocked you—*He'll be an easy case*—He mocked you! He threw back his head and laughed and said, "Oh, so you're worried about our competence, are you?" You said, "No," that it wasn't that. He stopped you there and told you not to fret. He said you'd find plenty you didn't like, but that it was all for your own good. "But the place to start is with your program coordinator," he said. You told him you didn't have one yet, at least not as far as you knew. You well could have, but not have been told. "You will," he said, "you will. One must be patient." His attitude was beginning to grate on your nerves, so you lost your temper, again—Careful!—Which was a mistake—Be careful!—I realize that—Careful, Wamblie!—But what could you do? "Look," you said, "I want to know when I can leave. What do you envision for me, two more days, two more weeks, what?" —*He still thinks he can leave soon!*—That broke him up—*He doesn't know about the power*—He was laughing uncontrollably and obviously enjoying it in a sadistic way— *But he will*—But he finally recovered enough to say, "TWO WEEKS! It'll be much, much longer than that!" "How long?" you asked. He shrugged and said, "I don't know because it isn't up to me." "Well, who's it up to then?" you asked. "It's up to you," he answered—Look out!—"Me!" you said, "if it were up to me, I'd leave right now"—He's one—"Perhaps you're missing something. Do you know you're headed for a deep depression?"—One of them—"You may not know it, but, if you leave, you'll only come back"—One of those against you—"But, by staying, you'll find yourself in a deep state of despair. It's just a matter of time"—Against you!—"How fast you learn to cope and get out of it is entirely up to you"—Because you're sick—"Suppose I don't want to go through it? Suppose I want to leave?"—So look out!—"Are you talking about a 3-day notice?"—And don't listen—"Yes"—Do you hear? —"You'll be back"—Wamblie!—"How do you know that?"—Are you listening?—"Because the same problems that brought you here will still be present"—Do you hear the voices?—"They won't go away unless you learn to deal with them"—Pay no attention—"So, in your opinion, I'm stuck here for an indefinite period?"—Not to him—"Yes, if you want to get better"—He'll tell lies—You stopped a moment to think. Maybe what he said was true. You didn't know. He was a professional. You wanted to believe him. You wanted to think somebody could help you. But they couldn't. "I suppose it wouldn't do any good to tell you I feel fine and completely ready to leave?"—*He wants to leave*—"No," he said, "because, inside, you're not well and that will soon show"—Another lie!—That answer didn't please you—A lie!—Especially since he seemed to know exactly what was happening inside you—All lies!—Your eyes fell to the floor and you began grinding your teeth—Wamblie!—"Mr. Wamblie," he said, "there'll be nothing left of your molars"—Do you hear?—Then he asked if there was anything else—Wamblie!— "There is something," you said, "I'd like to have my medication cut down"—*No!*—"Do you remember how you felt the first night you were here?" he asked—*Then he'd get better* —"Yes," you answered—*And want to leave*—"That's how you'd feel again without a full dose"—*But we'll get him to stay*—You decided not to pursue it—*There are ways*—You knew you'd get nowhere—*And he won't know*—At least not then—*He'll think it's him*—You had had enough—*Him that's crazy*—"Is there anything else?" he asked—*Then we'll have him*—You said, "No"—*Right where we want him*—He said, "In that case, good day, Mr. Wamblie." Then he got up and opened the door. You left and went back to your room—*What a case!*—There was no place else to go—*He's a very strange patient*—Besides, your room was a nice place, as nice a place as any because, since your roommate wasn't in it, you could be alone. That's what you wanted, to be alone. Seeing these people did nothing for you (if anything, it made things worse) because you couldn't seem to convince them you were fine and normal and everything was...well, fine. Instead, they kept thinking you were sick. Mentally I mean. Completely sick. Wamblie's going down the tubes, you're sure is what they thought and probably said, too, for that matter. And maybe you were, maybe you have. Maybe...but what are you going on about? You're just getting yourself worked up again.

Now, what was it I was going to say?....I can't remember....Well, anyway, it doesn't matter. After all, what have you been saying? Nothing in particular, everything in general, right? You're just rambling on and on. You can't stop. Why, I don't know. I thought you'd be tired by now, but you're not, not a bit. You still feel like thinking, like running it through the brain some more. On about the hospital. I guess it's not out of your system yet. But try to go to sleep. Put all this chaos out of your head. Just relex, it's not such a bad cot, and try to clear your mind. I'll try too. I realize I must. But, if I can't, don't worry. We can always go on if we have to, right? On and on. On about the hospital.

Development

I can't, I can't! There's nothing I can do. I'm just not tired enough to sleep. So get on with it then. There's nothing more to say. But what were you thinking about? It was the room we were thinking about....No, it was your program coordinator. That's the track we were on. By the time you met him you had been there two weeks. Two weeks! Can you imagine! That's how long it took. When you first got there, you thought you'd stay only a day or two. But you had already been there much longer than that without beginning a program, without even developing one. So all the restrictions were still clamped on because the procedure for removing them couldn't be carried out since you had no program coordinator. That's because the person they wanted was taking a vacation. No one else would take someone like you, so they thought they'd stick you on him. After all, he wasn't there to protest. And as for you? Who cares! You were a patient, so you could wait. He's got plenty of insurance, so what's the rush? It's better to give him quality treatment than fast treatment after all, isn't it? I'm sure that's what they said. Wait! Wait! Wait! That's all you did. At first, you thought you were waiting to leave, but it quickly became evident you were waiting to stay. I mean you were waiting to smoke a cigarette by yourself or take a shower or have a visit or make a call unsupervised. And you soon found out even these things would have to wait, "A bit longer, Mr. Wamblie," as they told you when you asked.

You did finally meet your program coordinator, however. I mean he did exist. You were beginning to wonder. He was another young man with a round face and bulbous eyes and a little elflike beard. I mean he was cute which was fine, but you didn't want him running your life. I mean he had nowhere near the life experience you did and that naivete was evident in his face. I mean he was nice and so forth, but just not very mature. Besides, he was probably only nice because he was assigned to work with you. They were usually nice to only their own patients because...well, they had to be to be therapeutic. But everyone else they kicked around like dogs. Not only that, but he was a staff member; something it was important not to forget because you didn't feel you could trust them or him, consequently. You were suspicious of their motives, of all of theirs', because, whether he knew it or not, he was a victim too. He was under their control without really knowing it. He was doing things he wouldn't do if everyone around him weren't telling him to. I mean it wasn't in his nature to be brutal to patients. But he was being told and they had him believing it was right. So you kept that in mind every time you saw him. Yes, you were careful to be conscious of everything you did, everything you said, every movement of your face that could reveal something you felt, every stride as you walked, every twist of your hand as you spoke and gestured. Everything! Everything! That's what you had to watch. And that was very distressing.

But here you've gone off on a tangent again. Yes. Now, what you wanted to think about was your very first meeting. It was in your room, remember? He came in one day and introduced himself. He was short and pudgy and had his hair tied back in a pony tail the way the young do these days and he looked like an elf. But, I guess I already said that. Anyway, he

126

sat down on your chair and asked how you were. "Fine, all right I guess," you said. There was nothing else to say. I mean you weren't going to get into it, so you just cut it short. He said, "Good," and asked how long you had been there. "Haven't you read my chart?" you asked positive he had. I mean they all did. But not him because it was his personal policy never to read a patient's chart until after he met them because he didn't want to become too biased. So you had a concerned attendant, wasn't that nice? Except the only way he could remain unbiased was not to work with them. But you didn't tell him that. The reasons are obvious. You simply answered his question like a normal human being. "Two weeks!" he said obviously surprised you had been there that long. "I wonder why they didn't assign you sooner." "I don't know," you said. He scowled at that, but what could he do? He had you and there you were, so he explained what a program coordinator does. He said his job would be to coordinate you program (that's obvious, of course, but that's what he said), to act as a kind of focus, to keep track of your schedule and know your appointments and see you get to them on time. There you stopped him because of the appointments, because you were wondering what kind. "You'll probably have psychotherapy and arts and crafts for leisure time," he said, "and gym and wood working and that kind of thing." He also explained if you wanted privileges changed or anything like that, you should go and see him. When he said that, you, of course, asked if you could get off supervision and all of those restrictions. He said it was possible, but there were things you'd have to work out. In other words, you had to negotiate everything with him from the visits to the phone calls to the medication which made you very impatient although you tried not to show it. In fact you tried to appear amiable and polite when you asked what you'd have to work out. He said things like how you felt, what condition you were in, your state of mind and so forth. He must have said it five different ways, at least it seemed like it to you. Maybe he didn't. But it was tiring. I mean you were getting bored. You didn't know it, it was unconscious, but you were gazing out the window in a sort of fog. You were thinking about how it was one thing after another I guess. You had been there two weeks without doing anything wrong. You were constantly told, when your coordinator came, you could get your privileges changed. Yet, here he was saying more was required. You were disgusted. That was obvious although you didn't want it to be. But you knew he noticed because you suddenly realized he was asking what was wrong. That's when you realized how you looked, that you had a listless expression on your face. But you slipped out of that and said, "Nothing!" as if everything were fine. He looked confused. His mouth was hanging open and, right then, a wind came up and blew dust all over the room. That started him choking and coughing; something that didn't please him too much. I mean he looked around the room as if it were a dump. It was a bit of a mess I have to admit. There were some papers on the floor and a lot of dirt. Your waste basked needed emptying and your dirty clothes were all over the cot. Not that that was your normal way of keeping things. But, since you had gotten there, you didn't feel like doing much, less with each passing day. At that point, he, like all the others, displayed his flare for the obvious. He said, "Your room could use a good cleaning," and picked up a paper as if that were needed for you to get the point. But he was right. It was something your roommate mentioned. But he (your roommate) was the cleanest person you ever met, even cleaner than you, before. In fact he used to walk with his hands on his chest to prevent what he called 'contamination'. It was strange. You knew that because one of the patients snuck into the records room and read his chart, then told everyone what it said. That embarrassed your roommate because it said, when he had sex with his wife, he would never allow her to touch his penis nor would he touch it himself. And, when they were finished, he insisted every item in the room be washed in case his sperm had gotten on anything. That was his problem. He had some kind of phobia about sperm. He was scared to death of getting any on him. Imagine! Because of that, he constantly washed his hands which meant the maid complained about the paper towels running out. She was getting sick and tired of filling the dispenser and the staff was getting tired of hearing about it.

But what were you thinking about?....Oh yes, your room. In comparison to his, your side was a pig sty. But you didn't care, not at that point, either that it was dirty or to hear about it. But what could you do? The attendant wanted to go into it, so you had to listen. It was that or look bad which you were still trying to avoid, however unsuccessfully. I mean you already left your room dirty which you knew would go in your chart, so you didn't want to make things worse. At least you asked him if he'd write it there; that your room was dirty I mean. He didn't answer, however, but, instead, asked why you cared. That irked you, so you said, "All of you do, don't you?" He said yes, but that he didn't see how that mattered. You simply stared at him as if to say, The answer is obvious. Which it was. But he didn't see that. All he did was stare with a silly smirk on his face. Finally, though, he dropped his eyes. Then another wind blew in and everything boiled up again. He commented it seemed a storm was coming in. "Guess so," you said indifferently. At that, his face sunk. It was almost as if he were embarrassed. No! It was as if you hurt him. Yes, that's it. And it made you feel bad. I mean you didn't want to ruin his mood. But you apparently did because he said, "If you don't feel like talking, I'll leave." You urged him to stay and promised not to be rude because you hadn't gone into the privileges yet and because you didn't want him to leave upset. After all, he was a kid with a delicate ego. He lowered his body into the chair reluctantly, looked at you dejectedly, then at the floor, then back at you and said finally, "I'm only here to help you. You might not like it, but you're here, so you might as wall get help. After all, it's one of the finest hospitals in the country with some of the greatest psychiatric minds." He said more, but I can't remeber what. It was a long, reverent speech, however, and, during it, you couldn't help wondering how old, exactly, he was. I mean he was sounding a bit starry eyed about the wonders of the hospital. So you asked him. He turned red and hesitated to answer, but he finally did and the answer was eighteen. Eighteen! A child! You were flabbergasted, but you tried not to show it. I mean you didn't want him to think you were concerned about his ability to be your coordinator. But you wondered what he was doing in a job like that, so you broached that subject too; politely, of course. He said he had been accepted into a premed program at some college or other and hoped one day to become a psychiatrist, but he was taking a year off before attending school to explore the field first hand. You later learned it was his father (a psychiatrist) who got him the job. You weren't too pleased because someone barely out of high school was going to be running your entire life. And you'd have to prove you weren't at all crazy which made you very angry, angry you had to. But you did have to. You had to get him on your side because his opinion might help you. At least you hoped it would. After all, he was your program coordinator. So you resolved to try, since you had nothing to lose and everything to gain, by looking as if you took everything seriously. And I think you did. Not take it seriously, but fooled him, I mean, because he appeared to think he had gotten across. I mean when he was finished he was obviously pleased, pleased with himself. So pleased, in fact, he offered you a cigarette which you took thanking him graciously. It was a good opening to what you wanted to say, so you asked him if you could get off supervision and start eating your meals at the cafeteria. He said you could if you made a contract. You asked what kind of a contract. He said, "I want you to promise you won't do anything to hurt yourself or others or property." You agreed, but that wasn't all. "I also want you to promise you won't run from the group on the way to the cafeteria," he said. You agreed to that too. I mean you're not the type to run from the staff, but he didn't seem to see that. Anyway, you asked when you could get them, but I guess you appeared too anxious because he said, "Now look, I want your solemn assurance. We're not playing games, ya' know." You said, "You've got it," as sincerely as you could and explained, no matter how much you wanted out, you wouldn't do it by running. He said all right and offered his hand. You grasped it with a smile, the first you had in weeks because you were finally going to be allowed to do things. Someone finally seemed satisfied you were honestly telling the truth. That made you ecstatic! Although he did say if you broke your promise you'd be back on hall restriction immediately. But you knew you wouldn't. You said you had no intention of doing anything like that and you asked if you could go to the cafeteria that night. He said, "No, it'll take longer to put through than that," which deflated your enthusiasm considerably, so you asked him why. "Because I have to bring it up in rounds," he said, "and then, if it's okayed, I have to get the doctor to change your orders. These meetings are twice a week; the next one being two days away," he said. "There's nothing I can do until then." You were disappointed because all your hopes were crushed again, at least temporarily. But how many times had that happened before? It seemed no matter how close you got to some minor change, it never quite happened. There was always something, some detail or other that had to be seen to first. That, in itself, could drive you crazy. But what could you do?

Anyway, it was then the heavy rain broke out. I remember the patter being very loud. It reminded you of the storm the day of the wedding. It was as severe and made you feel like curling up in a corner and dying. The attendant told you to put out your cigarette because he had to go close some windows. Then a nurse came in and said some man was there to see you. "Who?" you asked anxiously since you weren't expecting any visitors. She smiled and said, "You'll see," and left. So you crushed out your cigarette and left with the attendant. As you hurried down the hall, he said, "I enjoyed meeting and talking with you"; a courtesy these people usually forgot. You said, "Same here," which you knew boosted his ego and went to meet the man at the door. He wore a brown uniform and was obviously from a florist because he was holding a bouquet of flowers. He asked if your name was Wamblie and, when you said, "Yes," he handed them to you. You thanked him. He smiled and the nurse let him out. Then she asked if you wanted to leave the flowers in the foyer for everyone to enjoy. She was an older woman, the motherly kind, who would think of a thing like that. You agreed since it made no difference to you. She took them, handed you the card and said, "I'll put than in some water and leave them on the table." You nodded and then read the note. It said:

Hope You're Better Soon,
From Everyone At The Office

At first, you were startled because you couldn't figure it out. You glanced over it again and again: "From Everyone At The Office"? You couldn't understand how they knew where you were. Then it dawned on you you never called in. It had been two weeks, yet, you never called the office to explain what happened. It slipped your mind completely. But explain what? was your next thought. What could you tell them? What kind of an excuse could you make since you couldn't tell them the truth? Then you remembered they obviously already knew and that put your heart in your throat wondering exactly how much they knew. To find out, you went directly to the nurse's station and started pounding on the glass. Your program coordinator came out and asked what you wanted impatiently, I guess because your knock was too hard. But you were impatient too, after all, and you wanted some answers, you wanted to know who had pried in your affairs. You showed him the card and said, "I want to know how they know where I am." "How should I know?" he said. "Somebody here must have called them," you said. "That's out of the question," he said, "because there's a hospital policy that flatly forbids it." Then you thought and suddenly remembered your wife, thinking it could have been her. So you asked him to supervise a call. He agreed since all he was doing was writing up your interview; something that could certainly wait. So you hurried to your room to get some money. You were nervous about all this, about what they knew and what they'd do about it, if you still had a job or what. In fact you pulled out the drawer too far and spilled everything on the floor. Some coins splattered like a splash of water and rolled in all directions. You nosed around and found a dime and then went immediately to the phone. You dialed the number while listening to his breathing in the background. It rang eight times before anyone answered, but Henrietta finally picked it up. You told her the call was supervised and quickly got to the card. "Did you contact the office," you asked, "and tell them where I am?" "I did," she said, "but why? What's wrong?" "What's wrong?" you shouted. "Jesus Christ! I don't want them to know where I am" —*I can't stand this!*—"Well, I had to tell them something," she said. "Would you rather I lied?"—*He's angry*—"I'd rather you consulted me!"—*Always angry*—"Darling," she said, "you're too out of it to do anything about it, so I decided to take care of it myself." "Well, what did you tell them?" you asked. She sighed irritably—*I'd like to get off*—"I simply said you're going through a depression"—*It's awful to talk to him*—"Do they know where I am?" "How do you think you got the flowers?" she answered. "Well, if they know where I am, they also know it's more than a depression"—*God!*—"Look!" she said, "I told them you're there because you won't be back for months and they have a right to know that"—*It takes nothing to get him going*—"But you were wrong not to consult me," you said—*He's crazy!*—That made you boil—*And I dont want to talk to him*—You got very mad—*Not anymore*—You were so angry you couldn't speak—*Not ever again*—You just sat there breathing away from the phone so they wouldn't hear how rapid and loud it was. After a few moments, you calmed down, however; enough to say, "I'll be out of here in less than a month, so there's no reason for them to know. I mean don't you see I have a reputation to keep up?" you said—*He's got a reputation all right*—I mean how could you face people after having been put away?—*For being crazy!*—What do you say? Gee, I just went nuts there for a minute, but now, I'm completely well?—*He's so crazy!*—These were the things she didn't consider—*And paranoid*—She couldn't see why any of that was important. She just repeated, "Well, I had to tell them something because the social worker seemed to think you'd be there for quite a while." "For a while?" you shouted. "Yes, Dear," she said quietly, "for quite a while. But there's nothing to worry about because your boss has been here and we've talked at length"—He was there!—Can you imagine that!—That's proof!—He was there, there in your house without you knowing it—It's a plot—The man who demoted you was there—A plot against you—"He's been here several times," she said, "to give me support and encouragement and he promised, as soon as you're ready, he'll send a man out to talk about a job"—*That should quiet him*—That's what she said—Careful!—That he assured her there'd be a job for you—*At least I hope that'll shut him up*—But you weren't so sure—They're against you—"So you told him everything?"—Because you're sick—"Yes, but what are you so worked up about?" "You wouldn't understand," you said—*God, how I hate him!*—"That's ridiculous! He's very sympathetic"—She wants to get off—"The company won't let you down"—Because you know—"So you can forget about work and concentrate on getting better" —Know what they're doing—"You should be thankful for the flowers and the job and stop distrusting everyone so much" —Know about the plot!—You laughed at that little speech because she had no idea what she was talking about—She does!—No idea what a mess she made—She does!—No idea of the trouble you were in—She's created it!—She was just a busy little housewife who knew nothing of the world outside—It's her fault too—The only problem was she didn't seem aware of that. But you realized you were getting no where that way, so you asked about the social worker. You wanted to know what she had been told, but she didn't want to go into it—*You're crazy!* —"You should talk to the staff about your program," she said—*Crazy*—"That doesn't answer my question. I want to know what the social worker said"—*Out of your mind!*—"I already said no, Dear, so I want you to drop it"—*That's what she said*—At that, you lost your temper—Rebel!—But there, the attendant butted in—They're against you—"You better get off before you get any more steamed up"—Against you!—"Maybe I better get off everything including this planet!" At which point he cut you off—Yes, against you!—He terminated the call—See what he's done?—That made you madder—Don't stand for it!— You slammed down the receiver, kicked the door open and went straight to the nurse's station—Don't!—You could see him talking to your wife—Because he's evil!—You began pounding on the glass and yelling and calling him every name you could think of—Because he's evil!—You could feel the cords standing out in your neck—Evil!—Remember?—Evil!—When he saw how angry you were, he quickly got off, but you kept right on yelling—*He's hysterical!*—You couldn't stop—*I have to go*— You couldn't control yourself—*Your husband's gone wild!*—

That's why you should rebel!—Patients started gathering—Look out, Wamblie!—They started cheering you on—*He's mad*— Many were laughing and cheering wildly—*He's going to hit the attendant!*—They told you not to stand for it—Do as they say—Some said to hit him—Yes!—And, at that point, you were about to—Do it!—But you didn't—Do it now!—If you had, it would have gotten you into trouble—Before it's too late!—You would have gone into seclusion—Don't think—Imagine how that would have looked!—Don't hesitate—But no one cared about that—Because he'll have you—They just wanted entertainment —Hit him!—They just wanted a fight—Now!—They couldn't have cared less about you—Or you'll suffer—So when he said, "Mr. Wamblie, I don't want to, but, if I have to, I'll go get some staff members and put you in seclusion," you realized it was serious and that's where you'd end up—Suffer!—So you began to gain control. And when you did, he said, "I'd like to talk to you in your room if it's empty," which it was—empty I mean. He didn't want to go into it there, not there in front of everyone. Either did you. So you walked down the hall, went inside your room and sat down on the cot. "I have some serious reservations," he said very professionally. "About what?" you asked having recovered to the point where you knew not to be defensive and to admit you were wrong and shoulder the blame completely. After all, it was the only way to smooth things over. He answered your question with a question by asking point blank, "Are you contemplating suicide?" "Suicide!" you said, "what are you talking about?" He said he took what you said as a suicide threat; that about getting off everything including the planet I mean. You told him it wasn't a suicide threat and that you had just lost your temper and you apologized for that. You didn't try to explain it, excuse it or anything else. You simply said you were sorry. He said, "Good! Because, if it's a threat, you won't get your privileges," and then he asked why you were so mad. "My wife shouldn't have contacted my boss," you said. He seemed puzzled and asked why that upset you. "Because I'll lose my job," you said. "But lots of people have emotional problems and need to get away for a while," he said. "Employers, especially big companies like yours, understand that and treat it like a physical illness. It is, when you think of it." He also said he was sure the position would be open when you left. You acted like he was right and said, "Perhaps I'm more worried than I need to be," because you didn't want to say they'd like nothing better than to ruin your life and your wife was innocently helping them. I mean what would he have thought? He would have thought you were crazy! So you didn't go into any of that since he was a naive kid who wouldn't understand. And that answer seemed to satisfy him. He had no idea what you really thought. So you got off that and assumed it was over. But no. Before he left, he wanted to renegotiate your contract, he wanted to go through all of that again. He said, "In view of how you acted, I'm not sure it's right." So you had to tell him about all your agreements and promise you really wouldn't break them. You felt like you were begging and that wasn't easy, but you did convince him finally. If you hadn't, it would have meant more torture. You couldn't have stood supervised anything any longer without losing your mind completely.

Ha, ha! Losing your mind completely! I sometimes wonder if you haven't already. There are times when you feel like it, but you never know for sure. But it seems like it, here and there, especially after being in that zoo. Before you went, you thought you were in trouble, but that was nothing compared to how you came out. All those months and months and months of confinement; that's what drove you crazy. But you didn't think it really drove you crazy, did you? No, you didn't think you were crazy at all. It would have been hard to find anyone to agree. But you thought you were still...how should I put it?...dealing with reality. Yes, you thought you could see things other people couldn't, at least that's what you told yourself. But I don't know that you really believed it and that was your problem. After a few months, you didn't know what to believe which proved the doctor was right. I mean you did lapse into a deep state of depression. But you couldn't tell if it was something inside you, some deep psychological problem coming out or whether it was merely the result of being there too long, there in the hospital I mean. But, somehow, I think it was the hospital. I mean you tried not to change, but, eventually, you couldn't help it. At first, you told yourself you'd remain the same, capable person you always were and you didn't belong there, you were different and you'd be back to work in no time because that was the way to be optimistic, the only way to go on. After a while, however, after a defeat and another and another and another (and after realizing everyone around you thought you were crazy and had no intention of helping you), you sunk. I mean you began to believe them. Yes, you started telling yourself you were as crazy as they said. How could this have happened? you wondered. How could I be here if I'm not out of my mind? And that's when they had you. Once they convinced you of that, you were completely at their mercy which is exactly what they wanted. And that's why you didn't give in, not completely, because you still weren't sure. You still weren't sure you completely lost your mind. You still had periods, not many, but some, where something would happen, something positive would raise your spirits and give you new hope you hadn't gone completely mad. But it never lasted because something always followed that knocked you down and brought you to reality (yours or theirs, I'm not sure which), always without fail. And that was the only thing you could count on. Consequently, it got harder and harder to fool yourself into thinking things would change. But, somehow, you managed it from time to time. You still manage it now, otherwise you wouldn't be here. What else could have sustained you through all those months?

Actually, when I think of it, it could have been time, your perceptions of time I mean. In some ways, the past, your past life, seemed like it ended only a few weeks before. You felt, sometimes, it could have been retrieved with a little diligent effort. At others, however, it seemed like you never lived anywhere else and never would. The hospital service was your home, your hell. Because of that, you stopped thinking you were different, different from the others I mean. You were one of them by then. In fact you'd seen not a few come and go in your time there. You were as much a patient as anyone and you had pretty much given up trying to be different; not that you didn't want to leave. You certainly did want that. If you could, you would have left immediately, but, as things stood, where could you go? What could you do? Everybody you know would push you to go back because they couldn't think of you as anything but sick; not unless a doctor said so. If a doctor said so, there wouldn't have been any problem. But that wasn't forthcoming. So, what you finally learned was, to get the doctor's approval, you had to go along. You've said that before, but it seemed like a new thing, a deeper thing. You had to not just be good for a while and do everything you were told, but, rather, forget completely about life on the outside, forget you ever had one. You had to get totally involved with the hospital for an indefinite period of time. Conform and live only for it because the staff, that Goddamn staff, constantly interpreted everything you did as a symptom of your illness. They thought it was wrong for you to think you were healthy, that you'd do better to realize you were sick. And when you did, you became a patient psychologically; I mean in your own mind, that is, and only then could they see you as progressing. But that progress wasn't without it's pitfalls. Cooperating wasn't easy. You could never be alone for one thing. They always watched you, always inspected you. You had no privacy except what they granted. If you wanted to stay in your room and be alone, the staff said you shouldn't isolate yourself and then forced you out where you'd have to be with people. But if you were excited and feeling outgoing, you were told to stay in your room and calm down. In other words, whatever you wanted was wrong. They believed, since you were sick, all decisions had to be made for you and you were healthy to the extent you allowed it. Consequently, control of your life was lost and there was nothing you could do about it, not if you wanted them to think you were better. And, of course, you did. So you did what you were told and stopped asking questions especially about leaving because, to them, that was a sign of resistance. You even stopped thinking about it yourself, for a while, because you realized they were in control and there was no use thinking about something they weren't.

It was tiring, very tiring. But you went along anyway, week after week, month after month for quite a long time, a time that seemed endless. But there were little diversions, things to help it pass. I don't say it was total boredom or total depression either. For one thing, you were assigned a psychotherapist whom you saw twice a week. He was a funny old man who walked with a cane, constantly smoked cigars and talked in a droning monotone that would have put you to sleep if you had to listen to him much, remember? Yes, but fortunately, you didn't because he rarely spoke during your sessions because, "That's the patient's job," as he said so often. Because of that, however, you couldn't see any point in your meetings although you did go every time as agreed. Usually, you stumbled through them looking for something to talk about, feeling it was important for appearances to talk about something, but also feeling there was nothing to say. It was awful trying to fill up those silences. You dreaded it in fact. And you resented the doctor who never suggested a topic. No, he just sat there and stared. You never just talked like normal human beings, so, after a while, you didn't always try. Consequently, you had many sessions when neither of you spoke and you knew, when that happened, he wrote it in your chart. He wrote you weren't trying to get better and you seemed completely indifferent. I know he had that impression, but you could find no way to change it, perhaps because it was true. I mean the only reason you went was because the hall doctor recommended it and because it would look good, look like you were trying, whatever that means. But if it had been up to you, you would have given then up immediately. Not that you didn't want to profit from them. You would have liked to, you would have liked to talk to your therapist, you would have liked to tell him what was in your mind, everything you thought, all your fears because they were (are) many. But, somehow, you couldn't, just couldn't. You were too afraid, afraid he'd think you were crazy which is stupid, when I think of it, because he probably already did. But you didn't know it then, you didn't know which side he was on, you didn't know what he thought about anything. He never said, not while you were there at least. It's all so confusing. You couldn't figure it out. But maybe you were wrong, maybe he could have helped you, maybe, if you had let him know you, he would have known what you needed, maybe you wouldn't be here now in this awful, filthy room, maybe you'd be at home instead. But you tried that once and it didn't work. You did try, but only the once, never again, because he used it as evidence you were nuts. That's why you sometimes didn't talk because, when you did, the few times you were in a talkative mood, he was no help, no help at all. He was the same no matter what you did, no matter what mood you were in. But one time you tried, one time you spilled everything out. It was a time you felt like talking. Why, I don't remember. You just felt happy and, before you knew it, you were rambling on barely aware he was

141

there. You knew, afterwards, it was wrong, but, at the time, you couldn't stop yourself. So you told him a lot of things. For instance, you had come to the conclusion life should flow. You said you learned to flow and your life was flowing for the first time in years. You told him you finally learned not to fight anymore. When you were first there, you couldn't help it, but, by then, you knew not to resist. And you said you thought you were better because of it and you intimated you should leave. "Well, ah, ah, ah, Mr. Wamblie," he said, "why do you ah, suppose that's ah, ah, on your mind?" "Because I think it's true," you answered. "Isn't there another ah, ah, reason?" he said. You said, "No," and asked him what he meant. "Don't you ah, ah, know," he said, "that the ah, staff ah, ah, ah, wouldn't go along with your ah, ah, decision?" You said you hadn't thought of it, you hadn't been thinking about any of it and you explained the idea only occurred to you then as you were talking. "Consciously," he said and sneered. "I wouldn't know about that," you said. He said, "Well, ah, I wonder if you're not ah, ah, trying to ah, split the staff." You asked him what he meant by that. He said, if you got him agreeing with a decision to leave at a time when the staff didn't, it would cause some infighting. You denied that flatly and said the only reason you brought it up was because you really thought you were ready. He didn't, however. He made that clear although he never addressed the question directly. But he didn't have to. You knew how he felt. Instead, he asked again why it was on your mind. And you were stupid enough to answer honestly. You were stupid enough to tell him, for one thing, your wife and you had been abstaining, for a time, and you were anxious to get home and get things back to normal. He wanted to know why—You're scared—"I'm worried about myself," you said— Scared there's something wrong—You told him about your childhood fears and you weren't quite sure what they meant— Wrong with you—"You ah, ah, ah, have trouble if ah, things are ah, out of place?" he asked—Mentally!—"Out of place?" you said—*He's ill*—"Yes," he said—*Ill inside*—"You ah, ah, have a picture of how things should ah, ah, be"—*That's what he's afraid of*—"Doesn't everybody?" you said. "The ah, ah, point I'm trying to make," he said, " is ah, that ah, you're worried about yourself"—Talk!—"You ah, have fears because things ah, ah, aren't as you ah, think they should be"—Talk now!—These were the times it was hard to pay attention. It was so easy to fade listening to his voice. But you knew what he was getting at—He wants to know about the panic—He was intimating you had fears—The panic inside you—Fears about your tendencies —So tell him!—"No," you said, "I don't have any fears"—Tell about the panic—And that's true—And the fears!—You don't —The fears inside you!—It simply crossed your mind, so you brought it up—Inside your head!—It was just something to talk about—Inside your mind!—But you knew what he wrote in your chart—*He's crazy*—A pack of lies—*Crazy!*—Things to discredit you and make you look sick—*A paranoid!*—That's why he continued, to get more informotion. He knew you were talkative. That's why he said, "Oh! So you don't have fears?"—Wamblie!—"I was ah, getting the impression that's what you were saying"—Are you listening?—"I don't have any fears about that"—Do you hear the voices?—"About what?"— Say nothing—"About my masculinity!"—Not unless you want trouble—"What then?" he asked—He'll say you're crazy—And that's where you made a mistake—Crazy if you do—You tried to answer which I know was stupid. But then?....Hell! It didn't seem like a bad idea. Or it didn't seem like anything. I mean you probably didn't think. Your mind was racing, so you answered without thinking. "I think the big multinationals are staging a takeover and soon they'll be running the country"— Wamblie!—"There's the oil crisis and the economy"—Do you hear?—"Not to mention that Nixon might go"—Are you listening?—He said nothing, but he gazed at you intently—*The*

143

patient is nuts—But at least he didn't laugh—*Nuts!*—That was charitable—*And paranoid*—That's what most people did when you talked—Do you hear?—Because it was too frightening to believe—Wamblie!—They closed their eyes and bumped into walls—Wamblie!—That's how your therapist was. You could see in his eyes he thought you were cracked—Wamblie!—And that's when you knew you shouldn't have spoken. You should have kept your mouth shut. He couldn't let himself think the government might fall. It's too frightening. But here it happened, Nixon's out. And what do people do? They blame him (Nixon) because they don't know what else to do. But he tried to cope against unbelievable forces and all he got was flack. Figures! Well, I wonder what your therapist says now, now that you're right. I'd like to see him look you in the eye with the look he gave you then. Now he'd look foolish. Ha, ha, ha! That struck you funny which is nice because not much does anymore. I mean things look pretty ugly on the whole. But...but I don't want to get into that, I don't want to spew bitterness. That's what I have to get away from if you're going to put your life back together. So I better think of something else to go on about to fill up the time since you're still not tired, not a bit.

But what?....How about—no. That's more of the same.... But how about Henrietta—and her therapist? They had her seeing one too althought you didn't know much about it. All you knew is they said she needed support to get through the crisis you created. I'm sure they blamed the whole thing on you. I don't know what they talked about, however. You asked Henrietta, but all she said is it had nothing to do with you. "You've got your meetings and I've got mine," she said. "Do I ask you what you talk about?" You explained, if she wanted, you'd be more than happy to tell her although there wasn't much to tell: just two men sitting together not saying a word is all. But she always made you drop it. She'd just say forget it and walk out of the room. But what the heck, with all that interference you couldn't talk the way you used to. Of course, you hoped that would change when you finally got out, at least you thought it would which brings up couple's meetings, couple's therapy they called it. That was the hall doctor's idea, remember? He wanted your therapist and you to meet with Henrietta's therapist and her, her with the unit social worker that is; that bitchy woman you couldn't stand. They wanted to conduct these meetings once a week. You couldn't see the point because anything Henrietta and you had to talk out you could talk out better alone. But that's not what she thought. She wanted to do it. She thought it was great and, after all, who were you to disagree? Just a know-nothing patient. You asked the hall doctor why he had suggested it. "It'll give you a chance to work out some issues," he said. You didn't understand what he meant by that although it wasn't long before you knew. There were no issues you could think of except, maybe, what you talked over with your therapist. But that was nothing. Just a temporary reluctance on Henrietta's part; something that would pass as soon as you got home, at least that's what you told yourself. No, the problem was the hospital and its constant meddling, not the marriage. The only thing wrong with your marriage was you were never home. But the hospital wanted to go into everything. Nothing should be private in their pre-eminent opinion.

Ah! But there you go complaining! You do it too much. After all, it could have been worse. It always can be worse although, if it had been, you probably would have slit your throat. You couldn't have stood it if things were any worse. You were having enough trouble as it was although, in some ways, things were better, better than in the beginning. In the beginning, you were miserable. You couldn't have been worse. Well, you could have been worse. You always can be, but I don't see how. But what I mean is, things were a lot easier to take by then, probably because of the way you had been acting.

145

Because you were behaving yourself, a lot of your restrictions were lifted. It wasn't that the staff thought you were coming to terms with things, it was just that you weren't dangerous. So you could smoke unsupervised and you were allowed to use your razor blade and scissors and you could go to the cafeteria alone as long as you said you were leaving. You were never allowed off the grounds alone, but you were beginning to spend an occasional weekend home when you convinced them you were up to it and when Henrietta's therapist thought she could handle the intrusion. That's how they saw it, as an intrusion. But it made life easier and you thought (you were under the delusion) it helped Henrietta to see you hadn't changed, to see the hospital only made it look that way, to see you could think coherently just like always. But that's another story.

So that's how your life went. Therapy, therapy and an occasional weekend home. The rest was hall meetings and a small group session once a week. Other than that, there was basket weaving, the gym or woodworking to go to. Once in a while, you shot pool. The rest of the time you played cards on the hall, watched T.V. or just walked around and thought, usually about when you'd leave. You spent a lot of time thinking about that. For hours on end, you gazed out the window and thought about before, wondering how you got there. There were times when you couldn't believe it happened. But you went on and the months went by. You didn't get much better, but you didn't get any worse either. You knew the staff would like to have seen more progress, but you couldn't seem to create that image; the image of someone progressing I mean. But you tried, you tried hard, very hard. In fact you got to the point where you constantly wondered what it meant to progress or if it meant anything at all because, no matter what you did, they saw it as resistance. And that's how it went. You trying and them saying you weren't or, at least, not hard enough until they finally gave up or so you thought. To you, it appeared they were tired of trying. So they started taking steps to discharge you, at least that's what you imagined. You found out later you were wrong, but that's what you told yourself then. You told yourself they wanted you to leave. Finally! You thought you had outlasted them, broken their spirits rather than allow them to break yours. And that made you proud, didn't it? Yes, but you didn't tell anyone about that, but that's how you felt. You didn't realize they were going to bring you down and this was all part of it.

But you're getting ahead of yourself. So, as I was saying, all the signs said you were leaving. After being there as long as you, however, you can't just up and walk out. The shock would be too great. You were too used to the hospital and the outside was too alien. So they did it in steps. First, they let you go home, once in a while, then they let you go to work. Ha, ha, ha! Work! What a joke that was! You were sure taken in there especially by that company man in the meeting you had with him, the one you had in the hospital when you were supposedly ready to leave, remember? But it was just another plot. Don't go into it now. But it was a plot to ruin you. But think about it later. The plot that has ruined you. But it can wait. Anyway, you had the meeting in the hospital. You would have preferred it were at home where you could be more yourself and make a better impression. It was embarrassing to be seen there. You suggested that and explained whoever came couldn't help but think of you as a mental patient there. But the staff laughed and said he knew you were and it made no difference to him and you were overly sensitive on the issue. So what could you say? Nothing! It was all in their hands like everything else. You didn't even know who was coming, not until he got there. You were surprised to see who they sent especially since you trained him years ago. That was a slap. But what could you say? Nothing! You just did the best you could. You tried to make a good impression. You wanted to go in confident and self-assured. After all, it was your big chance to come back, that's what you thought, a chance to solve all your problems and get back on your feet. If you could come across and land a good position, the money would come and you'd be back at home. Then it would be a matter of sustaining it, of keeping going. You were sure you could do that. You already had for years. It seemed simple. So you prepared to make your appearance, another appearance. It was another opportunity to get back and get out. And that you wanted to do by looking the part. That was the important thing. Clothes make the man, they say, and you had the clothes. Your best suit and tie, not to mention a haircut and shave as well as a shoe shine. You also brought your pipe. It helped your image you thought, it made you look intelligent and responsible, much more dignified than cigarettes. By then, you had given them up, you had become a pipe smoker. All in all, you thought you looked good, like good executive material just like before. But the man who came seemed surprised when he saw you. He said, "Cripes! You didn't need to get that spruced up for this." You said, "But I thought"—"Na!" he said. "Don't worry about it. Relax." Then he winked. You were a little surprised at that, but you told yourself it was nothing, you were just a touch on the formal side especially since he was dressed well too. But, even so, there was an informal air about him and something amiable and relaxed. You remembered that instantly. He was the type that could turn anything into a joke and never get ruffled. You couldn't picture him ever being in the doldrums. Anyway, you met him with a nurse. The staff thought that was best in case you got upset. You were deeply embarrassed by it. You had no intention of doing anything wrong and it made you very nervous. But you didn't protest. It would only have made things worse.

When he arrived, the nurse let him in and explained about

the visit, about why she was there to supervise. He smiled politely and seemed to understand. You were afraid he wouldn't—*Is it safe?*—You thought he'd think you were dangerous, that he'd worry you might get upset and start screaming or cause a scene—*Will he attack me?*—What the nurse said about getting to know you, you didn't think he'd believe—*I don't want to get hurt*—You thought he'd think it was you, you were too unstable, mentally. You were scared of that, very nervous. But there was no need. He didn't seem to take it badly. That helped to calm you down. After she finished, he simply said, hi, and shook hands as if you were normal. You said, hello, and did the same. You didn't acknowledge you knew him, however, because it had been too many years since you had seen him. Besides, he didn't recognize you or, if he did, he didn't let on. He may have remembered. In fact he probably did. After all, you remembered him. But it was easier not to go into it. It would have been too embarrassing. Neither of you wanted that. Anyway, the nurse led the party to the day room. You went to a corner and arranged three chairs, then you sat down. There was no place else to go. All the conference rooms were occupied, so you had to meet in plain view of everyone. You weren't happy about that, but you said nothing about it because you knew the reason and that it couldn't be helped. Besides, where you were wasn't so bad. You were as secluded as possible and very comfortable, as comfortable as you could be. Anyway, the first thing was the pass. The nursed explained the reason for that and told him to show it if anyone asked. Then she asked him what he wanted to say. He pulled on his vest, repositioned himself, cleared his throat and said, "I want to get one thing straight right away, the company is behind you one hundred percent." That sounded good and you anticipated an offer; wrongly of course. But...well, go into that later. He said, "You don't have to worry about a job because it's guaranteed. I'm authorized to tell you we'll hold one open for as long as it takes. And don't worry about your hospital bills because the company will cover them in full"—Lying!—You didn't ask about your mortgage—He's lying—You didn't want to be snide —You know that—You just smiled although you were becoming leery—Don't you?—I mean all he said was fine, but it didn't address the question—Because he's one—The question wasn't a job—One of them—But which job—One of those against you— What would be open to you when you left?—So be careful—No one seemed concerned about that—Careful!—For all you knew, it would be a low position that didn't matter a bit—Do you hear?—And you knew that showed on your face because he was quick to reiterate you shouldn't sit and worry because a job was definite—*That should calm him*—"Forget about that and concentrate on getting better," he said with a grin and a wink, "and don't trouble yourself over the mill"—*Won't it?*— You were getting edgy—*But he looks upset*—You didn't know what to make of all that—*What should I do?*—He saw your confusion and tried to reassure you. He was trying to calm you down. "The company wouldn't drop you," he said, "not with all the money they've spent on developing your career"— Wamblie!—"Not with all your productive years still ahead of you"—Are you listening?—You smiled again—Do you hear the voices?—Or tried to—He's against you!—It was getting harder— Because you're sick—It was coming out strained—Because you're crazy!—Your anxiety was showing—So don't!—You couldn't hide it—Don't listen!—Because you thought he had come to talk about a job—Not to him—A specific job—You'll be sorry if you do—But that hadn't been raised—Because they're against you—It seemed he was there to encourage you, but not to make any plans—Both against you—The last thing in the world you needed —Because you're sick—But you didn't confront him because you didn't want to appear too hostile. You said instead, "That's all good to hear," as sincerely as you could. "Well," he said, "someone like you...I mean you've been with the company, what, twenty years? They don't just put you out to pasture just because you have a tough time for a while." "It makes me itchy to get back," you said to see if he'd suggest something concrete. "Well, yes," he answered fingering his watch fob, "I'm sure you are." Then he smiled and winked again; something which was becoming irritating. A tense silence followed. Then you asked directly if you'd get your old job back—You won't!—You were getting nowhere, otherwise, and you thought it would speed things up—Not that—"I beg your pardon?"—He won't grant you that—"Will I get my old job back?"—Because he's evil!—"Well...ah...I'm...ah...not sure"—Evil!—"I don't understand," you said," either I will or I won't"—And in on the plot—"Well...actually, I believe, they have you in mind for a selling job with salary plus commissions when you're ready to handle it"—So rebel!—"Ready to handle it? I'm ready to handle it now!"—Rebel!—"What did you come for if I'm not ready to handle it?"—Rebel now!—They looked at each other as if you said something wrong—Now!—"But, Mr. Wamblie," the nurse broke in, "you're not acting ready to handle anything." That made you realize you had to stop yourself—Wamblie!—Although you were furious, you couldn't show it. You knew not to challenge them—Wamblie!—After so many months, you at least learned that. So you lit your pipe and stared at the floor so they couldn't see you had flared up—Wamblie!—Then you became aware the man was calling you. "Mr. Wamblie? Mr. Wamblie?" you heard vaguely. "Yes?" "Should I tell your boss you're interested?" You didn't know what to say. It was enough to grapple with your disappointment, with the fact you had been kidding yourself, telling yourself you'd be offered something completely out of reach. You couldn't look at him, you couldn't let him see your face. So you covered it with your hands and suddenly found there were tears in your eyes. They had come again at the worst possible time. It was very embarrassing since you were trying to appear strong. And the nurse had to ask what the problem was which made it that much worse. You sniffled and said you were hoping to get your old job back. "Well, don't be so pessimistic," she said, "maybe you will, but the first thing is to get started. You can't very well expect them to saddle you with responsibility after all the things you've been through. That wouldn't be good for you or them. You have to break in slowly," she said, "and that's where they're giving you a chance. Then you work your way up from there." "That's right!" the man said—*I hope this will calm him*—Then she continued, "You know, Mr. Wamblie, you could probably arrange to work while you're here. You could get privileges for the job and come back at night. Talk to your program coordinator," she urged. And she suggested you start with one or two half days a week and work your way up from there. Then she turned to the man and asked if the company would accept that. He said he'd have to talk to the department head, but he didn't see any problem. Of course, he wouldn't because the department head wouldn't care. What you sold or didn't sell and the salary were nothing, a flash in the pan for a company like that. It wasn't exactly a risk and it was far from your old position. I mean selling wasn't what you did. You couldn't understand it because you didn't know the first thing about it although that's what you're going to try as soon as the weekend's over. So you weren't particularly pleased with the offer and that showed because the nurse said, "Now, Mr. Wamblie, why so sad? Things aren't as bad as all that." You said, "No," but you felt like screaming. She nodded and smiled and then turned to him and explained you would talk it over with the staff and call him that week. "Okay, Mr. Wamblie?" "Yes," you said. "Fine," he said repeating, "So you'll call me next week?" "Yes," you said. Then you shook hands, he got up and left followed by the nurse who let him out.

You went to the men's room. You suddenly had to go very badly. As you stood at the urinal, you thought about the meeting—*Can he handle it, nurse?*—After all you had been through, you were being given a second rate job—*I don't know*—You should have known—*Maybe*—You shouldn't have believed what everyone was telling you—*He better not do that with a customer*—They'd let you down, at least that's how you saw it. You finished and went to wash your hands. As you did, you looked in the mirror. You were surprised at your appearance. You didn't look the way you imagined, not a strong, dashing executive stared back at you, but a lonely and broken man. It was hard to realize, but I can admit it now. Your suit was baggy because you lost so much weight, there was drool on your shirt and your face flaked from a skin disease or, maybe, it was from nerves or medication. You never found out for sure, but the skin was dried up and peeling around your nose and eyes. You trembled too. You couldn't hold your hands still. But that had been true for a time. I mean you had gotten used to it and simply stopped noticing. So the outcome wasn't so surprising. I mean you had built yourself up into believing a fantasy. Yes, namely, your life would return to normal in just a matter of weeks. You had no one to blame but yourself. I mean when you looked at yourself, really looked at yourself, you knew the whole thing was a myth. Yes, you were being way too idealistic. So, during the meeting, you thought you lost everything, but, when you thought about what had been said, it seemed to make sense. In fact you found yourself wishing you said those things first because it would have made such a good impression. You would have appeared much better and realistically in control of your life. But you didn't, unfortunately. But, as you thought about it more, you felt much better because at least you had a starting point, at least you could begin to work your way out. All wasn't lost. You were foolish to think it could happen over night. After all, you weren't a good risk. It was true too much responsibility too soon would hurt you, the company too for that matter. So they were right not to come prepared with an offer, a specific offer. That's what you told yourself then, anyway, to get yourself out of the doldrums. And it worked. You started to feel much better. You began to feel like you could get your old job back, but it would just take longer than you planned. You just needed time to prove you could do it. You also felt it would lead to your discharge, that you'd soon be back home. If that happened, everything would be fine. And there was no reason to think it couldn't, no reason at all.

That thought made you very optimistic. And that's how you went home that weekend, that ugly weekend, feeling optimistic, very positive about yourself, your family and your life. Everything for the first time since you could remember. It was fantastic. But, of course, with every up, there's a down to follow and that weekend was no exception. Not that anything too terrible happened. That came later. Don't think about it now. It's an incredible story, what happened later. But the weekend itself was all right. You had a fairly good time although you wondered about things. Nothing important or so you thought. But there were little indications of things. To begin with, you were tense and irritable. Cranky! Cranky might be a better word. You always were when you went home because it wasn't easy to return and see how well your family was doing, to see them healthy and happy and going on as if you never existed. It filled you with despair and made you feel it wasn't worth continuing, you should simply give up. Why, I don't know. It was very selfish. But, to be honest, I have to admit, you would have been pleased if they had been struggling. Then you could have shared something with them. But, as things stood, you felt like an alien who just didn't belong. That accounts for your mood on the weekends I guess, as well as anything I can think of anyway. You knew it was no one's fault, just one of those things. You knew they didn't intend to hurt you, but, to someone in your position, that's how it appeared. And it did hurt you. It hurt badly! But I don't want to be self-indulgent. Self-pity produces nothing. But it wasn't easy to go home as much as you desired it. There were always little things, little irritants. Things that were of no importance to anyone, but were of monumental importance to you. For instance, that Friday Henrietta picked you up late—*I hate going to get him*—You scolded her when she got there and, on the way home, you gave her a lecture about how awful it was to wait and wait and wait—*I can't stand hearing about how awful his life is*—She showed annoyance and excused herself by saying she couldn't help it and she got there as early as she could—*He's so selfish*—And, when you got home, she went straight to bed saying she couldn't stay up any longer—*I've got to get away from him*—You thought that was to pay you back, you thought she didn't want to talk to you. It seemed like she just couldn't stand the sight of your face. That, combined with being in the hospital and being so out of touch, created a tendency in you to take these things as a sign she didn't care. It was very easy to do in spite of the fact she denied it. So you told yourself you were demanding too much. She was taken up with the day to day activities of running the house and her life wasn't like yours at all. She wasn't doing nothing, sitting around and waiting. Twenty four hours wasn't enough for someone with as much to do as she. That's what you thought. So she didn't get you until late and fell asleep when you got home, so what? It wasn't that she didn't want you, it was just she was preoccupied with too much else to do. That's how you rationalized. And you told yourself you could help by being more understanding instead of always thinking about yourself. You thought that was your mistake; thinking about yourself I mean. So you went to your room to see if she was awake. You wanted to apologize and try to explain why you acted so badly.

She sat and listened, but I don't know what she thought—*Here we go again*—She didn't really say—*More talking*—Probably, you were crazy. You probably said something you shouldn't that put that in her mind; things that probably were crazy. But you got wound up. Whenever you tried to explain yourself, you began to ramble, things got jumbled and the next thing you knew you were being stared at with a glare which is exactly what happened that night because of what you told her, mistakenly. But there were times when you needed understanding, times when you just wanted to talk. You weren't usually like that. Usually, you were quiet. But, that night, you were talkative, so you told her you were angry she had come so late. You told her you couldn't stand the hospital and all the anxiety it created in you. You said you had to get out, it was the only place you felt any anxiety. At home, you felt normal. Only at the hospital were you really upset. And that's why you had to leave, you explained, that's why you had to get away from the place before the anxiety overwhelmed you, before it engulfed you and drove you crazy. You were talking hysterically trying to make it clear, clear you had to leave, clear she had to get there. That's what you told her, but she didn't understand—*God!*—She was only listening because you insisted, but it was obvious she was bored, so you finally stopped and let her alone—*I'll be glad when this is over*—You were only making things worse by talking because she probably thought you were irrational—*He's such a nerd!*— But what could you do? Nothing!

The next morning, she got up early before you so much as opened your eyes. She always did whenever you were home. You sometimes thought she did it to avoid you and, now, you know she did. But then, you rationalized it was because she was busy and had a lot of things on her mind. I mean a woman alone with two kids and no husband? That couldn't have been easy. And it was all because of you, because you let her down.

Not on purpose. You certainly didn't want to. But it seemed you did again and again. Be that as it may, however, you can't scold yourself to much. That's not good. Guilt leads to guilt, nothing else....But you were thinking about her getting up and going to the bathroom and beginning to brush her teeth. You had gotten a good night's rest (the only time you did was at home), so you followed her in having been awakened by her leaving. You went and sat down on the toilet and said good morning happily because you wanted to make up for the night before. That was something (being in the bathroom together) you had done since you were married, so you didn't think anything of it, not at that time. I mean you took it for granted it was all right with her—*I can't stand him!*—Nothing had been said to the contrary anyway—*He's disgusting!*—But that was a mistake—*Disgusting!*—It's always a mistake to take things for granted because she responded distantly. It was as if she were repelled—*God!*—Not on purpose, but you knew how she felt —*How I hate this!*—She hated you! There was hatred in her eyes, so you pointed that out. "You despise me," you said, "don't you?" "Why, Darling," she said, "what makes you say that?" "Because I'm here," you answered. She said you were talking foolishly, reminded you to air out the bathroom, finished up quickly and left. It was a strange feeling not to be free to carry on as before, not to be able to feel like you lived there, to have to be so careful and sensitive in the confines of your own home. You weren't used to it and it made things difficult, but you could see how she felt. Your coming home must have been an invasion. After all, it had been many months, so it must have been hard on her, the whole thing must have been hard on her.

The rest of the day wasn't any better. Why, I don't know. It just turned out that way. You went shopping together that afternoon. You sort of wandered off and got looking at things—*There he goes*—That made her impatient, so it was really your fault—*What am I supposed to do now?*—But you felt hurt and rejected after what happened that morning and you wanted her to see that and pay more attention—*I'm not going to cater to him*—But she didn't. You wanted her to worry about you and to comfort you. I mean you wanted to see some sign she cared. But, instead, she got distant. You couldn't understand it, couldn't understand how she could be so cruel as to go back to the car without you. And you couldn't understand why you drove home in silence. It all seemed so needless and it brought you down. When you arrived, you began unloading the car. You did it slowly because you were feeling so bad. She went inside without a word—*I'm not going to try*—You felt like crying although it wouldn't have made any difference —*He's acting like a child*—So you went down to the basement. You were going to fix a few things around the house, some siding on the garage and a leaking faucet, but you couldn't find your tools. You always kept them behind the dryer. You were very careful about your personal things. But they weren't there nor anywhere else. So you called up to Henrietta to ask where they were. And she sounded flustered, as if she had something to hide—*Does he know?*—Then she said irritably she had no idea where they were, but it didn't matter anyway because she already had a repairman do the work—*I hope not*—Needless to say, that made you furious and it caused you to announce it was your house and you would run it. But it wasn't just that that made you so mad. No, it wasn't just she had hired a repairman. It was the fact she lost all respect for you, the fact she had come to see you as weak. You wanted desperately to prove you weren't, that you were a man, a real man who could run your house, your life as well as your wife. You knew she wanted someone strong to lean on, so you began by giving her a little of your wrath the way a man should when his woman becomes presumptuous. So you yelled. But she didn't cringe, not a bit although she would have at one time. "I have to take care of things since you're never here," she shrieked. You yelled louder the reason you were gone wasn't your fault and it was the hospital that made everything so miserable—*God!*—"They take everything away," you said. "Everything"—*Why do I have to go through this?*—Then she tried to calm you down realizing challenging your authority would only make things worse. But you didn't. You couldn't. You just kept at her and at her and at her until she screamed she had enough. "You've had enough!" you said, "what about me?" She was silent awhile, caught her breath, sighed with fatigue and said, "I know it's not easy for you, but it's not always easy for me either. I reach the breaking point too sometimes." Then she begged you not to worry so much. You repeated, "Not worry!" as if she were crazy. "Where's the money going to come from?" you asked. "How are you going to keep wearing those clothes, living in this house, driving that car if I don't make some money?" "My income is your income," she said, "so I'm aware of that too, but it does no good to argue." "Sweetheart, don't you understand," you said, "I don't know how things are going to get paid for. I can't come across with the customers." You had been selling in their little job for more than a few months by then. You explained you would meet a customer and everything would be going fine when you'd notice them giving you looks, funny looks. "So," you said, "I have to work harder to interest them in the products—*God!*—She interrupted you there and said, "That's what's wrong"—*If he could only calm down*—"You just can't see yourself or judge anything anymore"—*And not be so tense*—"You push too hard, Darling, you push too hard. You put pressure on yourself and overtax yourself too much. That's no way to recover from a depression." That set you off again because you heard it all before, over and over and over again. "That's all they say in the hospital," you yelled, "and I'm sick of hearing it all the damn time." She said she was sorry, but it was definitely true. You refuted that saying it definitely wasn't and, from there, you launched into a tirade, a tirade about work and a tirade about the hospital, too, and all their unwarranted meddling. You told her not to listen to them, to never believe what they said—*He's talking crazy*—And you said you wished the company would do that too—*And Paranoid!*—"They're in cahoots," you explained, "and they're always coming up with silly ideas"—*Again*—As evidence, you cited the training program, the one they wanted you to take—*I wish he'd stop*—It was the same program the twenty year olds took. "They act as if I just joined the company," you said. "That's their solution to my problems? But I have no problems," you added, "that idea is all part of the conspiracy." "But you just got through saying you're having trouble coming across," she said, "and now, you're blaming it on them? But that doesn't matter," she said. "The thing is, you're being ridiculous and your boss is right. Less selling, less pressure is a good idea, at least for a while." "Two days selling won't buy a day's worth of groceries," you snapped. "I need to stay at four. Two days training will diminish my salary as well as commissions. I need five, to be honest, if we're really going to make it." "Well, if you're not selling with the time you've got," she said, "maybe something else is needed." "Yeah," you hollered, "for the hospital to get off my back!"—*The hospital! The hospital!*— "Now what kind of a crack is that?" she said—*That's all he talks about*—"Don't you think I know they discuss me, my boss and the hospital?" you said. "He parrots them all the time." She told you you were silly. "I may be silly," you said, "but I'm not going to be trained for something that has nothing to do with administration. And that's that!"—*I give up!*—She stamped out in exasperation—*He's hopeless!*—You lost her again—*I don't want to see him*—It seemed every attempt to communicate failed. I don't know why, unless it was because you were so anxious, anxious to make things right I mean.

Sometimes, the thing you want most is the thing hardest to get. But maybe the fact it's so hard is what makes it so attractive. I don't know, that or anything else.

All I know is you were attracted to Henrietta as much as ever, more probably. You wanted her. And the feeling of wanting her worried you because it meant she wasn't yours. I mean she was your wife, but, somehow, she didn't belong to you, not like before and that was hard to accept. In fact it terrified you just to think of such a thing. So you wanted to make yourself more secure, you wanted to patch things up and get them back on track again, you wanted things to be more like before when you didn't have any problems. It was with that in mind you got into bed that night. You asked if she were awake since she had gotten in sometime before you. She said, "Just barely," and asked you why. You said you had been thinking about the weekend and apologized for the unpleasantness. "Don't worry about it," she said. "But I do" you said—*I have to go through this again!*—She said nothing, but sighed with irritation—*And again!*—"I wish I didn't have to go back," you said—*And again!*—"Back?" "To the hospital," you said. "I know," she answered, "but if you don't follow your treatment, you won't get well." "I know," you said, "but I'm so tired of it." Then you told her you liked being home and you rested your head on her arm—*Not that!*—She said she knew you did, put on a light, got out of bed and put on her robe—*I won't give him that*—You asked what she was doing. She said she could see you wanted to talk and, so, was rousing herself by sitting in a chair. Otherwise, she'd drop off, she said. You thought she was going to leave the room as she so often did when you tried to communicate. But that wasn't it. She seemed annoyed, but ready to listen. You were pleased by that, so you told her about your plans beginning with spending Fridays at home—*Oh no!*—You said the only time you were calm is when you were there with her—*Here we go again*—"If

161

the only time you feel anxious is at the hospital," she said, "that probably means you have more to work out there." You explained you weren't sure about that. "All I know," you said, "is, here, I feel good and, there, I feel bad." She shook her head and said, "I don't know what to say if you're going to run away." You said, "It isn't running away. Besides, I think my coordinator will support the idea and I'm asking you to do the same." She reminded you you had a session coming up and suggested you discuss it there. You repeated your question and pointed out she hadn't answered it. "What question?" she said. "Will you support me?" She said she couldn't. "Why?" you asked. "To be honest," she said, "you're pushing too hard." She said she thought it was better to wait and it seemed to her the hospital could support you, but not if you weren't there." "You sound like them," you said. "They're not always wrong," she replied. You agreed, but said they couldn't help, not as much as she anyway. She looked puzzled and asked what you meant. "I've been doing some thinking and I've made some realizations," you said. "One is that a relationship between a man and a woman is the best kind of therapy there is. If things are right with one's wife, all the rest falls into place. When there's no wife, that's when you substitute a therapist. So what I've realized is you're the most important thing to me and only with your help can I really get better. But I can't do that unless I'm here." Then you told her you wanted to take a trip and you wanted to come back and begin living at home—*No, no!*—"It'll be like a honeymoon," you said, "and we'll start all over from there"—*Not that!*—"But we haven't got the money!" she said. You said not to worry, you would figure that out. How, you didn't know, but you would have thought of something if she agreed. But she wouldn't agree. No, she was incredulous and she couldn't think of anything to say. But that was understandable, I suppose, since you were giving her so much to think about. After all, she didn't have many ideas of her own. But then, she was a woman. Anyway, she finally said she thought, since things were going so well, you would, if anything, be spending more time at the hospital. You said you were sure home was the best place for you. She said she had reservations about that and couldn't go along and it was important to see what the staff thought. A typical answer, but you were used to that. After all, she was influenced too. That hospital got it's hooks in everything which is why you didn't blame her for hesitating. It's much easier to believe something if everyone else does too. With the hospital's okay, she would have gone along immediately, but, without it, she couldn't consider the idea. You asked her not to judge it only on what the doctors said, but to give it some thought on her own. She said it made her uncomfortable discussing it without having them there for advice. "Why?" you asked. She didn't know, she said, but she was positive it was wrong. That's how much they had manipulated her. She couldn't have a talk with you without feeling she had done something wrong. And that's what you explained to her. She denied it, of course, and said you were silly. You said, "Okay, deny it if you want to, but promise me one thing?" She looked at you expectantly, so you went on to ask she think it over between now and then. She agreed, but said she could come to no decision. You said all right because at least there was some agreement, an agreement to deal with it again. That was something, somewhat of a gain especially since you convinced yourself she'd come around because the sense of your plan would be so clear if she just stopped to think about it. That's what you told yourself then anyway. You were wrong, of course, but you're getting used to that. But, be that as it may, she came and got back into bed. You put the light out. She curled up and tried to sleep. You laid on your back with your hands behind your head mulling over all you talked about. No matter how hard you tried, you couldn't understand her. Something was different. She wasn't the same woman you knew and loved. So you started wondering why she changed and you began to get ideas—*Hello!*—For one thing, you couldn't find your tools—*Can you come tonight?*—Where were they?—*And do some repairs?*—For another, the sink was fixed and so was the siding—*Some repairs on me?*—Who had done it?—*Okay, Sweetheart, bye, bye*—A man, that's who, another man. Your wife was stepping out on you. That's what you thought. And what else could you think? She treated you like an intruder, like a stranger. It was as if you didn't belong in your own house. It could have been your paranoia, but you couldn't help wondering what, exactly, was up. And you were beginning to fear it was something although, at the time, you could barely believe it. But these things happen even in the best of homes. However, you were hurt, deeply hurt to think it had in yours. I mean it never occurred to you things were that bad. You never thought she'd do such a thing. In fact, as you thought about it more, you couldn't believe she had; not your wife, you told yourself, she's too good a woman for that. And then you felt guilty for having imagined such a thing. You told yourself it was the pressure and all those other things. You made excuses for her because you wanted to believe she was good I guess. After all, she was all you had. And you just about convinced yourself she was. But now you know, know it was true. But then, you tried to prove it wasn't believing, or half believing, it wasn't. Otherwise, you would have gone nuts. You wanted to believe it was your imagination. Everything else was of your own making, you were told, so why not this? Yes, it wasn't true you told yourself as you rolled over closer to her, rubbed her arm affectionately and said, "You don't know what goes on in there, Darling. I've got to get out"—*No!*—She said she supposed she didn't with a deep, listless sigh—*Not that*—You stroked her skin several more times—*I won't do it*—She rolled over to look at you and said softly, "Honey, not tonight. I'm

just not in the mood." "You never are anymore," you said—
God!—She turned from you and let her head fall on the
pillow—*What can I tell him?*—"I know, Darling," she said, "I
know"—*How can I get him to leave me alone?*—You were
disappointed, but you could understand how she felt. She had
been through a lot. Besides, for a woman, it's just not as easy.
Conditions have to be right. I mean you could see, or thought
you could, it wasn't that she didn't care. It was simply that she
was worried, perhaps a bit pensive and unable to relax and tired
too. That's what you told yourself because you didn't want to
believe the other, that about a man. It seemed too outlandish.
You believed she was faithful and you didn't want to push her
if she wasn't in the mood. It would only create more problems.
So you laid back and apologized for your advances since it was
more than she could handle. She was tired, as I said, and she
couldn't understand you. You were asking too much to expect
her to. And you were afraid you may have frightened her with
all your incoherent ramblings. You even asked her a question
to that effect. She said it did make her uncomfortable to hear
you work yourself up all the time. "All this talk about coming
home," she said, "we just have to wait and see." Then you
realized the impression you were making and then tried to
reverse it by telling her you were fine and there was no reason
to worry. "It's all going to turn out right," you said. And you
told yourself exactly the same thing because you thought, once
you were home, she'd get used to having you around and
everything would get back to normal. The only problem was
your being away so much plus the effect of the hospital on your
personality. So you had faith it would all come right soon
enough especially if she'd support your plans. After settling
that, you tried to sleep—*What's going to happen?*—You
couldn't stop thinking, however—*Will everything be all
right?*—Your mind was racing with thoughts—*Will he come
home as he wants?*—And Henrietta cried quietly for a while

which made you feel very bad. It was so unnecessary. There was no reason for her to go through all that. It was all because her husband was away. That's what you thought. But what could you do? You were trying everything you knew—*I've got to get away!*—And still she was upset to the point where she finally got up and said she just couldn't sleep—*I can't sleep with him anymore*—She said if she went to the guest room she thought you'd both do better. You agreed and told yourself it was just one of those nights. Nothing serious. Anything to help her get to sleep. You certainly didn't want to keep her up. Besides, you knew you'd be awake for a while yourself. But you were used to it. If you're not, it's awful. So she put on her robe and slippers, pulled off a blanket, took a pillow and left. You looked after her feeling sorry she was upset.

That lasted until the next day; your feeling sorry for her I mean—*I've got to get him back*—Then you began to wonder again because she was so anxious to get rid of you—*And call him up*—Is there another man? you kept asking yourself—*And see him tonight*—Then you'd answer, There must be—*Tonight!*—Why else would she want you back so early on a day you had privileges until ten at night?—*Otherwise, I'll go crazy!*—Her explanation couldn't have been the truth. It couldn't have been she wanted to be home alone to get ready for the upcoming week. You couldn't believe that. I mean what was there for her to do? Shopping, cleaning, cooking, a few things of that sort, but nothing monumental. She wasn't so busy, things weren't that bad. Next to you, her life was paradise. She didn't have to put up with living in a room with constant surveillance of everything she did. She didn't have to eat in a crowd every night. She wasn't confined to a few acres of land day after day, week after week, month after month as you were. So what was she complaining about? Nothing! She was just complaining for its own sake. If anyone had something to complain about, it was you. Your life couldn't have been worse. Everything, absolutely everything was wrong. You got no respect from anyone, you lost your career and things were deteriorating with your family. You were stuck in a place that wasted all your time and took you further and further from everything you cared about, a place bent on destroying your life no matter what you did to reverse it. And she complained? How could she, how could she be anything but nice? After all, you had done nothing to her. You were innocent as much as she. None of it was your fault, yet she blamed you for everything. And that's why I said things couldn't have been worse. Well, they could have been worse. They always can be. But I don't see how although I try. But, sometimes, they're so bad your pessimism can go no deeper. That's when you try to find reasons for hope. Usually, you can whether real or not. Usually, you can find some justification for going on. Things aren't that bad, you tell yourself. You have plenty to live for. You're main problem is you're too pessimistic, too ready to see the worst in everything. All you have to do is get going at work. Function there, progress there and everything will fall into place. You'll be home and happy and fine. That's what you told yourself. That's what you tell yourself now. And you want to believe it. You want to believe your life will be better, as good as before. You want to believe you can get yourself out of this. You want to believe it desperately. And I suppose you do. I mean it's not impossible, is it? You still could. You could start work on Monday, do well, progress and, in time, start living at home again. It's not totally impossible. I can't believe that.

Ah, but see it? There it is. You're constantly trying to convince yourself things'll get better. But it's just an excuse to go on, to evade the terrible truth that life is ultimately futile and anyone who believes it isn't is naively fooling themselves, nothing more. That's the joke of existence. We all strive to be happy, yet to be happy is to be a fool. And why do we want so badly to be fools? Because it would be too terrible otherwise. Otherwise, we'd give up and die. What's the point in that? Ha, ha! Ha, ha, ha!....Excuse me! Ha, ha, ha!....Excuse me, but I can't help laughing. Ha, ha! It's all so absurd. You ask what's the point in giving up and dying? The answer is the same as going on. It's all equal, it's all nothing and it's all pointless, totally pointless. Your sitting here talking, trying to explain it, is pointless or trying to explain it's unexplainable! That's equally pointless, yet we continue, you continue. And why? Because the thoughts keep coming, the words keep coming or, perhaps, it's because there's no way out. I mean what could you say that wouldn't be pointless? What could you say that has any meaning? Nothing! Absolutely nothing! So should you be silent? Of course not. That's equally meaningless and more boring besides. And that's why we try to make sense out of life. That's why we trick ourselves into believing there is sense. Because it's entertaining and it keeps us occupied. As long as we're occupied, we don't realize the meaninglessness of it all. We don't have to admit we're wasting our time. And that's healthy. So most of us do it. Most of us are occupied telling ourselves it makes sense and, therefore, persevere or survive or exist which is what you should do. Persevere! Exist! While you're existing you'll go on, you'll remain occupied. You couldn't go on otherwise. If you dwelled on these thoughts, you'd die, you'd simply perish. That doesn't seem right, not just yet anyway. So you will occupy yourself since it's your only alternative. You'll occupy yourself with more stories since you're still not tired, not a bit.

Ironically, all you can think of is how optimistic you were. Here I'm saying it's absurd. Yet, then, you believed it; after the weekend home I mean. You had yourself convinced everything would turn out fine especially if you could live at home. You were good at it then. You're less so now and getting worse all the time. But then, you thought that would solve all your problems and it was a solution close at hand. At least I think you had yourself convinced of that. Maybe you didn't. Maybe I only thought you did. Maybe, in actual fact, you didn't convince yourself at all. Maybe you knew deep down it would all come crashing to a halt. Maybe it's impossible to kid ourselves. Deep down, we probably know the truth no matter how much we try to deny it. Yes, I think that's true, that much is true although none of this was conscious at the time. Consciously, you thought everything was fine or soon would be. That's what we have to tell ourselves. We can't allow ourselves to think the worst even if the worst is the truth. So we find ways around it. That's where optimism comes in, to pick us up as it did you then; consciously, anyway, as I say. I don't know a thing about the rest. But, consciously, you were optimistic. And that's how you met your wife in the office of your therapist's; at the administration building for couple's therapy I mean. You were feeling optimistic and you made no secret of it in greeting her. You said, "Hello, Dear," warmly and confidently. She was cool, but said, "Hello." You said, "Should we go in? I'm a little bit late." "No," she said. "They're talking and asked we wait out here." "I see," you said as you sat down beside her. She looked at you with repugnance and moved to the end of the couch—*He's disgusting!*—You didn't know what to make of that—*And repulsive!*—She could have been upset about something, but you weren't sure—*And I hate him!*—But you were anxious to hear her decision and you asked her about that, about your vacation and your coming home. She said coldly she had nothing to say. "Oh," you said with confusion, "I see." It sounded serious, whatever it was, but you thought it wasn't the time to press her. It would only have irritated her more. So you said nothing and waited. A few moments passed, then the secretary motioned you to go inside. You sat down in your usual spots, side by side, facing the two of them, those two blank faces. You all said good morning, but nothing more, not for a while. Henrietta was a little apprehensive. She was fidgety and nervous and she didn't look anyone in the eye. You wanted to start, to talk out all your plans and come to a decision, but, somehow, you couldn't. The time wasn't right. Consequently, you, several times, began to speak and then stopped yourself. You just couldn't get up the nerve. Neither the doctor nor social worker uttered a word. They just sat there staring at you both the way they usually did. Things must have gone on that way for at least a half an hour. Then the social worker said, "Nothing to talk about? All the problems solved are they?" Henrietta said nothing. You answered her, however, by saying you had an idea you thought would be good, good for both of you. Then you explained your intention to take her away for a while and then to return to begin living at home. You said you thought you were ready to leave. "What about money?" the social worker asked. "You can't afford that." "We can't afford not to," you said, "because we need some time alone." She commented it all seemed so sudden. "No," you said. "We talked about it last weekend and agreed to settle it here." Then you turned to Henrietta and asked her what she thought—*I don't know*—But she looked disgusted—*But I don't want to do it*—Her face was scowling —*Not with him*—You couldn't say anything. You couldn't get a feel for what was in her mind, but your heart was beginning to pound. Finally, however, the social worker asked the question you couldn't. "Mrs. Wamblie," she said, "do you have some feelings about your husband's ideas?" "Yes," she answered, then, "No," then, "I don't know. I mean I don't care. I mean...well...I have something else to say." Then she started to speak, but stopped. She said reluctantly she didn't know how to say what she wanted. "How ah, ah, ah, can we help?" your therapist asked. "I don't know," she said appearing extremely frustrated. Then tears started rolling down her cheeks. A moment later she seemed composed, however. Looking directly in your eyes, she said, "I don't know how to tell you this, so I'll just tell you. I want a divorce—A divorce!—"WHAT?" you said—That's what she wants—"I said, I want a divorce"—Because you're crazy!—You were a bit stunned—Because you're sick!—The word reverberated in your ears. "Divorce!"—Because she hates you—You weren't expecting anything like that—Hates you now!—Sure there were problems, but divorce?—Hates you!—It seemed terribly brash—For being insane—"You want a divorce?"—Insane!—"Have things gotten that bad?"—Insane!—"Yes they have"—That's what you are—You didn't know what to do—Insane—You were totally at a loss—Insane—Numb would be a better word—Insane—You were numb—That's what you are—Not feeling a thing—You're crazy!—"I don't know what to say"—Then you caught yourself giggling nervously—Wamblie!—I don't know why, but you said again, "I don't know what to say"—You're crazy!—"I mean what can I say?"—Crazy!—"How do you feel about what your wife has said?"—Crazy!—"I don't know, but I know she hasn't been happy"—Because of you!—"I haven't been terribly happy myself"—That's why it's happened—"I mean no one's terribly happy"—Because of you!—Then you got confused—You've ruined it!—You lost your train of thought—It's you—You stammered, but finally got out that it was a little unexpected—Your fault!—That irritated Henrietta—And that's your punishment—"You're so blind!" she said—So cry!—That brought tears to your eyes—Cry!—You couldn't help it—Cry, Wamblie!—They just came—Cry over what you've done!—"Honey, what did I say? What did I do?"—That's your punishment—"You're so good at deceiving yourself"—For not seeing—"You see nothing of what's happening around you"—You deserve it—"You think I've enjoyed ironing your shirts?"—Deserve it!—"Washing your underwear?"—Deserve it!—"Cooking your meals year after year after year?"—For what you've done—"You think I've enjoyed sleeping with you?"—Done to her—"You're repulsive!"—Done to yourself—"Repulsive!"—Done to you both—"Repulsive!" she said—And now you're paying—"I can't believe it!"—Paying for your mistakes!—"That's what I mean"—Paying for what you've done!—"That's how blind you are"—Because you don't see!— "This thing has been eating and eating and eating at me!"—Not what's around you—"And you, you simpleton, never noticed a thing!" "It's another man, isn't it? You're seeing another man." "YES!"—Another man!—"You should have told me"—That's what it is—"I did tell you!"—A better man—"I told you in a thousand ways!"—A man who's sane—"But you were too preoccupied"—Sane!—"But now you know"—Sane!—"Now I know"—Not like you—You could barely comprehend it—Not insane—Things can't have eroded that far—Not driven crazy— They can't have been advising her to tell you and working with her on how—Crazy by a plot!—They can't all have known— That's what this is—All but you—A plot!—All knew for months —A plot against you!—That's evident—Against you!—All behind your back—Because you're crazy!—That's too much—Crazy!— Overpowering!—Crazy!—I'm paralyzed!—Crazy, Wamblie!—I can't move!—Crazy!—There's the social worker calling you!— That's what you are—"She's only kept this from you because she didn't want to hurt you"—For believing her—"She cares about you deeply, but, with all that's happened, she was afraid to burden you with anything more"—For believing them!—"I see"—For believing anyone!—You were phased out—And now you'll stop—But then you snapped out of it—Won't you?— Somehow, you smiled and felt good—And only listen to us—Nearly euphoric—Won't you?—"If that's what she wants, I guess she should have it"—Won't you, Wamblie?—"If it'll make her happy"—Won't you?—"I want her to be happy, that's for sure. I wouldn't want her sad"—Won't you?—"I wouldn't want that for anyone"—Won't you?—"Well," you said, "we'll have to settle about the house and the boys. We'll have to get lawyers too. It'll be strange facing our friends, won't it, Dear? I mean how will we tell them?" You were rambling again, like you are now, saying whatever came into your mind. It didn't seem there was anything else to do. So you went on and on until the doctor stopped you suggesting perhaps you were planning a bit ahead of yourself and now was the time to focus on feelings. "Yeah, yeah," you said barely capable of understanding him. "But now, what do we do, now what do we do?" you asked over and over and over again. Then you talked about other things. I can't remember what. But Henrietta was crying uncontrollably, so they took her out in the hall. Then the psychiatrist came back and tried to calm you down. "I'm all right, I'm all right," you were saying as you fumbled with your pipe. "I'm not so sure," he said, "wouldn't you like an escort to the hall?" "Sure," you said, "okay, if you want," as you put your pipe in your mouth. But you unrolled your pouch and spilled tobacco on his carpet. Then you went to pick it up when the pipe fell out of your mouth. And you drooled a little too. Just a drop. But it landed on the pile of tobacco. "Whoa, Mr. Wamblie," the psychiatrist said. "Just lean back and ah, ah, relax. I'll pick it up." And so you did while he cleaned up the mess. "I think you need an ah, ah, escort," he said and called the hall as if it were an emergency. It seemed no time passed before an attendant came. They must have been worried to come so fast, worried you'd do something, something crazy. After all, they all knew what was going to happen. All but you that is.

Coda

Henrietta had gone. You didn't know where they took her. But she wasn't there. The social worker either. They probably went to her office to talk. But I'm not sure. You were sitting on the couch in the outer office. That's what the doctor said to do. He was in his office writing. I don't know what. Probably about you, about what happened. You said nothing to the attendant when he came. You didn't acknowledge him in any way. You were too dazed. Everything was upside down. Or, maybe, it was right-side-up and had been upside down before. I don't know. Be that as it may, he asked you to come back to the hall with him. You said nothing, but you got up and started walking. He asked you to wait, but you kept going. I don't know why. You just did. It was like being a machine that, once activated, cannot stop just because someone commands it. The secretary gave him your hat and coat, at least that's what I assume happened. He had them when he caught you anyway. He again asked you to stop, but you didn't, you couldn't, not until he forced you. He stood in front of the door blocking your passage, otherwise you would have gone outside hat and coat or not. It was very cold. Dead of winter. He was worried about your health. You weren't. You couldn't have cared less. But then, that's why he was there I suppose. You allowed him to put your hat and coat on you, but you didn't speak or look at him. You just left your arms limp and let him do what he wanted with them. Once he was done, you began walking back. On the way, he tried to get you to talk, talk about IT; what happened I mean. He was told to, trained to to get information. You said nothing—Just go on—You just kept walking with your eyes fixed ahead—On to the hall—"Well, what happened? How did it go? How do you feel?" he kept asking—Say nothing—But you kept ignoring him, so he finally gave up. So you tramped through the snow with your hands in your pockets for the rest of the way back. The only time you spoke was on the hall to ask if you could go to your room. "If you're sure you're all right," he said. "I'm all right," you said. "I just don't feel like going into it"—Because you're crazy!—"Your program coordinator will be in at three," he said. "Maybe then, you'll feel more like talking." "Okay," you said. Then you went down to your room. You got your hat and coat off and sat down on the cot by the window. You felt crazy—You're crazy—Anxiety that goes beyond fear—Crazy!—Anxiety that goes beyond panic—Crazy, Wamblie!—It's hard to understand—That's why the anxiety—You can only feel it—That's why the fear—It's strength—The fear you can't master—It's impossible to dominate—The anxiety you can't control—When it comes, it comes—The overwhelming flood!—There's nothing you can do—The flood of panic!—It gives you thoughts—Panic!—Bizarre thoughts—Panic!—Thoughts of retaliation—That's what it is—Thoughts of killing—It's panic!—Bloody, gory thoughts about the hospital—Because you're crazy!—The company—Insane!—Your wife—Out of your head!—Terrible, terrible thoughts—You're nuts!—And what is the cause?—You know—Them!—You're sure—There's no doubt—You're positive—Some things you know—Positive!—Just know—It's them!—And how does it happen?—The same—They're injected into your head—They do it—They're not from you—Wamblie!—They're from them—Are you listening?—It's too upsetting—Do you hear?—Don't let them!—They're talking to

175

you—Push them away—And they want you to listen—They're too overpowering—Listen good!—And what's the cause?—Listen to the voices—The doctors!—They're all that can save you—They do it with the devices they carry—Save you from losing your mind— Carry to be paged—Save you from insanity—But they're not for paging—They'll command you—They're used to create static and jumble everything in your brain—So get the foil!—That's what they're doing—The tin foil you bought—Making me think you're crazy—With it, you can interfere with their waves—Making me believe you're sick—So make strips and line the door jamb—That accounts for the anxiety—The windows and the heating vents— That's why you want to melt and disintegrate—Do a careful job—They're doing it to you—It'll keep out the waves—They've done it to you before—It'll give you some relief—You know that—Push all the furniture in front of the door—There's no doubt—Securely block the entrance—Although you're not completely sure—You don't want them coming in—You may be wrong—Because they'll force something on you—But you'll never know—Curl up on your cot in the corner—How could you?— Clasp your hands to your ears—You have no way to know—Stop the sounds!—It could be you—Piercing, high pitched sounds!—The thoughts are your own—Sounds you can't tolerate!—If true, you should obey—Sounds you can't stop!—Maybe it's the forces giving you commands—You're trying to stop the invasion!— Maybe you should kill someone—Their invasion of your mind— You feel like it—But nothing works—It takes all your energy not to—Nothing!—But you can stop it—The sounds and jumble are still coming in!—And not give in! Finally there's a knock—They're telling you not to—But don't answer—Obey!—You're too afraid! The knob turned and the door hit the furniture—Them!—But it's not open enough for anyone to see in—It's them!—Whoever it is pushed it some more—You're terrified!—That makes you afraid— You're being driven out of your skull!—"No! No! No!" you're yelling. "Go away! Leave me alone! Leave me alone!"—You have to follow the voices!—Whoever's out there has left—The commanding voices!—But only for a minute—The voices you're hearing!—He's returned with several others—Above everything else—They're working the door open further and further and further!—The all powerful voices—They've got it wide enough to enter!—Before it's too late!—Get under the bed and cover your face!—Too late!—Disappear if you can!—Because they're after you!—That's all you can think of!—After you!—Because they've found you!—After you!—"No! No! Go away!"—Because you're crazy!—They're telling you to calm down and asking if you want seclusion—"No! No!"—Crazy!—"I don't!"—Crazy!—"Not that!"—Crazy, Wamblie!—They're saying you should, that it's best because, there, you'd feel secure—Security!—"Come on, Mr. Wamblie"—Security!—"It's all right"—That's what you want! —"We'll all walk down together"—But that's not what you'll get —"NO!"—Not from them!—"All I want is for it all to stop!"— Because they're evil!—They're saying you have to—Evil, Wamblie!—That they'll force you if you don't—Evil!—So get out from under the bed—So don't!—And stop bawling and sniveling —Don't listen!—Stop mumbling about devices and channels— You'll be sorry if you do—Stop your mouth from going—Very sorry!—Before they ask you what you're saying—Sorry!— They're asking if you'll walk down quietly—Because they hate you!—Say yes and start out—Because they despise you!—And stop sniveling like a child—Despise you, Wamblie!—You can stop—Despise you!—Stop with five of them around you— Because you're sick!—By one door on the left, another on the right, another on the left and so on into the foyer—So rebel!— Run, Wamblie!—Rebel now!—You have to get out!—Don't let them force you!—Lunge for the door!—Don't!—Before they restrain you!—Before it's too late!—Before they're on you!—Too late!—You'll be face down with your arms and legs behind you before you know what happened!—I said it's too late!—You can try to break out of it, but there's nothing you can do—I said it's too late!—They're carrying you into seclusion!—Do you hear?—

You're face down on the mattress!—Hear the voices?—You're completely incapacitated!—The all powerful voices?—They're emptying your pockets and taking off your belt and shoes—Wamblie!—They're pulling down your pants and giving you a shot!—Are you listening?—Now they've left and locked the door—There's nothing you can do—So bang your head!— Nothing! —They're telling you to stop—Nothing in the world!—But keep it up!—Because your mind is gone!—So they'll put you in restraints!—Completely gone!—Like they're doing—Gone!—Like they've done—Forever!—Your hands and feet are strapped to the bed—There's nothing you can do!—So you can't move—Nothing!—You'll never move—You're powerless!—Never again! —Your limbs are bound like an animal's!—So don't!—Fighting makes the straps dig in—Don't try!—So relax—Because there's nothing—Let the drug take effect—Nothing in the world—You'll be better off—Forget it—Let your mind go—Forget everything—Go—It's fading—Into oblivion—Fading—Wamblie!—Fading—Do you hear?—Fading—Are you there?—There's nothing—W a m b l i e — N o t h i n g — W a m b l i e ! — N o t h -i n g...nothing...neeskuuaach!...— W a m b l i e !— ... peeeeeeeewww!...And that was the end of that...skeek...—Wamblie!—She left—Do you hear?—Or the beginning of the end...skeek...skeek...—Wamblie!—I mean Henrietta divorced you—Do you hear?—...skeek...—I mean you lost her—You shouldn't fall asleep—But then, you lost everything—So wake up!—You just hadn't known it—Wake up!—That's when you learned the truth—Wake up!—And you've been miserable ever since—I said up!—What?—Up!—Huh?—Get up!—Oh...God!

I must have dozed off for a minute. Yes. That's the first time in days. But what was I thinking about?....Oh yes, I remember now...but I better not burden you with that anymore. That might make you leave. Besides, you better get more sleep. That little bit was far from enough. I don't know if you can, but I know you should try. Otherwise, you'll go crazy! I think perhaps you did. But don't worry about that. You've been thinking for a time, an awful long time. You undoubtedly need rest. I do too by now. After all, it's the middle of the night. We've thought into the middle of the night again. It's not a good habit, but I suppose you needed it. To understand your predicament I mean. I mean that's what we're trying to do, isn't it? Understand? An absurdity from which there seems no escape.

But let's not get off on that again. We've already agreed. We'll get some sleep, then see about tomorrow. At least I hope we'll get some sleep. You've been having a lot of trouble lately. It's been most difficult. But then, so has everything else. Life, for instance. It's never easy, is it? But go along now and let me sleep. I've had enough talking. You can't expect me to go on forever. Eventually, I have to stop. And I will if you can get comfortable again....So good night....Good night! Good night! Good night! Goddamn it!

Movement III

Introduction

Again you couldn't sleep, not a bit, not a wink. It's useless to try. I don't know what to do about anything! This lack of sleep will kill you! I can't stand it anymore! Why can't you sleep, why can't you sleep? I keep asking over and over although I find no answer. It seems there is none, none that I can see. You're tired heaven knows, yet, every time you try, you can't fall asleep. You're alert. Energy is exuding through you. Rest is the antithesis of your state of mind. It's been like that for hours. Since last night in fact. It's been horrible! So what did you do? You paced. All night and into the day. You paced. The sun came up. You paced. Knowing nothing beyond the room. You paced. The shades were (are) drawn. You couldn't face the day, not in your condition. So you paced. You needed rest, but you paced. That's what you've done. You couldn't do anything else. The anxiety came every time you tried, so you've been going on all night, all day I mean. At least I assume it's day. It must be by now. Afternoon even, perhaps even dusk. I suppose that much time has passed. And all you've done is pace, all you've done is pass the time, passed it off into nothing. That's what you've done, nothing! You're not a step closer to your goal. The room's in worse disarray than ever. You won't be ready for work tomorrow, but what can you do about that? Nothing! And that's probably the best thing.

Perhaps you worry needlessly, perhaps you should relax and take things as they come. But that's not so easy for someone like you. You tried, tried all weekend. But you had not one moment of success. So you tried harder, yet the moment of relaxation moved further away. In other words, it had the exact opposite effect. I mean you felt more tense. And the more you tried to relax, the more tense you became. If the converse were true, you'd be happy. But no. In either case, you're tense. If you try to relax, you're tense, if you try not to relax, you're tense. And that's your dilemma. But what is the way out? Not to try? To give up? No! That results in catastrophe and everything goes down the drain. It already has in fact. It's completely destroyed, you're completely destroyed. So why do you try? Why not give up? I can't explain it, but something simply won't let you, something keeps spurring you on which brings us back to rest. You don't need to be spurred on so you don't give up, no, you need rest. It's not a matter of being too lazy, it's a matter of pushing too hard I think. Or it's the other way? But I'm not sure now. Either you push too hard and get too tense or you don't push hard enough and accomplish nothing. Ha! Accomplish nothing. That sums up your life. You accomplish nothing. Try or not, relax or not, lazy or not, you accomplish nothing. This weekend is a perfect example, this year too for that matter. I mean nothing's come out of it. Nothing! And I was determined this weekend would be different. Determined! Yet it hasn't. It's the same, exactly the same. Or worse if anything. And what can you do? Stop trying? Try? I don't know anymore and I'm beginning not to care. I know I've said that before, but then it was out of spite. Now, I mean it. I do! You're at that point because there's nothing left to care about except yourself in a vacuum totally unrelated or connected to anything or anyone. And why should that make a difference? Because you're nothing, not alone. I can't think of you out of this world, yet you are. You suffer completely alone. So it doesn't matter if your efforts are futile. I mean if they were successful, they would be the same. If the room were clean and you were rested, what would be the difference? Would your wife want you back? Would the President be reinstated? Would a bum in the street reform? Would you be any happier? The answer is no. It would make no difference to anyone. So you've not failed, you've merely gone on existing that much longer and I guess you can take pride in that at least. But it's got nothing to do with success or failure, nothing to do with accomplishments, it's got to do with comfort, so I don't know why I pretend anything else. The whole thing is for your comfort. That's all. You need sleep to be comfortable because it feels better and so does a clean and orderly room which is why you want these things. It's got nothing to do with the rest of the world, it's only got to do with you. But why can't you accomplish that? I guess it's a chain of events beginning with sleep. That's the problem. Sleep! Not sleeping leaves you tired, being tired leaves you preoccupied and totally unable to work and, consequently, the room stays dirty while you contemplate sleep and the reasons you're awake which is where it all goes wrong. So the problem is sleep. Why can't you sleep? It all goes back to that. It's not because of medication. I can't believe that because it does you no good. It would be a false slumber. You discounted that long ago. Then there's the dark which you've had a lot of since the shades have been down all weekend. That might be the reason. I've thought you needed daylight so you'd feel you'd been through a day. But I discounted that too because, before you can go through the day, you have to go through the night sleeping. It all goes back to that. So you've remained in the dark attempting to do it although it hasn't worked at all even though you hold out in the hope it will because you can't face a day until you sleep, just can't. The only other reason could be food and the fact you've had none whatsoever since Friday noon. Couldn't that keep you awake? I don't know. But I tried a remedy, not because you're hungry (though I know you are. I mean you don't feel it, but you must be), but because it might help you to sleep, so I thought you'd go out for a snack, but you couldn't get the door open, couldn't budge it a bit although you tried the knob and lock several times each, you banged it, kicked it, but it still wouldn't open although it did give you a headache right behind the eyes. I'd like to think you could have mastered it, but you couldn't, not by trying at least, so you finally decided to leave it alone there being no other way whatsoever. Accepting that is accepting reality. I mean you're not one to defy fate even though it left you without food and, therefore, without sleep. But being unable to stop, you thought some more about it. You came up with a solution too that will work in time. Alcohol! There's another reason too, but I'll save that for later. It's a clever idea. I hope it works. It always does in movies. But anyway, you pulled out your bottle of scotch and thank God you remembered that on the way. It's a fool proof method if you drink enough and it shouldn't take much since your stomach is so empty, so you've got nothing more to worry about until you wake up which is when you'll have a day to face. So it's better than food because you don't have to go out and you don't have to bother with the door which is probably just a hallucination there being no other explanation since there's no reason why an unlatched, unlocked door shouldn't open. Therefore, it's not in the door, it's in you which I can accept now. I mean it wouldn't open, so you're drinking instead although it's not making you feel anything but nauseous. In fact you'd better go lay down. Yes, traipse through the water to the cot....There's a lot of it now. See it? Yes. The pipe's been leaking for days. But there's no one below, so it doesn't matter if it all runs into the basement.

Ah! There. It feels so good to lay down. But I wish there weren't so many cockroaches. I guess the water forced them out. You've grown so used to the dark, you can see them on the walls, thousands of them it seems, so the little episode on Friday apparently didn't work since they're not scared in the least. But that's all right, isn't it, Wamblie? Yes, that's all right. I mean this is more their place than yours. Yes, of course it is. After all, they've certainly been here longer than you and, besides, you'd be more lonely without them, true? So don't be nasty and say, hello. "Hello, little roaches. How are you? Nice day, isn't it?" Go ahead! "So what's new with you guys? Anything?" That's right. "Nothing's new with me either. Nothing's changed in a year in fact. My life has stayed the same. Because of my wife and the hospital, not to mention the company. But you don't want"—Yes! "Well, anyway, things haven't been the greatest. I've been pretty depressed. I don't know why exactly. Well, yes I do really. It's my wife. She's the one, the one who's deserted me and for no good reason" —Wamblie!—"No good reason at all"—Listen!—"She's a no good bitch and I hate her!"—Listen!—"Hate her!"—You're talking—"That's all"—Talking to roaches—"Because she doesn't care"—But roaches don't comprehend—"Not about you"— Besides, they're very filthy—"She's just a wretched little creature" —And you should get rid of them—"With brown kinky legs"—So beat them!—"Legs that are creepy!"—Pulverize them—"And disgusting!"—Now!—"And that's sickening!"—Wamblie!—"And gross!"—Do it!—"But that's how it is"—Do it now!—"I think"— Now!—"But I don't know"—Before you're raving!—"Don't know anything"—Before you're crazy!—You're breathing hard—Crazy! —"Why, I don't know"—But don't get anxious—You can't slow it down—Not anxious!—It's getting faster and faster!— Not now!—Why an anxiety attack?—No!—"Why?"—Not now!— The sweat is dripping—It's bad!—It's not the heat—Because you're scared!—Maybe you should go back—Terrified!—Back to the hospital—Hysterical!—Maybe that would save you— Wamblie!—Maybe you should go call and go back—Do you hear?—They wouldn't be surprised—Do you?—They'd like it in fact—You're hysterical!—Like to see you've failed—Hysterical!—It would give them pleasure—Do you hear?—So why not?—No!—It could save you—Do you hear the voices?—Because of the door?—No!—You must be able to get that open—Do you?—I'm sure you could—No, I said!—But why bother?....You're starting to feel calmer now. If you ignore them, the crises passes—Wamblie!—Panic sets in, but then it passes—Wamblie!—It's like a wave. It rises like a wave that rushes over you and knocks you down, it builds, crests and recedes like a wave, as always; that much you can depend on if it always will which is an unknown quantity like everything else which is all that's known. You can think you know, for years you thought you knew, you thought your life was perfectly patterned, you thought you could predict it all and that gave you comfort. There's nothing like stability to make life a breeze. But then it all collapsed and everything went wrong. I don't know what you left out, but I know there was certainly something, something like the future and the fact it's so unknown which is what you can't accept; that you had (have) no control over your destiny, no control from one minute to the next which is all that is for certain; that much you've learned. The minute you think you have things figured out, it will probably all go wrong which probably means, if you don't think you understand things, everything will go right which there's a chance of, more of a chance than if you think you know, anyway, which is when you'll suffer the greatest disappointment which is what you did that day, the day that guy came into your office. Before that, everything was fine. Everything! Your marriage, your career, everything. Then he told you that.

But I've already told you. At least I think I did. If I remember correctly, I already explained everything that happened and went over the whole sickening mess which is probably why you can't sleep since just thinking about that makes you bitter and want to...want to...want to what? I don't know. Disappear I suppose which would be a luxury although it'll never come even if you killed yourself since the body would remain. Besides, it's out of the question since there's no reason to want to since you're perfectly content here; notwithstanding your bitterness, your anger toward them for what they've done. But that's another story. Besides, I told you all about it I think. But no matter because it does you no good to dwell on it since it only makes things worse, since it only makes your disappointment greater and it makes you wonder if you're losing your mind which you've wondered a lot especially because of the voices, those voices you've been hearing all night or think you have, at any rate, although you're really not sure since it all runs together with the voices, the thoughts, a conversation here, a conversation there, all becoming one huge fog you can't distinguish; not only whether they're voices or not, but whether you're thinking or not. But who knows? Who knows? And what does it matter? It's your head and what goes on goes on, so why try to control it or even consider doing that? We watch the sun come up and go down, why not our minds since they're just a force, just another force to observe, so why try to make it our own since they belong to someone else or something else controlled by higher powers which is what you've finally come around to. They function on their own with no regard for us and that's true of all of them, of everyone's because we're only allowed the illusion they're ours to avoid unnecessary conflict. But, as long as we perceive that illusion and assume our minds are ours, we can proceed as if we're normal as long as we don't challenge that or try to use our minds independently since that they don't allow. Try to own your mind and they'll crush you in fact. You do it their way or suffer. That's all there is to it. Except, of course, you have the satisfaction of an attempt, you have that. If nothing else, at least you can take pride in trying, in trying to understand. I mean in not just accepting, but attempting to grapple with the meaning of life which you've done, you've forced them to force you which is why you can't win. That's why it's absurd to take any satisfaction because they can force you. The power ultimately lies with them, not with you, since they can make you conform no matter what you do. So there's no way out....Well, there's one way out; a way that would take you out of their hands, so perhaps you should, perhaps that's the alternative although it seems absurd to get born and kill yourself. What sense does that make? None that I can see. And it's got to make sense. What matters if nothing makes sense? Nothing! Nothing matters without reason and logic since they are the ingredients of truth. So there's got to be sense for things to have meaning. Therefore, the suicide idea is false because to kill yourself can't bring freedom because there'd be nothing left to sense it, to enjoy it, so why do you think of it so much, why is it constantly on your mind if it has no validity? Maybe it's not from you, maybe these ideas are being planted in your head, maybe that's just what the powers and the forces want; for you to kill yourself and save them the trouble, maybe that's what they're aiming for although you won't give them the satisfaction if for no other reason than spite. See? You can exert some control after all, some power, it's not all theirs I don't think although one never knows for sure since the truth is impossible to discern even for the smartest, even for the greatest because even they debate life's true meaning and can't agree since no thought process will bring them to it, no amount of reason and logic will take one to the truth; that much you've learned: that it can only be deciphered on an emotional level. I mean you can feel truth, but not...wait! You were just saying the opposite. You've got to stop this thinking before you become any more confused. You're running around in circles this way saying one thing, then the opposite and believing it just as much. But it's so hard to know anything since logic and

189

reason don't come easily to you although you can still make sense of something can't you, maybe, if you try? All night, you have your hardest to understand, to understand...what? I don't know. Maybe it's nothing. But you've tried to understand something. At least you've done that although nothing made sense including your thoughts which flutter from one to another like butterflies which made you think you sunk into oblivion since you couldn't do anything about it and you thought you'd never get back, back to where you are although time has passed and you haven't gone anywhere except exactly the same place doing exactly the same thing which, perhaps, is a blessing in disguise. But where did the time go? Where did everything go? You've been up all night, but you don't know what happened. Nothing I guess. You thought, that's nothing, and you paced, that's nothing except movement to no particular purpose although movement, nevertheless, which is something, anyway, you shouldn't disparage since it's all you have, all you've done. You've paced, so why not take pride in it? Paced! Paced! Paced! It sounds like something. Besides, you couldn't do anything else there being nothing else to do except stave off the void. Pace...or sleep! I thought you'd do that, but the answer was no, you're not allowed or, rather, wouldn't allow yourself. I'm not sure which although it doesn't matter since the effect is the same. The effect, the suffering. You were made to suffer instead, but you're used to that. But then again, you're not. I mean, you've had your share, but you haven't grown used to it since you never do unless you're crazy. But you're not crazy. On the contrary, you're sane. At least when you're not alone which explains what happened last night which explains why you paced. But you've already said that. Pacing, you go in circles, talking, you go in circles, thinking, you go in circles with no way out just as last night, day I mean, last day, last night and day it was, I think, although I can't remember for sure although I know you've been going in circles for sure since, no matter how far you go, you stay in exactly the same place with it all coming back on itself like everything that leads everywhere and everything that leads nowhere, nothing that leads everywhere and nothing that leads nowhere which is exactly the same and yet completely different which explains precisely your return which I never should have doubted since it couldn't have happened otherwise, not if everything comes back on itself which it does although it doesn't, too, sometimes although it does, too, so it is your destiny to return and, therefore, it's not surprising you're out of the void or appear to be, feel yourself to be, momentarily at least, with some meaning which has to be imposed however arbitrarily since you can't go on as you have all night, all day, spewing garbage that means nothing to no one, pacing and thinking and rambling like this which is all a waste of time which is all you have and that's all you've done with it. I mean time on nothing, nothing on time in spite of the matter of choice, the right, the ability to choose something constructive which is what you want although how many times have you thought how to do it which is the question you can't answer since there are no answers you can see because you're too tense which is probably your problem. You're too nervous, too tired, too drugged....No! You're not drugged like before which we've talked about. But you're too...what? I don't know. But here, I'm going on again just as I was when you left. It's been a long night, I mean day. Night and day actually. Whatever. It's Sunday afternoon and tomorrow is Monday I hope. I sometimes wonder since you haven't slept in days. Yet you must be refreshed tomorrow or you'll give a false impression (again) which you wouldn't want. So get going and don't say you can't. You've done it before and you can do it again, right?—No! Too tired. Too lazy—That's an excuse—I've been through a lot—An excuse—We've all been through a lot—Wamblie!—That's no reason—Are you listening?—Yes it is—

Why?—Wamblie!—Because every time I try, every time I do what I've done all night, every time I think of what I have to do and think about doing it, my heart starts to thump harder and harder and harder, my lungs expand and contract, expand and contract more and more and more until my chest feels like bursting or collapsing—You're getting overwrought!—One or the other—Do you hear?—Every artery, every vein, every capillary swells with the flood and the panic rises—You're working yourself up—Then I have to ebb the flow—Are you listening?—Somehow!—Wamblie!—So I pace—Do you hear the voices?—You pace—You must calm yourself—I pace to slow it down—Calm yourself now!—If you get overwrought, it'll let go—Because it does no good—It's a slim connection— No good at all—To what?—So don't!—To everything—Don't do it!—That's why I can't bear it—I'll only hurt you—There shouldn't be this intensity—Hurt you more—And why not?— Then you'll be sorry—Because you're too delicate to withstand it—Very sorry!—But what can you do?—Sorry, Wamblie!— Pace—Sorry!—That's right—Because you don't listen—Pace— Do you hear?—That slows everything—Wamblie!—So the night isn't wasted—Do you hear the voices?—At least you're alive— Do you?—Stayed alive. At least you've managed that—Do you?—But is it right?—Wamblie!—I get tired of that thump! thump! thump! thump! thump! thump! eternally—Wamblie!— And the lungs. Larger, smaller, larger, smaller, the same, over and over, ad infinitum. I can't bear this sphere! Can't stand it anymore!—But you'll have to—Why? What can I do?—There's something—Kill myself?—Yes!—That's a little extreme—You can kill yourself—But it would stop my awareness—Put an end to it all—Stop the heart and lungs—An end to the misery—Yes, but is that what you want?—Yes!—Not to be crazy?—That would do it—Crazy?—That would certainly do it—What's that?—Then you'd have no problems—When you're different—Then you'd be dead—Different from what?—But not crazy—From others—Not anymore—Which others?—You wouldn't have that problem—Other people—Not anymore—Everybody—So do it!—Anybody—Do it now!—But there's no others here, so who are you different from?—Don't listen to them—All the others you've known—The other voices—Compared to them, you're crazy—Let them go—In whose eyes?—Let them go!—Theirs—Let them fade—What about yours?—Wamblie!—In mine, I don't know—Do you hear?—And that's the problem—Do you?—You can't make up your mind— Let them go—Can't make it up—Go now—Can't put it together— Then go and do it—Can't invent it—Do as they say—They're there—Do it now—They exist—Now, Wamblie!—But...but you're getting dizzy and you'll come apart this way. But what was the question? The question is, should you kill yourself?—The question is, are you crazy?—That's the question—Am I crazy?— And the answer is yes—Yes!—You should—No!—You shouldn't —Don't jump to conclusions—Do it now!—I'm not—Why suffer needlessly?—I was saying yes to the question, not the answer— Unless you're afraid—Don't conclude anything before you understand—Is that what it is?—About?—Are you afraid?—My meaning—Afraid of the other?—Your meaning?—You should be—About craziness—You should be afraid—I wasn't and I already know—Because it's completely unknown—About?— Unknown to you—Craziness!—But death is the only way— Yes—The only way—How could you be crazy if there's no one here to think so?—To know—There's me—To know the other side—No matter—You want to know the other—No matter?— Don't you?—Not in this respect—You want to know oblivion— Insanity exists only in relation to others—Don't you?—Others?— Wamblie!—Others must deem you so—So stop!—And if they don't?—Stop listening!—You're not—Listening to them—And if they do?—They'll get you nowhere—You are—Going in circles —And me?—That's all—You decide according to them—So don't listen—Why?—Not to them—Wamblie—You have no strength to—Listen only to us—No belief in yourself—And do what we say—And why?—Do it!—I don't know—Don't push them!—It's a power I've given up—Don't try to crush them—Gave up?—Don't!—Shut up!—Don't—No need of that—Or you'll be sorry—Two talking's too much!—Wamblie!—Too much confusion—Wamblie!—Too much talking!—Do you hear?—Go on alone—Hear?—Of course—Hear?—That's fine—Hear, Wamblie?—Get control—Don't crush them!—Of what?—Don't!—Yourself—Please!—Then go ahead—Wamblie!—I will—Wamblie!—Start! —Don't push them!—Start where?—Please!—With freedom—Wamblie!—That intrigues you—Wamblie!—But what can be said? It's nice. Freedom! It's a Godsend although you don't know that until it's gone. I've lost it, it being the first thing they strip you of by watching your every move. And why? Because they were afraid of you because you didn't conform and because you still don't which they can't tolerate and I'll give an example to prove it. The President—ex, I should say. They couldn't control him—They've gone—He had a moral sense—So don't worry—A sense of justice—Just keep pacing—And he exercised it despite what they said—Pace and they'll leave you—Yes—Sit and they'll come—Result?—Think and they'll go—A loss of freedom—Yes—Not just for him, but for all. So relax—If they can level public officials, they can level anyone—Relax—And they've leveled public officials—Relax—The President, the Vice President and their entire administration are gone, all gone. And why? The press which is controlled by...by...by someone, someone we can't see. But they have people believing what they print and what they see, nevertheless, to the point where they wanted him out and, so, he is which makes me wonder how he feels. Fear, depression, pressure and no support from anyone? Probably, which is a lot like you. You've been through a common experience. They're no help, no help at all and so what happens? You crumble and fall and everyone says I told you so never thinking they could have caused it since they're always playing the victim and saying it's always being done to them, it's always Nixon's fault, always Wamblie's fault is what they say which leaves you both wondering what happened, wondering what people think, wondering how you got here, how he got there. But there's the difference; your surroundings I mean. He doesn't have to suffer in a dingy room, no, he gets a palace and he's with his wife while you're a nothing who's thrown away except...but...but there's talk of jail and it could go that far just like you. After all, you're locked up, so why not him? Because he's the president? That could make a difference, it makes a difference now since he is the president or was two days ago which he's suffering for since he has to listen to those who've betrayed him say he destroyed himself while they shirk their responsibilities and blame it all on him as they do on you which is the Christ story all over again exactly because, when you're a saint, they destroy you because they're jealous you see so far, see the evil so well and that's why they try to blot you out. So he could easily end like you in a hospital too which wouldn't be a surprise because that's what they do with people like him and with people like you, they throw you to the wolves and watch you get eaten calling it entertainment which gives them something to do, something to look forward to even though it gives you nothing which they don't think of, no, they don't think it takes everything you have mentally, materially, spiritually, not to mention your dignity. They don't think of that. It's entertainment to them at your expense; Nixon's and yours, so he has nothing to look forward to, you have nothing to look forward to except a dead end street for you and for him.

Dead end!....I don't know why, but that reminds you of the boy, the one you saw today. Or was it yesterday or the day before? Yes, it was the day before on the way here when you went down the dead end although you didn't know it at first....Oh! That's why you thought of him. You saw him on a dead end street as you were walking very fast feeling uncomfortable being out in the street exposed and...but that's another story. Anyway, you saw a child, a little boy playing in a pile of dirt with trucks and tractors building a road, a miniature road when he saw you and gleefully ran toward you and asked who you were which caused you to pretend not to hear and simply hurry on since you didn't have time for a little boy's questions which apparently disappointed him because he turned around and went back to his toys, but with much less enthusiasm. Shortly after that, you realized where you were, that you were on a dead end, so you turned around and went back and the boy, seeing you, approached again with a smile on his face and asked again, "Who are you?" "Just an explorer," you answered without stopping since you didn't know what else to say since it seemed there was nothing very meaningful, not your name or career, nothing like that. I mean how do you say who you are? I don't know. But you hoped what you said would satisfy him although it didn't apparently since he kept running beside you repeating his question and appearing very interested in knowing and, when he did, you said, "My name?" having no idea what else he'd be after although, by then, he had tired and stopped causing you to shout, "Wamblie!" over your shoulder suddenly feeling it paramount he know your name as if your existence would end if he missed it, as if that were the only way you could live. It was funny how that struck you. I guess strange would be a better word. But I'm not sure if he did or not, remember your name I mean because you kept on going since you weren't prepared to stop. But the incident left you slightly unnerved, I guess because you couldn't answer, you couldn't really answer since everything you thought of was artificial and superfluous and seemed like an insult to say which was all the more true since his question was so genuine, so genuine you didn't want to be ungenuine yourself since it would do no good. But you could think of nothing to say and that provoked anxiety although, at any other time, you could have answered that question without a moment's thought although then you couldn't which made you too fearful, fearful of the future. I mean what were you and what would you become? Rich? Famous? A bum in the gutter? That seemed more likely if you live that long although you probably won't....I think you need a drink, another drink. That could help calm you down since something has to before you go completely out of your skull. No pun intended.

Exposition I

You remember being that age; five or so like the boy? Yes, it was a happy time for you, very happy—A lie—It couldn't have been better—Don't listen—Your parents, your family were great, all great and they gave you an excellent upbringing. You have absolutely nothing to complain about there, not there—All lies—It was only later things got bad—Don't pay attention—I can't explain why, but your early life carried none of the seeds of what came later—Not to them—But...well, it's another unanswerable, so why try?—Just go on—But, at least there's some consolation in that, your childhood I mean—Just go on—At least that was a good time of life since, right on through, there were no problems—More lies—None whatsoever —That's all you're telling—Not that I say there weren't a few minor things like in any family, but nothing abnormal—That's not true—There were none in your teens either or in your twenties or thirties either for that matter—Don't answer—It all went fine with no outstanding occurrences—And it's wrong—But now, there are many—Don't!—Now, it's one thing piled on another until your back breaks with the strain—Wrong to lie—Actually, it already has—Don't listen—Long since, otherwise you wouldn't be here—But you are—You wouldn't be suffering like this—Not to them—Are suffering—You wouldn't be trying to hold back tears—Because they're evil—Suffering for lying—Your nose wouldn't be wheezing—Evil!—For what you've thought—You wouldn't be so sad and so miserable—Evil, Wamblie!—Thoughts that are false—You would't be ready to give up—They want to hurt you—So that's what you should do—I don't know what comes over you—That's all they want—Give up!—But then again, I do—Nothing more—Now!—It's a wave of despair—So don't!—Now, Wamblie!—That's what it is—Don't listen!—Before you suffer anymore—No matter what you think about—Not to them—Suffer with your thoughts—Good things, bad things—You'll go crazy if you do—Your tormented thoughts—They all cause depression and leave you vanquished —Do you hear?—Thoughts of suicide—But that's not true, Wamblie, what are you saying?—You'll be sorry—Some things leave you ecstatic, some things leave you soaring—Very sorry—I can't describe it, but you can be uplifted—Uplifted!— Sorry, Wamblie—That's still possible—Yes!— Although it's not what you're feeling now—Unless you get away from the voices—Now you feel—The haunting voices—You feel—Crazy! —I don't know what you feel—That's what it is—Not glad—It's sick!—Not happy—And deranged!—Not miserable—And crazy!— Not despair—Do you hear?—But like crying?—Do you?— Crying!—You're crazy!—You want to cry—Because of them!— Yes—They've done it—But you can't—And there's nothing you can do—Not fully—Nothing but suffer—I don't think—Or kill yourself —Wait!—There's always that—You're confused—That for relief— You want to cry—So do it!—Yes—Do it now!—No!—Now!—I can't!—Now, Wamblie!—But you want to?—Before it gets worse— Like those two days—Worse and worse—You've cried this year —Worse and worse—Many times—Do you hear?—But not enough—Are you listening?—You want release—Wamblie!—You don't want to fight anymore. Not like those days—Wamblie!— But that's not good, it's not good to cry like a child when you're a man—Wamblie!—Unseemly. That's what it is: unseemly. Yet, you want to like you did when you were five and like you did in the group—They're gone—Those are the occasions on which you cried though you've felt like it many other times—I think—But what gets in the way? I don't know. It just won't come. But then, you could do it? Yes. And why? I don't know. The tears would just flow. And now, you can't? Yes. But you could then. Yes. You did in the group. Yes. You cried like a baby although it wasn't until the end. In the beginning, you just sat there like everyone else—I think you've weathered them—The leader was that nurse—Yes—Remember?—Good man—The one who forced medication on you the first day you were there—Now you can relax—Yes—Relax—It was she and you and a handful of others—Relax—You were sitting in the conference room like you did every week only, then, you had just been let out of seclusion—Relax—Yes. It was the evening of the day you were put in seclusion. They didn't want you to go, but you insisted, yes, and they agreed, yes, so you were sitting there doing nothing. Ten minutes passed. There was silence. Fifteen. Still silence. Then the nurse asked if anyone had something to say. But all of you sat there like lumps and didn't speak a word. Not one of you so much as looked at her. "I don't know why you bother coming if you're just going to waste your time," she said. Then a patient, a young man, said, "We have to come, remember?" "Well then, why don't you use the time?" she asked. "We pay a hundred and ten dollars a day just for our rooms," he answered, "this is nothing but an overpriced hotel with bars and lousy service!" She told him he was angry and she challenged him to talk about it. "NO!" he yelled. But his anger didn't phase her in the least. She just told him calmly his attitude was useless. "You're here for a reason," she said. "You couldn't handle your life. There are others here like you. Why don't you take advantage of that?" "Because I don't want to," he screamed. "I don't need this place!" "Apparently, you do," she said. So he started in. "Locking people up doesn't help them, taking away all their possessions and all their contact with the world and regulating their entire lives doesn't help them a bit," he said. "It sounds like you've got complaints against me," she said. "YES!" he screamed. Then he explained why he was there, that he tried to commit suicide. He said he didn't agree it's unhealthy to contemplate death, however, and that he had been locked up against his will. "People who run around and never give suicide a thought are the ones with problems. Someone who never gives suicide a thought is someone who never thinks of their life. It's always an option to be considered," he said, "and I'm sick and tired of being prodded to talk about it." The nurse glared and shook her head as if his ideas were insane, totally insane. But she didn't attack him. No. She let someone else do that by asking a woman, a middle aged neurotic alcoholic, what she'd say to his remarks. She thought a moment, then asked him if he thought someone who's potentially dangerous to themselves or someone else ought to be put away. "NO!" he answered without hesitation. "Even if they're homicidal?" But there, another patient jumped in who explained the evil and insidious forces of society had taken away all choice. He started raving that everything is measured and predictable and that's the problem. "We're sick because the hospital has decided we're sick and, therefore, programs us to be sick. But we're only sick if we believe it." From there, he went into Hitler. He said, "The hospital makes patients conform like a dictator." Then he brought in the President—ex, I should say. And that's where you disagreed. Yes. On that point, he didn't understand. There, he equated Nixon and Hitler, so you took issue with him on that. Yes. "The President is good," you said beginning your explanation. But the nurse wouldn't let you. No. She broke in and said, "The reason for the group is to talk about feelings." So the first one piped up and said, "What do you think we're talking about? What we're saying is our personal feelings. Technology and science are what's wrong with the world, can't you understand that much at least?" She (the nurse) sighed listlessly and said, "You're intellectualizing again. Those are thoughts, not feelings." But he sloughed that off as if she sounded stupid, so she looked straight at you—Why?—You were ready to cry—You don't know—You don't know why—You just were—But you were overcome with grief—That's all—Maybe because your wife was leaving you, maybe because of the talk in the group or maybe it was having been in seclusion that day—It's all those things—You just did't know—And more—But you were very low and there was moisture in your eyes—It's because of you—You had your hands over your face and you were sniveling some—You and your problems—But you caught her looking at you and, when you did, you looked back—That's why—She asked what you were feeling—Why you want to cry—"I don't know," you said—Cry with grief—"Glad? Happy? What?" she asked—Because you're powerless—"Like crying"—Powerless to act—"But you can't cry for some reason?"—Powerless to progress—"Yes," you said—Powerless —Then, "No"—Powerless—Then, that you didn't know—That's what you are—But you said you'd wanted to for a long, long time—And that's why you want to cry—Since coming to the hospital, you'd wanted nothing else—But you can't cry—You said you teared a lot in recent months, but hadn't had a good cry since you were young—No—"What gets in the way?"—Can't really cry—"I don't know"—Not really—"It just won't come"—Because you're afraid—"But it did when you were little?"—Very afraid—"Yes" —Very fearful—"When what?"—Because it would mean you're weak—"When my father got mad"—Very weak—"What was he mad about?"—Weak like a child—"He was mad I blew my nose"—You'd look like a child—And that you cried—Not a man—Yes—No—"It made me very unhappy"—But a child— "Why?"—You wouldn't want that—Because you didn't know— Not that—You didn't know what they were doing—Would you,

Wamblie?—They didn't tell you—Would you?—But you were scared—No, you wouldn't—Yes—Because everyone would know— Not at first—Know you're scared—But later, on the table—Know you're afraid—At first, you were happy—Know you're fearful— When your mother came in and smiled and took you by the hand, you were pleased—Then what would they think?—You had never been to your father's before—They'd think you're a coward—You didn't know where he went—You a coward—He always took care of you at home—Imagine that!—But this time, you were going to his office and the prospect filled you with joy—But you don't have to cry—So you got ready quickly and left—No—But there, your mother helped you out of your clothes—You don't have to—She didn't say why—Because you already are—She simply undressed you—Are a coward!—And you didn't ask because you knew she'd be impatient—Are scared!—You knew when it was time and when it wasn't—Are afraid!—Then she put you in a gown—Aren't you, Wamblie?— Then she brought you into a room with a bed and table full of surgical tools—Aren't you?—Then she told you to lay down— Aren't you?—That's when you first got scared—Yes, you are— Especially when she left and you were laying there alone— Scared of what'll happen—Then your father came in dressed in a cap and gown—Happen if you cry—That scared you more—That's it, isn't it?—He was cold and distant—Isn't it?—He didn't say, hello, but, instead, fussed with the tools—Wamblie!—The only time he acknowledged your presence was to tell you to look at the wheel on the wall—Are you listening?—You did as he asked with intense trepidation—Do you hear?—It was a bunch of black and white circles that spun and spun and spun—Do you hear the voices?—It reminded you of a nightmare—Wamblie!—Then he pressed a cloth to your face—Do you?—A damp cloth that smelled and made you dizzy—You should—You wondered if he was trying to smother you—Wamblie!—You weren't sure whether to fight or not—You should!—Then everything went blank—You're breathing too hard....Three hours later, you woke up in a crib with an extremely sore throat, remember? More sore than before, but you still didn't know what happened, you didn't know he took out your tonsils because he didn't tell you because he wanted to see if you were a man, he wanted to see if you could act like a man and so you did. Your mother didn't either; tell you I mean, because she did whatever your father said. She came in saying you'd have to vomit before you could leave. You told her you couldn't, but later, a big gray lump came up which made you feel better although you still felt sick. It was like the worst hangover imaginable and your throat hurt badly, yes, but you didn't say a word because you wanted to be a man—It hurt—Your mother took you home—Hurt badly—She didn't say a word—The pain was intense—Either did your father—The wicked pain!—But that night, you sneezed and blew your nose which started to bleed along with your throat—The overpowering pain!—You were scared and screamed and that brought your father in—But it's wrong—He bawled you out for forgetting what he said—Wrong to scream—What he thought he said, but didn't—Wrong to show it—About not blowing your nose I mean—You're not being a man—You tried to explain you didn't know, but nothing would get him to listen—But a baby!—He just got madder and madder and madder—Do you hear?—And he called you a baby—Are you listening, Wamblie?—And so you cried—You're a child!—You cried and cried and cried—A child!—That was the last time—Do you hear?—That time and in the hospital telling it—Wamblie! —You've never cried again—But you want to—Wamblie!— Yes—Want to, but can't—Yes—Wamblie!—Can't...can't, can't. What a funny word. Can't, can't. It seems to mean something. Can't, can't. Can't, can't. You can't...can't what? Can't anything. Can't anything anymore. But you could once. Yes. Could. Could, could. Could cry, could play, could be happy, yes you could, you were, very happy, when left alone, when left alone in the basement, when left alone to play with your village. Then things were nice, then you were happy because you could be in your world—Why?—Not in theirs—Because you were God—That's why you liked it—Leave me alone—The God of the village—Liked it so much—Please!—The village you created—And so you were there—Please!—Created like God—There alone—I can't stand it!—Created out of clay—Away from everyone—I'll go crazy!—First a man, then another and another and another until there was a village—Alone and away—Absolutely crazy!—Day after day you made the village—That's how you liked it—So stop!—And all were yours to do with as you pleased—Isn't it?—Stop it now!—You were careful with detail—Isn't it?—Wamblie!—Stop hammering!—Careful to make them right —Wamblie!—Or I'll go crazy!—Because you wanted a perfect village—Are you listening?—Crazy!—A utopia—Wamblie!—I said crazy!—A perfect place—Do you hear?—Crazy now!—And it was—Wamblie!—I mean it!—Until your father ruined it—I will—Until he smashed the figures and threw them in a heap—If you don't leave me alone—Until he accused you of being a baby—So stop!—So you gave it up thinking you were too old—They have—And you think your father was right—Don't worry—You were too old for such things—Just go on—That's what you thought then—Go on thinking—He had you convinced—Go on pacing—Convinced of a lot of things—That'll keep them away—Because you believed whatever he told you—And relax—A father's word was God's—Relax—That was an absolute rule—Relax—At least in your house. And that's why you believed him no matter what he said and, I suppose, you've suffered because of it, because of what he said, I mean, since he probably misled you although you don't know for sure although some things he told you couldn't have been true especially about IT which can't have been the reason although, according to him, it was although, in reality, it couldn't explain your condition, you can't be this way because of that since you haven't done it that much your being very careful about that although the pattern fits with everything he described coming true like the pimples like he said and like going crazy, too, which is exactly what he predicted, I think, I think you've gone crazy but, then again, perhaps you haven't, perhaps that's a fabrication on the part of...but don't go into that because it's a waste of time. But he did warn you that time on the couch, the time the roof leaked over your bed and forced you to sleep on the livingroom couch early in the morning when you didn't think anyone would be up, when you had the urge, yes, and couldn't resist since it was the only way to get back to sleep, so you did it into the blanket which you, then, threw on the floor when your father came in unexpectedly and picked it up and started to fold it, but then noticed it was damp and said, "What's all over the blanket?" which caused you to cower because you didn't know what to say. "Well, if you're masturbating, you should do it with some knowledge," he said. "For one thing, it'll give you pimples. And, if you continue, it'll eventually drive you insane." You must have looked horrified because he said, "Yes, insane. Now you know what you're fooling with." Then he threw the blanket down and left and, sure enough, you did develop pimples, a very severe case and, later, you went insane with a collapsed life, so perhaps he was right although you haven't done it much although it could be the case since you could be this way because of that, because you went against the powers which is always bad since the signs seem clear. I mean you've gone against the forces and now you're suffering. It's a simple equation and perhaps true although I'm not completely convinced since everyone in the hospital couldn't be there because they sought too much self-gratification, could they? I don't know. I mean there's no way to know since the answer will never be revealed, at least not to you, so around and around the questions go like walking a Mobius strip on which the further you go, the more you find you're stuck in place with still the desire to go on, with the desire to progress even though you're not which is what your father said although it took so long to happen since, for years, you were fine with no sign of problems. In fact, if anyone had problems it was them, not you, since they were the ones whose lives were in turmoil or so it seemed since they were quite unhappy after you left although they tried not to show it your mother always claiming everything was fine, she was happy with her life and loved serving your father although there was a scotch bottle hidden in the pantry which doesn't really matter since she probably wanted it out of your reach. Her life was great. It couldn't have been better. She happily cooked and baked and cleaned all day and had friends to have coffee with and listen to the soap operas with and play golf and bridge and gin with, so there's no reason to think anything was wrong because so what if she did take a drink? There's nothing so bad in that although she did get a little tipsy on the occasions when you came home although you don't know how long that had been happening since you never noticed as a child although it probably started shortly after you left since your leaving probably provoked it since you were very attached which means it couldn't have been easy for her to see you go, it couldn't have been easy to have her only child leave which perhaps was the reason she was a little out of sorts getting used to having no child to take care of although it was probably a temporary thing, yes, that was it, nothing serious, nothing to get alarmed about although you did talk to your father or tried to. And why? Because you were worried, worried about your mother and wondering if she was an alcoholic and wondering why he seemed not to care since, when you asked him about it, he slammed down his fist and screamed, "My wife doesn't have a drinking problem!" which made you shut up. I mean his certainty convinced you because you reasoned, if there had really been a problem, your father would have done something although he didn't which caused you to tell yourself everything was fine even though your mother was there serving Christmas dinner with glazed eyes, a worn out smile and wobbling on her feet which embarrassed Henrietta when you brought her to visit especially since you told her of your parents, your great and wonderful parents who could do no wrong which caused you all to act (you, your wife and your father) like nothing was wrong, like it was a happy family reunion in spite of the fact you knew there was something wrong, you knew there were problems and your parents couldn't talk which probably started right after you left, after you went away to boarding school I mean; that boarding school with it's little rooms that were cramped like boxes with four small walls which had a front which had a door which led to a hall full of other doors opening on other boxes with two sides having a cot, a desk and chair and a chest of drawers, in that order, with also two closets and a window overlooking the grounds which is where you spent your school days, the days you spent away from them, your parents, your parents who had many problems, your parents who couldn't talk....But no. Don't say that. It was just a little thing which you're blowing up out of proportion as usual. Your mother had a little to drink, that's all, because it helped her to feel a little better and there's certainly nothing wrong with that since people do it all the time like you who's doing it now which doesn't make you an alcoholic, does it? No! So get another drink and relax.

Exposition II

I wonder if you should kill yourself. Seriously. I wonder that. It could be a viable alternative since a good argument can be made for taking that course since, perhaps, it's that bad, your life is that bad. I mean it couldn't be worse since, physically and mentally, you're a wreck and have been for months which I can't seem to change which, I guess, I've pointed out many times. So what should you do? Kill yourself? Yes. Kill yourself because things are that bad although you don't want to believe it since everything tells you to reject the idea; your entire life reflex is to try to preserve what you are which is natural although the truth is things are that bad, bad enough not to go on in fact, so why don't you give up, why do you keep hanging on and on and on when things are so awful? I don't know. I can't understand it, but there's just something inside that won't let go like the forces which tell you to do it, yes, although you won't—They're telling you—It's ordained by God you do, yet you won't—Because you're not listening—And why?—Not to them—No answer—And that's your insanity—So why look?—Insanity!—The same—Insanity coming out—So stop! —Coming out—Stop looking, stop asking, stop everything— Coming out—That's best and equal to death. Yes. It's all equal to death. Yes. It's the sum of everything, yet there you sit attempting to stave it off. God, what a pack of fools we are!

You and everyone else, I mean, because the only answer is death. It's all! It's everything! That's an insight! The truth has sprung to light as it always does if you look hard enough which, I guess, is what crazy people are for. To look for truth I mean. That's your purpose in life since no one else can do it. Therefore, you do have a use, a purpose, a contribution to make even in your current state. In fact, perhaps it's your current state that makes your worth so great since all great men suffer, they say, and I guess that's true of you who has arrived at these fantastic insights through a great deal of suffering although there is a barrier left to complete understanding which is? The fear of death of course. Yes. You're afraid to die before you learn to understand it. That's the only reason you don't kill yourself. You've learned enough to know it doesn't matter, but you haven't overcome your fears. That's your dilemma, your hell, your punishment. But for what, I don't know. Don't know? Unless it's seeing! Yes. Perhaps you're being punished for seeing. You don't know. Perhaps the forces or God or whatever it is is punishing you for presuming to see the truth, for presuming to enter his domain, for having the audacity to enter His province. Yes. Thus, you are placed in this predicament as a test. That's what it is. A test of your loyalty. So you should be subservient. Will you stop searching independently and owe all allegiance to him?—It's the way— Will you stop questioning and do as you're led?—The only way—Maybe then you'd be released—So do it!—Maybe then you'd become normal or kill yourself!—Do it now!—Either one would be better than this—Now!—You'd settle for either one— Now, Wamblie!—Anything to relieve your suffering—While you can!—You'd cut yourself off from reality if it'll work—Can do it!—You'd cut yourself off right now if He shows you how—Do it!—If He gives you a sign as to how—Die, Wamblie!—HOW!— Die now!—HELP!

Nothing except the one thing you learned. That is: people

who are crazy aren't out of touch, they're not the ones who have broken from reality. No! They're in touch because seeing the truth puts them in an altered state of consciousness which no one else can comprehend because they haven't gone through the suffering which brings insight which brings suffering to crazy people who are, therefore, insightful seeing the truth, feeling the truth every so keenly while the rest steer clear remaining ignorant and happy, but crazy and out of touch because it's not all beneficial being crazy and seeing the truth when you take into account the suffering which cannot be discounted since there's also a selfishness involved which results in gaining understanding on the part of crazy people who are the most selfish of all since they can't share a moment of experience with anyone, no one, because they're totally involved with themselves recognizing nothing else which is how he was, I think, which would explain your suffering, your punishment as well as anything since you're being punished for being so selfish, for being so within yourself although you're not, not completely because, if anything, you're outside too much, outside yourself since inside it's turmoil in which you get lost while outside the picture is clear, where you stand with the others is clear, who's against you and who's plotting is clear, all clear with no doubt or very little all of which means you're not the crazy one, but sane like everyone else who isn't total chaos inside, who can say they completely understand the depths of their souls, who has complete and total understanding of life? No one. Not while alive, at least, because, to be alive, is not to understand since that's a necessary condition although, perhaps, when he's dead he will although, for now, it's out of his realm which means you're not crazy after all since you're one of those whose realm it's out of and since to understand that really is to be crazy which leads back to the question which eternally comes back like everything else because understanding that realm is not only crazy, but it's not crazy, too, since there's a reason you're that way; why you see things as you do is for a reason, is explainable, is comprehensible and, therefore, is sensible and understandable and something that's understandable isn't crazy. And how is it understandable? Because you were driven to it by those who plagued you or tried to, but couldn't since you wouldn't give in and go along, but instead fought them every step of the way which is what makes you sane with the brains to fight instead of simply going along like a dog on a leash which means you established something, which means you finally figured out you're not crazy, that it's the others who are crazy since they close their eyes and do what they're told like little lambs who are nuts. Ha, ha! That's a laugh! Sane? Insane? They're all out of their heads. They can pretend they're not like most do successfully although they are since it's a simple fact of life to be crazy while thinking you see something, while constantly striving for that and thinking you have attained it in spite of the fact you haven't, it being a condition of life not to in fact, one of it's most profound underpinnings since any question has multiple answers all equally valid depending on the argument you make which is why the hospital called you paranoid and made a good argument you are since you hear voices and think people are against you etcetera, etcetera, etcetera, like sick people who do that because there could never ever be any truth to all they said since it's all delusions which explains why they said you were sick and why you said you weren't since it was they who were sick and they who were irrational and they who were paranoid! And why? Because they were so afraid of you, little old you. They were afraid of your thoughts, your fears, your feelings and your perceptions and saw nothing in them at all and didn't even try to because they so greatly feared insanity. That was so pervasive in fact, they locked you up when you showed any sign of it which is when you had a hold over them who were so afraid, more afraid than you since you could make them jump when you wanted to since you could make them put all their energy toward you just by causing a ruckus which is why they pounced on you in a pack if you did anything not to their taste which was the difference between you since, when you did something they didn't understand, they pounced whereas, when they did something you didn't understand, you tried to understand by asking questions and wondering about it, by considering every answer although the fact you often didn't find one was no reason to think of you as crazy since, the point is, you looked, you searched which was different and, therefore, crazy since anything different was wrong although, in spite of all that opposition, you kept going, kept searching for answers with great tenacity since you were pursuing the truth which no one else could understand, not what you understand at a high price which is to be thought of and called crazy within, without although it's they who are crazy and you who is sane which describes the problem exactly, which is the nature of being sane inevitably makes you insane which is why everything comes back on itself with no way to get off a continuous circle, a sphere like everything that is. Everything! His babbling being a perfect example of a circle which always comes back on itself like logic in its nature or you who have a set of conflicting beliefs which, every time you try to unravel, lead to more confusion than you had before like a concept thought through leads to another which leads back to the first and, therefore, contradiction. So everything comes out the same if not in result, at least in process. Yes, you've hit on something there which is the sum of the parts may not be the same, but the process by which we arrive at the sum is always the same which is the bind all mankind is in of continuously living and reliving again the same thing over and over and over which means, therefore, our fundamental approach to the basic problems of living must change if we're ever going to be salvaged and saved though I don't see how or in what way, but knowing the idea, the method, the process leads us in continuous circles with no break must change.

Ah! But are they all led in circles or is that only you? Maybe you are crazy, after all, since you're probably the only one going in circles which explains your insanity while the rest of the world doesn't appear to be, only you who appear to be to them which is why they incarcerated you unless it was because they're going in circles, but refuse to see it and so despise you for trying to bring it out in which case either they're going in circles or you're going in circles since it's got to be one or the other or both which must be the case since there's no way it can be said you're not going in circles for the simple reason you are whether or not they are which is unknown although you can see arguments that say yes and arguments that say no with the truth being indecipherable though probably the same since it's probably the truth in either case meaning one side is as true as the other depending on how you look at it which is all that can be said since there's nothing else which solves the problem, his problem finally because you've found an indisputable answer that takes everything into account which is it depends on who's looking as to what's true there being no ultimate truth for all which reminds me of an example that just came to mind about whether or not one person sees color the same as another or only thinks they do because they call it by the same name the reason being, of course, because, when they were little and pointed to a color, a particular color, their parents said it's...say brown causing them to, whenever they saw that color, call it brown and dark etcetera even though they, in reality, may have seen yellow which means, if that's true, there's no way to know because that person would always call yellow brown and brown yellow, what is yellow or brown to them, I mean, which leaves the truth of what is yellow and what is brown a mystery that can never be solved since you can only see yellow and brown or anything else for yourself since you have your truths and they have theirs although the fact they don't see yours doesn't mean it's without validity stemming from circles as it does with the one you've just gone around on again being proof there's no escape since, every time you talk, that's where you're led as if you're cutting the lawn and going in a curve by starting on the outside and going around and around and around until you're in the center and left with finding another to go around on which results in the same effect which you never realized before how much the same everything is in process, I think, though it could be otherwise which is exactly your problem isn't it? That you can't find boundaries that leave the North Pole and move ahead, always ahead, yet end at the North Pole just the same because you don't know when to stop, you don't know when to say, I've come to a sane understanding and, if I go any further, it'll be insane again because you always go further and further and further until things become senseless and then sensible again whereas, by themselves, they wouldn't be so crazy without you making them that way by going on without knowing where to stop or how to tell sane from insane which is a perfect example of the problem, as far as I can see. The thoughts get muddled, so you can't distinguish a thing let alone your perceptions which sometimes get to the point where it's chaos there, too, what with the sound of a voice talking, talking and thinking to the point where you can't tell which is which, which you thought, which you said and which others said or thought which explains why the thoughts of a voice and a voice are the same and can't be distinguished which you're getting tired of doing anyway since it makes no difference if you're crazy or sane which means you should accept yourself and stop questioning so much because the questions lead nowhere which I've already explained; that and that insanity is a reality of life since sanity only exists when you choose to impose it and take things out of the realm of chaos you're in which is exactly what you've got to do, yes—The chaos—And get ready—The confusion—Tomorrow—Which plagues you—But how?—From them—That's the question—Who?—Unanswerable—You know—Unsolvable—Don't you?—So go—So do something—Just go—Do what?—I can't—Go—Too weak—Without worry—Weak?—Not about them—Just go—Not about anyone—To work—Since it's useless—Clean up—So useless—And go—So don't—To work—Don't hesitate—Tomorrow—And don't worry—But he can't—Or you're done—Why not?—So get up!—Can't cope—And go!—Why not?—Go now!—Not capable—While you can!—That's false—I said can!—You can—And must—No!—Go!—Not no—Do it!—I'm afraid—Now!—A coward!—Go!—Afraid!—While you can—A coward!—Can do it—Don't waver!—Tomorrow—Why not?—Don't hesitate!—Because it ruins you—Don't think!—You're saying that—Just act!—No—For once—You're lying!—Just do it!—That's paranoid!—Wamblie!—No!—Obey!—It prevents you—Wamblie!—From reaching—Obey!—From touching—Do you hear?—You're isolated—Are you listening?—And alone—Do you hear?—Cut off—Do you?—Completely—End it—You're in danger—Forever—Alone—Thinking—So suffer—Forever—The aloneness—Talking—The isolation—And for what?—Completely—To live?—Why?—Fading—Life—You're fading—Because it's nothing—You touch—Life's nothing—And don't touch—And why?—See—I don't know—And don't see—Anything—Feel—Anymore—And don't feel—It's over—It's illusive—It's not—And gone—Not what?—You invented it—Not over—A hallucination—It will be—It is—If you do—You talk—Do what?—You hear—It—So you're real—What?—But you're not—You know—Not real—What?—But delusional—What I mean—But you're there—So?—You're real—So do it—I'm real—End it—He's real—Now!—But not reaching—This minute!—He's isolated—Why?—And unreachable—Aloneness—He won't try—Aloneness?—Though he wants to—Which is good—So it happens—Why?—Since he likes it—No worries—He does?—None—Yes—So do it—Why?—Now!—I

don't know—It's the way—But we're talking—If you want—
Why?—And you do—I don't know—Don't you?—Since you're
lonely—Don't you?—Since there's no one—Wamblie!—So you go
on—And end!—Pretending—To the suffering!—There's someone
—For good—With you—And ever—To talk with—And ever—And
share—Don't you?—Which is nice—Don't you?—It's not—So do
it—Why?—Now!—Their hallucinations—Because there's time—
Not real—Plenty—But fantasy—To suffer—Yes—And be
miserable—He invented—If you want—All of it—Which is the
question—Do you hear?—Yes—Wamblie!—To be crazy!—Do
you?—There's nothing else—Do you?—No!—Are you listening?—
Crazy!—Are you?—Yes!—Are you?—Feeling delirious!—
Wamblie!—Yes!—Wamblie!—With liquor—Wamblie!—Yes...

Development

...he doesn't know anything as well as what to say since he doesn't have much and he doesn't feel much like talking anymore since it's such a bore to jabber on and on about nothing especially since its too hot to talk or do anything else what with him sweating just walking across the room where everything is oppressive, but particularly the heat it being August again and over a year since he went to the hospital where nothing worked, where everything failed completely leaving him exactly where he was when he went in except for two differences one of which is he no longer has a family and the other of which is he no longer has a job. Well, he does have a job, but not a good job, not his old job which brought him down on the ladder which he tried to get up on again when he first started working while he was still in the hospital when he thought the forces were against him because he got nowhere which led him to, rather than continue in a futile effort, quit for a time. So, for several months starting about Christmas, he didn't work at all since he was in no condition to as you're in no condition now either, I guess, since your condition seems the same as then except now you have to work because there's no alternative which isn't so bad since the company will stick by you or so they say. I wonder sometimes. But they have, throughout this mess, kept a job open for you which isn't his old job, but a job, nevertheless, which is some comfort at least, isn't it? especially after they, at the hospital, through that period after Christmas, through that period after he was informed of the divorce, tried all kinds of things to revive his interest in anything they could, but primarily work which they said they wanted him to go back to although he couldn't believe them in view of the part they played in keeping him away although none of that phased him in the lease since he had given up and so was assigned an attendant to watch especially over him everywhere he went on the hall which he was confined to for over two months which he didn't care about really because he was happy having nothing to do and nowhere to go including home which he stopped going to since he couldn't see any point in it anyway because she didn't want him there which was right on her part since she was better off without him because he flopped completely and stopped caring about everything since he didn't want any demands or pressure or responsibility because his only problem in life was they wouldn't let him sleep which was all he wanted to do which may be hard to believe, but you only knock your head against the wall so many times before you pass out which is the point he reached in spite of the fact they still wouldn't let him sleep which would have made him extremely happy. But no, not them. They were too dutiful to allow such a thing, they were too concerned with his welfare to give him what he wanted, so they only let him sleep at night the rest of the time keeping him locked out of his room so he couldn't go and lay down which, as I say, he would have if he could although it didn't much matter since he went and laid down on the couch instead, usually in the day room in front of T.V. where they weren't so apt to find him although they always did sooner or later and, when they did, they always woke him up even though he didn't care since he could just sit there until they left and then lie down again, not really caring if they harassed him or not since it made no difference to him they told themselves they wanted him to feel there was someone there who was reaching out and, consequently, every shift assigned someone to spend time with him or talk to him which was the same, always the same, however, which he quickly got tired of since one of the attendants or nurses would come in and start a conversation in spite of the fact he didn't say anything as if that would help lift his spirits and make everything all right again whereas, in actuality, they paid no attention to him at all, but went on enthusiastically trying to make things as congenial as possible which was nice, I suppose, except they seemed not to notice if they failed or not since he wasn't really talking much, but instead watching them, one after another, as they spoke without ever saying he was bored out of his skull although it did get to him when they came in and started questioning him without letting him answer, I mean really answer which caused him to say as little as possible to avoid prolonging things until he got to the point where he stopped talking altogether which didn't take long and didn't matter either since they didn't care either as demonstrated by the fact that, no matter what he said or didn't say, the attendants and nurses started giving him advice on the subject because, I guess, they didn't know what else to do what with him being so reticent which gave them the illusion of a conversation since the space was filled with the sound of their voices which passed the time and meant they could write in his chart a conversation had taken place which would make it appear they fulfilled their responsibility like before when he was on escort being run ragged in an attempt to rouse him out of the doldrums, before when his program coordinator had every minute filled since he thought, with enough activity, he'd sooner or later come out of it though he was wrong since nothing could have gotten him out of it it being too late for that, not volleyball, arts and crafts, painting, the library, nothing! He used to walk to these things although he was tempted to make them drag him, but never do anything when he got there but watch from the side no matter how much they urged him until later when he did make them drag him to the floor where he lay like a bag of sand it being the most comfortable place although, in spite of that, they kept dragging him, however, although, eventually, he tired them out since they were disgusted with his complete refusal to move and so restricted him to the hall to give him a real dose of it and see if that wouldn't make him cooperate since they didn't know what else to do although none of it worked because if was exactly what he wanted since it didn't seem like punishment, but rather a gift since he liked it even better because he could just sit on his ass and pass the time watching everyone else pretend there was some justification for activity.

And so it went, the time I mean although it felt like it had stopped although he paid no attention one way or the other since, to him, it was nothing more than one gigantic mass of oblivion he waded through with his eyes closed because to open them would have meant he'd see nothing but darkness anyway. So it all ran together until he hardly knew what day it was and hardly cared either and only wore clothes when they put them on him and only ate a little and only when they shoveled it into his mouth and only peed and shat on the floor and stopped going to all meetings unless they dragged him and then only lay on the floor in a heap since he cared about nothing including himself and felt, if it could have been done with no effort, he would have put an end to it all since nothing they did seemed to matter anymore which brings to mind the dream he had in which he was nothing but a carcass lying in a desert with no eyes, but rather holes in the skull where they had been and with rotting flesh around his mouth and ears when the hospital staff came to him in a pack, each with the head of a hyena, and tore off what flesh was left with their teeth gnawing and ripping until he was nothing but bones which they cracked open to suck out the marrow which he didn't mind as long as he could lie there in peace since all feeling was gone leaving him insensate like the fifteen year old girl who was starving herself to death in spite of the fact they forced her to eat saying she'd die if her weight dropped any lower in front of everyone to show her they felt no shame in what they were doing. So four attendants went into her room and dragged that sixty five pound hunk of pure bone kicking and screaming to the foyer where they laid her on her back on a couch and held her there until the hall doctor came out with pleasure on his face to the point of sadism holding a length of plastic tubing which was dripping with a thick, oily fluid at which the girl began screaming hysterically and attempting to wrench free at which the psychiatrist made a mocking face and told her how much she loved it saying, "If you didn't love it, you'd eat to avoid it," and no one cared how much she fussed because no one wanted to see her die whereupon he took the tube and rammed it up her nose and down into her stomach at which she gasped, stiffened and closed her eyes as if fading into unconsciousness while they attached the feeding bottle with her breathing heavily as if plunged into cold water all of which did nothing to him who was calm as could be feeling nothing for her and nothing for himself because he was dead inside which they all knew since he didn't give a damn what anybody thought, not after he was told about the divorce.

But they went on supposedly trying to help him —No!—They were too stupid to give up—Not helping—They started saying he was in mid life crisis or middle aged depression or some such thing—Not a bit—Then they began talking about electro shock therapy as a possible treatment to lift his depression—You know that—They said it would lift his gloom, get him out of the doldrums and make him feel like himself again—Don't you?—They always came up with something to try—Yes—They couldn't admit there was nothing to be done—You do—They couldn't admit they failed. But I don't know what made them think he was in the doldrums since he was simply seeing the truth which they were too afraid to see—You were—But he didn't care one way or the other—Were seeing—Whatever they wanted was all right with him—Yes—They could have cut out his brain and it wouldn't have mattered—Do you know that?—So, shortly after that, it began with them saying the chances were good, by early the following month, he'd be back at work and ready to leave— Yes—That would have made him laugh if he could have laughed—You do—But actually, it came true—True?—Not that he's back to normal—You're not—I think I can safely say, he's not—Not at all—But he did feel better after the therapy and he did start back to work which I'm supposed to continue Monday...tomorrow! It's already Sunday and I haven't done a thing. But that's another story.

Anyway, I was saying how the therapy helped or, if it didn't help, at least it got him out of there which was help in itself even if he lost his...his what? Personality? Sort of...but I should go over this which is interesting to think about, more interesting than that other dribble.

Anyway, they took him for treatment three times a week: Monday, Wednesday and Friday which wasn't very pleasant since he missed breakfast which he usually liked to have although, come to think of it, he also missed medication which he consistently hated which made it all come out even in the end like everything else since one cancels out the other. However, the reason for missing breakfast and medication was vomiting since, during the treatment, he could vomit and choke and die since the gag reflex wouldn't be working. Why, I don't remember although it was explained to him several times. At any rate, the first few times he was scared out of his mind although he soon got used to it, used to walking over with an attendant, a different attendant each time so all of them would learn about the procedure. That was morbid and eerie, walking over, because the attendants were glum and apparently apprehensive, at least he thought that was true since they didn't talk much and didn't seem to know what to say since he was about to have his brain shocked which left nothing to say past good morning and nice day. So the walk over was always quiet and somber to the point where only their footsteps and the sound of the wheelchair moving over the pavement could be heard, the wheelchair they used to bring him back that is. Not that he couldn't walk, he always felt sure he could, but, for some reason, they'd never let him. They always made him ride in the chair. When they got to the administration building basement, the place where they gave the treatment, they were greeted by two doctors and a nurse all of whom said, "Good morning!" happily. "Step over here please." After that, they put him on the table. "And lie down." Then one of the doctors would examine his chest organs. "Just relax while I feel around." At least that's what he said he was doing. "I'll only be a minute." But he didn't know for sure. "There." Then the nurse would take his blood pressure and strap him to the table. "Why the straps?" So he wouldn't fall off. "To hold you." You can fall off when your body jumps. "The treatment produces a convulsion." It jumps from the shock. "So we use these to secure you." Quite violently. After he was harnessed, the nurse would put a needle in his arm attached to a plastic tube which was attached to some bottle of something—I don't like this —Run!—He didn't know what—I don't like what they're doing —Run now!—But they were mounted over the table the way plasma bottles are—They're going to hurt you—Before it's too late—The nurse would then drip something (whatever it was) from one of the bottles into his arm—That stuff'll hurt you —Too late!—And the doctor would put an oxygen mask over his face—It'll hurt your body—Too late—All of which made him relax—You shouldn't have agreed, Wamblie!—And the next

thing he'd know he was fading—Wamblie!—Fading—
Wamblie!—Fading out—You shouldn't have... ... ...
..."Mr. Wamblie?" "Oh!" "He's coming to." No memory. "It
went well." You don't know where you are. "How are you?"
And you don't remember a thing. "All right." But you don't
care. "What's your name?" You're in too much of a daze.
"Help him up, nurse." "I don't know." So they're making you
sit up while the doctor explains. "Mr. Wamblie." But you can't
remember. "Wamblie?" Not from one minute to the next.
"Yes." A thing he says. "Now what is it?" So he repeats it over
and over...."I don't know." Your name. "It's Wamblie." Your
occupation. "And you're a salesman." Your wife's name.
"Your wife's—ex, I should say, is Henrietta." How many
children you have. "You have two children." Where you work.
"Now, can you tell me your name?" Your children's names. ....
"No." The name of the hospital. "It's Wamblie." Your age.
"Wamblie?" What treatment you just had. "Yes." All over and
over and over again. "Now, what is it?" And now, he's asking
your name again...."I don't know." But, although you just
heard it, you can't remember. "Wamblie." Just can't.
"Wamblie?" I don't know why. "Yes." Now the attendant's
starting it. "You can take him back now." Since you're fully
revived. "And keep on filling him in on the way." At least
enough to go back to the hall. "Let's go." But he won't let you
walk. "In the chair, Mr. Wamblie." "What?" He insists you be
pushed back in the wheelchair. "In the chair." "But..." "I'm
sorry." That makes you angry. "Please, I..." "I'm sorry, Mr.
Wamblie." You're sure you can walk. "But you have to be
pushed." But there's no use arguing. "Now, can you tell me
your name?" You're not up to fighting...."No." So do what
you're told. "It's Wamblie." And go along with his chatter.
"Wamblie?" Your name. "Yes." Your occupation. "And you're
a salesman." Your treatment. "You've just had shock therapy."
Your age. "You're forty one." All the way back to the hall.

"So, what's your name?" That's all he'll talk about...."I don't remember." Yet, you still can't remember. "It's Wamblie." So he's going to continue inside. "Wamblie?" Until you can recall—"Yes."—The simple facts of your life. "Now, what is it?" But the more treatment you have—"Wamblie?"—the harder it gets. "That's right....Again?" Being guarded is hard too...."I don't know." He's watching you. The attendant has to stay with you—"It's Wamblie."—Watching your every move, every time—"Wamblie?"—Your every thought for at least an hour and a half. "Yes"—Because he's evil—After the treatment. "And what do you do?"—Evil!—They always act like you're crazy. "I don't know"—So rebel!—And about to do something dangerous. "You're a salesman"—Rebel now!—I don't know why. "A salesman?"—Jump out the window—Unless it was the treatment. "Yes"—Jump now!—You've had it a lot. "And what is your name?"—And end it—For weeks in fact...."I don't know"—Now!—You're smiling—And that's why you get that smile. "It's Wamblie"—While you can—Like an idiot—It causes you to smile sometimes. "Wamblie?"—While he can't stop you—Can't you tell?—No matter how you feel. "Yes"—Jump! —Can't you feel it?—You look at someone and a smile springs to your face. "And how many children do you have?"—You should have jumped—It's there—You suddenly realize you're smiling for no reason...."I don't know"—While you could— Making you look stupid—Like a child. "You have two children"—But it's too late now—And foolish—It's embarrassing. "Two?"—It's too late—And ridiculous—And uncomfortable. "Yes"—Too late—So stop it—Because you don't feel anything like you look. "And can you tell me your name?" But you look happy...."No." And I guess that's important. "It's Wamblie." Important because they let you leave. "Wamblie?" They finally let you leave. "Yes." And now, here I am...here...someplace....I think I'll get a drink.

Recapitulation I

...because life is something clung to by a very slender thread. Yes, isn't that the truth, for those who cling, that is, since not everyone does when you think of those who kill themselves. But for those who hang on, it is by nothing more than a slender thread. True. That much can be said since they can be finished off in any of thousands of ways at any of trillions of moments unpredictably when heart attacks, choking, a chance meeting with a psychopathic killer or a car accident are considered as well as millions of other things any of which could happen without a moment's notice—To you— So it's amazing any of them live to maturity—They could happen to you—Or what is called maturity—In an instant— Adulthood is actually what I mean—You could die—If that can be called maturity—And be gone—In most cases, they're not reached together—Forever—But they like to think they're immortal is what I'm trying to say—And ever—They like to think, Well, nothing'll happen to me—And ever—But that's not true since anything can happen to anyone and sooner or later does whether they're prepared for it or not—Because you're not—But there's no real preparing since the forces are so unpredictable —Not prepared—There's no way to judge them which is why they must accept what happens happens and be content to live their lives for the flash of existence they endure, come what

227

may, since a flash is all the time they're here when you take all time in total—Flash!—And that connection is a thin, a supremely meager one—You go on—So, despite their feelings of importance, they're actually the most delicate of creatures tied to existence by almost nothing—Flash!—Because it could all come to an end so easily—You go off—A life can be snuffed out so simply—And that's the end—Take him for instance—Flash!—He could kill himself—You could—You go on—He could go get his pistol right now and put an end to his existence—You could—Flash!—He could put a bullet in his head right now and end it all—And should—You go off—Or, if not all, at least the consciousness part—Why not?—Again—That's the part he'd stop because that's the part that's plaguing him—Why not do it?—Flash—Consciousness, that is—Do it now—You go on—Thinking!—Now!—Flash—It drives him crazy, so why doesn't he stop it?—Now, Wamblie!—You go off—Why doesn't he stop the pain?—This minute—And that's the end—There's no reason not to—This instant!—Why does he go on living?—While you feel it—To what purpose?—Why not?—Again—What difference would it make to the universe?—None—Flash—The universe wouldn't care—None whatsoever—You go on—It would be just another wave slapping the shore and receding into oblivion—And it would stop the pain—Flash—Death is a gift—The misery—You go off—Since things are so awful on earth—The suffering—And that's the end—So, since it makes no difference if he lives or not, he might as well kill himself—That's the way—Flash—Yes—Why not?—The world wouldn't change if he died—Do it!—Flash—Even if it were premature—Do it now!—It would be the same manure heap one way or the other—Now!—Flash—Therefore, his death or not makes no difference—Now, Wamblie!—He's far too insignificant to have an effect on the larger order—Why hesitate?—So he might as well kill himself—Why falter?—I can't see why everyone doesn't—Why not do it?—I don't know how others avoid it—Do it now!—Apparently they do, however, since not everyone commits suicide—Now!—Flash—Not as far as we can see although living is a suicide since it leads to nothing but death—Now, Wamblie!—I guess the reason more don't, however, is because, for some people, other people would be hurt—Since that's not true in your case—Other people matter—Not in your case—And that's where he's different—Your case is different— He doesn't matter to anyone and no one matters to him—You don't—So the only reason anyone lives is because they matter to others—Not to anyone—Yes—No one—But no one would be hurt if he died—No one—So he'll kill himself—So do it—He's determined to do it since he can no longer find a reason not to—Do it now!—So that's it—Now!—He's resolved to do it—Now, Wamblie!—Do it now!—Now, Wamblie!—For the same reasons as Christ—Why don't you?—Who didn't kill himself—Why don't you?—But knew he would soon come to an end—I'm not sure— And so does he—Sure I should—As I say—Should do it—For the same reason—Why not?—Because of so little insight into the mystery of things which gets thrown out of balance being weighted way to far for Christ who died to balance them out since it was necessary, given the nature of things, to maintain the balance between good and evil since there's got to be as much of one as the other since they go hand in hand like night and day, summer and winter, the bottom and the top which is all there is to it. Given that, why does he go on since, if he killed himself, it would be because he's supposed to, it would be to maintain a balance, it would be because, like Christ, he's no longer fit for this world?—Don't know—He's seen too much, seen too deeply, he's penetrated too far—Nothing— Consequently, he must die—At all—Wamblie!—Because the balance is of more importance than him and because it's the only way he can have an effect—Anymore—Wamblie!—Alive, he makes no difference—So I can't!—Are you listening?—None whatsoever—Can't do it!—Listening to the voices?—So he'll do

it—Not now!—They're calling you—He'll die!—Because of fear!
—And they want you to obey—Like I said—Fear inside!—They
want you to do it—Because he's Christ—The panic!—Do it
now!—And can't avoid it—Panic inside!—While you can—Not
any longer—It's overwhelming!—Wamblie!—So he'll get the
gun—And I can't!—Wamblie!—Then he'll do it—Just can't!—Do
it!—At least I think he will—Not now!—Do it now!—Although the
thought of dying is terrifying—I can't!—Now!—Why?—Because
he doesn't know what's to come—Wamblie!—There's no way to
know where he'll be after the fact which scares him terribly
especially since he got so close to doing it—Wamblie!—He was
right on the verge of doing it just now even though it's risky
since it could turn out there's a heaven and a hell as he
believed growing up even though there's no way to know. But
if there were, he could end in hell since suicide is a sin
although, if he knew he could go to heaven, you wouldn't see
him hesitate. But what if he went to hell?—What then?—What
would you do?—Damned for eternity!—Suffer—That's what
he'd be—That's what—Yes—Eternally! He loves the thought of
heaven, but he's filled with dread when it comes to hell—So
don't—So maybe he better reconsider—Don't do it—Maybe he
shouldn't kill himself—Not now....

What are you saying? Of course he shouldn't! How can
you think such a thing? It would be a waste, a terrible, terrible
waste and what would it be for? Nothing! It's a stupid self-
indulgent idea and he should be put away for thinking such
things since people like him need to be controlled because
people who can't control themselves should have it done for
them and be stopped even though it's not his fault, it most
certainly is not, but rather the world's since it's the world
who's out of control and so in need of a highly developed,
highly ordered structure. That is, it's the world that's missing
control. He doesn't know where or how it went wrong, he can't
answer for that since all he knows is it's got to change so

people like him, people who merely reflect what's going on because they're too attuned not to, no longer suffer in the face of this senseless insanity. He's suffered too much at its hand since all his problems can be traced to it which means, if the world were right, none of it would have happened and he'd be all right. But no. The world had to disintegrate and take him with it. Well, that's going to change and it should start with children since the only way to control the world is to control the children, for their own good, since we need order so badly because we need to stop the spread of immorality from sex to drugs and back again which is why the children should be stopped since, otherwise, it'll continue. But no. They stick someone like him in the hospital while his child runs around like a nut and for what? It's not the adults that are running wild, it's the children which is why his son would have been better off in the hospital than him which means the hospital was wrong to take him since he's not the one who needs to be controlled! It's not him at all! But they took him anyway and dealt with him all wrong by treating him like a child, an adult like a child, and by constantly trying to control him even though, with an adult, that's wrong since an adult can be reasoned with and understand more than just force which means they should have tried to be gentle with him, they should have tried not to threaten him, they should have tried to make him relax and feel good about himself, not to mention them. But no. The staff in the hospital was so insecure and so threatened by the insane, they had to strike them down before they were struck down themselves even though the patients would never strike them down. Unless it was to build themselves up. I don't know. But it was probably both. Whichever. The point is, they felt better or safer or something when the patients were low and so concentrated their efforts on keeping it that way which, I guess, is in the nature of things since whenever, in human existence, an individual or group has power over others, they abuse it attempting to prove to themselves they are more powerful which is exactly how power was used in the hospital all of which explains why he hated it so much. I mean there he was suffering enormously for no good reason, suffering at their sadistic hands. Although it could have been his fault—It was—Perhaps he was wrong to go there—You were—Perhaps he was wrong to submit—You were—Perhaps he never should have given up his autonomy—You shouldn't—In that sense, he bears responsibility for everything—You do—I guess everyone does—Wamblie!—Bear responsibility—You do—All people are totally responsible—Do you hear?—For what they are—It's you—And for what they do—Your fault—So there's no one to blame—Yourself!—Do you hear?—Which is crazy—It's you—The whole thing is crazy—Wamblie!—You!—And it makes him angry—So suffer—Angry to the point of—Suffer!—Of—Suffer!—Of—Suffer now!—Violence!—For what you've done—So I'll get them back—Violence!—For what they've done—It's the answer—Revenge!—So send the doctors a message—Now!—For what they've done—From a patient—Now, Wamblie!—Done to you—Which says they'll soon be killed—Do you hear?—They deserve it!—Send them messages—Hear what they're telling you?—Deserve to die—From all over the country—They're telling you something—For what they've done—Saying that soon they will die—What?—Done to you—Saying that soon you will kill them—To seek revenge—So many times—That when they least expect it, you'll be there—To seek it now—While you were there—Then you'd be an animal—For what they've done—They're under their power—Preying on them like an animal the way they preyed on you—Done to you—Helplessly under their power—Like animals—While you were there—With no way out—Trying to survive—There in the hospital—Except rebellion—Clawing your way to live—Under their power—So it's right—By violence—With no way out—And good—So do it—But violence—And just—Go to your boss and pull out your gun—So do it—Do you hear?—And shoot him in the face—Do it now!—Wamblie!—Right in front of who's ever there—Now!—Do you hear?—Then go to the secretaries—While you can—Hear the voices?—And shoot at random—Wamblie!—Do you?—Because they deserve to die—Are you listening?—Wamblie!—For their obliviousness to others—They deserve it—You should do it—Then go into the street—Deserve to die—Do it now—And shoot people down—Die by violence—Now!—Since they're all worth nothing—Violence now!—Do you hear?—Since all they want is to persecute him—Wamblie!—Persecute him by being oblivious—Wamblie!—Because they won't act—Are you listening?—Because they follow so blindly, he has to suffer—Do you hear?—And that can only change if he makes it happen, if he lashes out and stops it, if he forces them to open their eyes—Wamblie!—Then they'd see what they're doing—Wamblie!—With a bullet in their head they'd realize they'd been wrong, realize it because it wouldn't have happened otherwise since, in the larger order of things, he'd never shoot them if he weren't supposed to. Therefore, if he does it, it's because it's right, right and justified....The breathing is so hard....The only problem with the plan is he doesn't have a gun in spite of the fact he said he did which was only a joke, a joke on himself because he wanted to think he did because pretending that meant he could imagine all that violence which does him so much good as long as he's imagining, but not really doing it since he could never, ever actually kill someone or himself either, for that matter. I mean he was only joking when he said he could while, in actual fact, he had no intention of killing himself or anyone else primarily because, if he did, if he did kill at the office or in the street or kill himself, how could it be fair? In anger, it sometimes seems it is while, in actual fact, he knows it's not since God or the forces or whatever it is divides things up so they eventually balance out which allows nothing in the world to swing too far. Nothing!

Which is why killing people could be right since it could be just a swing of the pendulum since it could be merely the forces evening things out. After all, he suffered, so why shouldn't others suffer too? Why shouldn't the suffering be distributed evenly? Why shouldn't they all share in the load? There's no reason why not. But no! It won't be that way, it hasn't been that way. I don't know why unless it's because he can see the larger picture. But it seems to me he suffers too much. Like Christ, he carries a disproportionate load of the misery for the simple reason he can carry it, for the simple reason he can open his eyes to the miserable truth and not turn away in fear. That's why Christ was chosen to die and that's why he was chosen too. He's taking the sins of the world on his shoulders and, in that way, he's saving the world although I think he's dying in the process, dying for the sins, all the other's sins, that's what'll kill him eventually. Eventually, he'll die under that load unless it turns out he's different, unless Christ and he aren't alike which is entirely possible although they're the same, in many ways, which is positive, but still could be different, in others, in the sense that, while they both suffered for the sins of the world, Christ sought no revenge, he made no attempt to balance things out, none whatsoever. Christ just took their evil into his heart and let it kill him and the world's been unbalanced ever since. But this time it should be different, this time the sins shouldn't go unavenged, this time it should be balanced, this time people should die to pay for their sins, to pay for their violence, the violence done to him which is the same as the violence done to Christ! He can make up for all of it, all of the centuries of sin. He can bring it all into balance and atone for the evil just by killing all who refuse to see the light, who refuse to share the suffering, who refuse to carry their rightful load. He can put it all right by striking back, by saying "NO" and rejecting their excuses. That would change things, that would certainly change things, change them for the

234

better. And it appears to be his destiny to do so....The breathing is so hard....Or, at least, it would be if he had a gun which he doesn't meaning he can do none of this....I don't think....Oh well....A little rest is needed now.

The water's still dripping all over the floor which doesn't matter even though it's spreading everywhere. But it'll all drip into the basement, so it really doesn't matter. It's very dirty water, isn't it? Yes, mixed with the dust and grime in here, it makes for quite a mess. So, I suppose something should be done about that although there's nothing to pick it up with...unless...the bag hasn't been unpacked yet, but there might be something in there to use, perhaps a handkerchief or something like that. Oh, but it's already been used, hasn't it? Yes, but...a shirt would mop it up! Yes, a shirt to soak it up and wring out in the sink a few times. That would get it dry by tomorrow. Yes, that's what to do....Now where's the shirt?.... Oh! There it is right on top. So in it goes to soak up the water, out it goes into the sink and in it goes to soak up the water. This is going to be a bit of a job, it's going to take a lot of time. But no matter. Just keep on working until it's done, until the floor is completely dry. God, it's hard to walk! It's more comfortable on the knees even if they are in the water. Not that it's really walking since the legs aren't steady enough for that anymore. Yes, a prop is needed to keep the body up straight. It's as if death had set in which might be it. I don't know. I suppose you could be, I suppose you could be dying or dead. I don't know anymore, so you could be in the grave. If true, I wonder what your grave is like, I wonder how it represents you. Did you die a bum in the gutter or in glory the same as Christ? You don't know and I guess you never will since you're already dead. Or, if you're not already, you will be when it comes. Your grave site I mean. When you're brought there, you'll be dead, so it really won't matter since no one sees their grave after they're gone. So we have no idea how the world will see us or if the world will see us at all. None whatsoever. So...so you better get this place cleaned up because time is running out. Soon, you'll have to go to work, soon, you'll have to leave this place, so you better be ready, ready to leave by cleaning up, by mopping up the water which is exactly what you're doing, isn't it? Yes, and it'll probably take all night, so you better have another one, another to see you through.

Recapitulation II

What a weekend! It's never going to end, at least it seems that way although much of it has passed finally! In fact, soon, it'll be Monday (technically, it already is) and the whole ordeal will be over. That's a short time away since dawn won't be long now and he's wasted all the time, the entire weekend is gone. I don't know why. These things just happen. They're beyond our control, his control although it started out all right, he left the hospital and came here all right although it's been downhill ever since. Or, maybe, he didn't leave all right since the ending could have been shaky. In fact, I guess it was although I don't know why. Just one of those things, I guess, going far back. I mean the end was shaky for a while, the last few weeks were rough, because it's not easy to leave a hospital, not easy at all because they said he was too dependent on them for one thing. Imagine that! He too dependent on them! That's crazy since he spent the entire year trying to get out from under their thumb only to have them turn around and say he's too dependent. That's outrageous! But so was everything else. Not that I want to get into it although there are lots of examples I could give. But there's no reason to. It's boring anyway. But it did utterly amaze him when they told him he was dependent and he was initiating nothing on his own; not that that wasn't true. It was. However, he stopped initiating on his own immediately upon his arrival because they labeled everything he did as some sort of psychopathology, so he immediately began trying to please them by doing everything he could to convince them he was sane, but none of it worked although he continued since there was nothing else to do, not that he could see, until the divorce at which time he broke down and simply stopped caring since he was entitled to that after all he had gone through although, after shock therapy, he went back to his old ways, he started trying again, he started caring again. Since he wanted to leave, he tried to show he was ready by of course doing what he thought they thought was positive, by cleaning his room and eating and so forth which is when they told him he was dependent on them. He said baloney and explained how he had wanted to leave every minute of the entire year which is when they said, "But you never initiate anything. All you do is try to see what we want. You never decide what you want." He was a little indignant at that. I mean there he was being told, for an entire year, everything he wanted was bad (to go home, to go to work, to be with his family, everything!) only later to be told he was dependent because he looked on them as models or pretended he did, at least, which is crazy although he did find a way out which was actually more of the same in the sense that, when they told him they wanted him to initiate, he initiated which, in actual fact, wasn't initiating at all but, rather, doing the same old thing which was doing what he thought would please them. Only, that time, they didn't think he was doing it to please them, but, rather, it was initiating, really initiating, so, instead of calling it pathological, they praised it as a sign of health; the fact he was starting back to work, that is, since, for some reason, they thought it was good without assuming he was rushing things, so they gave him their blessing I guess because they were sick of him and because they had tried everything they had from drugs to shock treatment and back again although none of it worked leaving nothing left to do but get rid of him which they did although, while they wanted him to stay, everything he did was crazy while, when they wanted him to leave, everything he did was a step toward health. Except one thing which was his goodbye which they didn't think was so good because he was so happy, happy to be going at last, at long last he was going to leave the place although they didn't think that was good; not that he was leaving, but that he thought it was so good, because they thought he should have been unhappy, unhappy to be leaving because of all it meant, meant to him since they didn't realize it meant nothing to him, he couldn't have cared less about any of it. But, actually, that's not true either. It meant everything to him. But to be out, not in. That's where they made their mistake. They made their mistake when they accused him of not dealing with his feelings, his feelings of separation—You didn't—Because he was acting glad to leave—Didn't deal—They thought he should be sad—Not at all—Sad to lose them—Since you didn't want to go—Sad to go from people to aloneness—Wamblie!—Although he told them he wanted to leave—Are you listening?—But they didn't believe him—Listening to the voices?—Since you didn't want to leave—They were sure he should be sad—They're calling you—Not at all—And that made him mad—And you should listen—Since you felt so secure—Mad they told him how and what he felt—Listen closely—And afraid of being alone—Because, if he was mad, he didn't want them to see it—To what they're saying—Afraid of being alone—But they didn't think of that—Since they're saying the truth—Alone in the world—They wouldn't—The truth—With no one to turn to—But he did—The truth, Wamblie—No one to go to—Feel mad—The truth of your fear—No one but yourself—Because they pushed him out—Of your panic—Alone!—Once they were through with a patient, they said he was resisting if he didn't want to go—Panic inside—Do you hear?—So he didn't show them he didn't—

Panic at being alone—Wamblie!—He didn't let them know he didn't want to be alone—Alone forever—Do you?—That he hated being alone—And ever, Wamblie!—Because they would have said he was resisting progress—As you are—Or so he thought—Are now—As it was, they claimed he was saying goodbye in an unhealthy way—This minute—Which means there was no way to win—Aren't you?—Whatever he did was wrong—Aren't you, Wamblie?—So he gave up trying and decided to leave—Aren't you?—Just get out—Alone!—That was easier—Alone now!—And so he did—Now!—With little fanfare —Wamblie!—Which is what they thought was wrong— Wamblie!—They thought he wasn't saying goodbye, he wasn't dealing with the goodbye, he was avoiding the emotions asso- ciated with goodbye—You did—It was obnoxious the way they harped on that—Didn't you?—They just assumed patients couldn't do it—Didn't you, Wamblie?—That none of them could say goodbye—Avoid them?—That none of them could go through the anger of the loss—Avoid the goodbyes?—The loss of all those people—Avoid the hurt?—Of an entire unit of people—And the loss?—They thought all that had to be dredged up for a true goodbye to have been said—And the pain?—It's true—Otherwise, it was avoidance—Of goodbye?— Isn't it?—That's how they felt justified in digging for that— Because you're scared—Isn't it, Wamblie?—Because it was therapeutic—And afraid—What they're saying—They thought it was therapeutric—And terrified—It's true—To continuously say —At the thought—Isn't it?—That he was avoiding the hurt—Of the loss—Since you are afraid—Of the loss—At the thought—To leave—By acting so glad to leave—Of aloneness—On your own—And every time he showed anger—Because you're a coward—On your own—At their silly assumptions—A coward— Forever—They told him it was misdirected—Wamblie!—And ever—They told him he was angry—Do you hear?—And ever— At losing all of them—Hear what you are?—It scares you—Not at what they said—A coward—And frightens you—They said he would soon be in touch with that—You're a coward!—And panics you—But then, he was avoiding the issue—A coward!—With no break—And they said he was angry—Wamblie!—None whatsoever—Because he was being told to go—Wamblie!—In the suffering—He said, baloney!—In the torment—That he really wanted to go—That's driving you crazy—He didn't want to stay—Crazy!—Not there—Crazy, Wamblie!—Not with them—Do you hear?—Not after all that happened—Wamblie!—He didn't want to be alone—Wamblie!—But he didn't want to be with them—Do you?—How could he?—Do you?—How could he want them after they treated him so badly?—Do you, Wamblie?—Jesus! He couldn't wait to get out of the place, to get away from them, them and their control. It's a blessing not to be there even if he is alone. After all, loneliness is better than abuse, it's much better than abuse. He'd take it any day and so would a lot of other people like everyone there and like Nixon, too, which is why he left since being alone is better than abuse. That's why, on Friday, he stepped down. He had had enough abuse. When he did (when he left), he thought the world would come to an end, he thought it would all be over, but he didn't tell them that because he didn't want them to know what he thought because then they might have kept him, they might have made him stay which he certainly didn't want. No. He wanted to be rid of the place, so he didn't say he was worried, worried about the world, he just said his goodbyes and went out the door since it was the only way to get out quickly which he would have done if it hadn't been for that kid, if it hadn't been for his program coordinator who stopped him at the door as he was leaving, as he was on his way to the taxi that brought him to the bus that brought him here and for what? Because he wanted to say goodbye, he wanted to tell him how much he enjoyed him and how much he'd miss him now he was going to which he replied by accusing him of lying saying he knew he felt none of what he said since it was all part of his job which made him look surprised and caused him to repeat he really did mean it. But he said he really couldn't believe it. He said, "Why? Are you such a bad person that no one could miss you?" He said, "Well, I'm pretty bad, I'm pretty crazy. After all, I've been here longer than almost anybody." He said, yes, but that didn't mean he couldn't like him. "Besides," he said, "you're doing a lot better now, better than when you came." He said sarcastically, "Yeah, I must have gotten a lot out of being here." He asked him what exactly that was, out of curiosity, he said. He said, "Seriously?" He said, "Seriously." So he thought a moment, but could come up with nothing although he finally remembered the smoking, that he had finally quite smoking that past year and so said, "Well, I'm not polluting my lungs anymore." He said, "Is that all you can think of?" He said, yes, and went out to the taxi, yes, because it was true that was the only thing that happened or, at least, it was the best thing that happened since nothing else mattered, nothing mattered a bit. So he should have been glad he said something he could run and write in his chart, that he could go write down he was avoiding again, avoiding right to the end which is something he apparently has a knack for, that and drinking which he'll do one more time before it's time, time for work or the other if that's what he decides to do since he very well could since we never know what comes next, not for sure anyway.

Coda

...but maybe he committed a crime unwittingly. Could that be it? A crime not subject to law, but to...to...to something else. I don't know what. I suppose he could have, however. Whatever. The main thing is, he's through it, he's through the year and through the weekend; a terrible weekend of being alone. I'm certainly glad of that, glad because he couldn't go on, not like this. Something's got to change. I don't know what. I don't know how. Not yet. I only know it has to. He got through the weekend, but he couldn't get through another, not like this. That's impossible, simply impossible although he did find a way to pass that time, at least he did that, at least he can be happy about that, but I'm not sure he can continue passing time since it gets harder and harder and, if it keeps getting harder and harder, soon, it will get impossible and I don't know what he'll do then although I fear that time is soon, really soon. If only time could be stopped since, if it could be stopped, he'd be safe. If time could be stopped, he could rest and relax which is what he needs to do. He'd like to remain suspended and not have to cope, not have to cope with anything. Not work, not family, not himself. He wouldn't have to cope with himself. He could rest and refresh and begin again. If he had this weekend, that's what he'd do. After all, that's what he should have done, the fool. He shouldn't have spent it getting into this state, this

243

decrepit state because, now, he can cope with nothing, the idiot, now, he's good for nothing, not unless he can get through that too. Maybe he can, maybe he can get through work, one day of work, that's all he'd have to get through. Then maybe he could refresh and get through another. I don't know. But nothing is impossible, not if he tries, tries to stop time which is the only way he could do it, the only way he could go to work or probably the only way anyway. I don't know. Perhaps there are others, other ways, but none that I can see. But we'll see anyway, won't we? The time will come since it can't be stopped, since time can't be stopped as much as he'd like to because time is absolutely in motion, it goes on and on and there's nothing he can do to stop it although that's what everyone tries to do, they try to stop time or they try to pass it. But, sometimes, one is involved with the other, isn't it? Yes, it is. Sometimes, he tries to stop it by working on ways to pass it. But then he realizes it goes on, the motion is still there, the terrible motion is there in spite of his efforts to stop it. Yes, he looks in the mirror and sees age since life is a process of seeing the age, of seeing the age he doesn't want to see. So with the age comes fear and with fear comes the past, memories of the past which is the only way to lessen the fear. He lives in the past as age sets in more and more and more. He tries to hold on to a moment, a good moment and thereby force time to stop. But it doesn't. It just keeps on going and going and going and there's nothing he can do about it since he's powerless in its grip, except draw the good times near and push the bad times away, push them out of his consciousness. That and death is all he can do. Those are the only ways to stop the motion, stop the energy, stop the force of time or, at least, to give himself the illusion he has stopped it. And that's why his life is so disjointed. That's why it doesn't flow smoothly with the force. He's lost his nerve to let it. He's afraid to trust it—Afraid!—Afraid to let it—You're afraid—Afraid he won't have control—Aren't you?—But that's a silly fear—Aren't you?—Because he doesn't already—Aren't you, Wamblie?—He's not in control at all—Afraid of the loss—And he never will be—The loss of control—Not unless time can be stopped—Control of your life—But it's stupid to try—Control of your future—Instead, he should get in the rhythm—Control of your destiny—The rhythm of time—That's what you want—Don't!—That would be much smarter—Control!—Don't try—Smarter than trying to stop it—Control!—Not control!—But no—That's what you want—That's what hurts you—He's too stupid—Control!—That's what ruins you—Too stupid to know that—Control!—Do you hear?—Too stupid to do that—That's what you want—Wamblie!—He tries to evade it—To make things easier—Do you hear?—Instead of living within its bounds—To make things simpler—Hear the voices?—So he suffers—To make them the way you want—Wamblie!—Suffers more because of his mistake—Isn't it?—Do you?—Because of his evasion—Isn't it?—It always happens and it always will—Isn't it, Wamblie?—Time wins in the end. Oh well.

Better get dressed—It's so still—It's almost time for work—And silent—He has to be ready for work—Suddenly—It's that or lose his job—Empty—And if he loses his job, he loses everything—Very empty—Everything he has—Empty—Because it's all he has, there's nothing else, not anymore.... Now where the hell is the suitcase?

One shirt only, that's all he packed? I guess it is since there is no other. He must have left the others at the hospital, the ass. He was in such a hurry to leave, he forgot to do his packing thoroughly, so he's only got one shirt, one dirty shirt since he used it to mop the floor. Oh well. I guess he'll have to wear it even though it's damp, that and a suit, a suit without a tie since he has no tie since he forgot that too, like a stupid idiot. Oh well. Who gives a damn anyway? It makes no difference how he looks. It's all the same in the end or so he thinks. But he should care how he looks, he should be concerned about impressions. But you're not are you? No. If I'm going to be honest, I have to admit I'm not, not concerned a bit which is why I've dressed so haphazardly—Wamblie!—Yes, your shirt is a mess, your suit is wrinkled and the collar's not lying flat—You're talking—But what's the difference?—Talking to yourself—I'm not going to worry, not about that since I'm too exhausted and since I've had no sleep and since I've had nothing to eat, not for several days—Which is strange—Yes, that's like you—Do you hear?—So he'll go like that thinking there's nothing else he can do, since he's got no more time, and let come what may—Very strange—Yes, that's so like you especially now—Wamblie!—He's thinking there's no reason to worry, none he can see anyway—Do you hear?—After all, he can't distinguish illusion from reality, not anymore, not after this weekend—Are you listening?—For all he knows, his clothes look perfect. He's simply too far gone to tell—Wamblie!—I mean as far as he's concerned, he could have imagined the story, he could have made the whole thing up—Wamblie!—Crazier things have happened. Yes, my entire vision could be a lie. It could be a product of my own twisted thinking rather than the truth which is probably what my paranoia is from. Illusion, not reality. It could all be an illusion. It makes me wonder if the world is really out there or if I made the whole thing up, simply imagined my entire life. I suppose you could put up the shades and find out. I could. I mean they've been down all weekend and you've spent a long time in the dark. But if I put them up and see the outside, will that really convince me? I can't promise it would although it would follow it's there (the outside world) given the pattern of your life. Or my death if that's what this is. As I say, I don't know about that. But why don't you try it and see what happens. You've got nothing better to do.

It's a bright sunny day and he's standing there in a daze

gazing out the window with that silly smile on his face. You'd think he'd never seen a city before or an alley which is really all he's looking at. But maybe it's the light that's so blinding it stings his eyes that makes him look that way. They hurt very badly, so badly, in fact, he can barely stand it although I guess he will since he's smiling so obliviously. He'll stand there and absorb the pain and, once his eyes are used to it, he'll leave and go to...to work or home? We'll see which. But I know he'll go someplace since I've convinced him to leave. Besides, it couldn't be otherwise, not any longer...but enough of that! You have to get going...but where did I put the bottle? Under the cot, under the cot! Oh! I'd better get it and take it along. That and my razor just in case. I mean you never know. Yes, you could change your mind and, if you do, you want to be prepared. Yes I do, but why does that thought make me want to cry? Why am I suddenly so sad? Just leave it alone and go, can't you! You've got everything you need. The bottle, the razor, left pocket, right pocket, check. Yes....

The street is a dirty place and full of nothing but motion —Motion!—The trolleys, the trucks, the busses and the cars not to mention the people rushing around like ants on an ant heap —That's what it is—It's all so disturbing—It's motion—And disorienting—Motion!—But it's essential to the flow—And it's disturbing—Essential to the motion—Very disturbing—To the universe's motion—Can you feel it?—The universe which is head over heels in passage—Wamblie!—Movement—Can you?— That always comes back on itself—I can—That always moves, but never changes—Can feel it—Never progresses—Feel the disturbance—Never gets anywhere—The anxiety—But back where it started—And the fear—Wamblie!—It's a wheel that way—At the motion—Are you listening?—A circle—The terrible motion—Do you hear?—A ball—That I wish would stop—Do you?—A skull—Stop now!—Wamblie!—A consciousness—Stop moving—Do you?—Circling and circling—Moving now—

Wamblie!—Because that's what life is—And remain—And the universe—Stationary—No matter what side you're on—But that won't happen—You always come back to the other—Won't happen—Then go back to the first—Not to you—And so on—Not ever to you—In a smooth progression—Since time can't be stopped—That never indicates anything has changed—Can never be stopped—The road is the same—Just like the universe—Always the same—In constant motion—Yet, one day he wakes up—In terrible motion—And finds he's some-place—That can't be stopped—Some new place he never expected to come to—Do you hear?—That's the shock—Are you listening?—The same as when it goes back—Wamblie!—He tries to contemplate it—Wamblie!—But he can't. He can't give credence more to one than the other—Do you hear?—They both make as much sense as either—Do you?—And that's the dilemma. Although there must be a way to comprehend it. This abyss he's in can't be all—It isn't—There must be more—There is—There's got to be—There is—A ring!—Is more—A ring of life—Since it's endless—A solid ring—Endless!—That's what it is—Since it's endless—It's a solid ring—There's more—With infinite breaks—There's more—A solid ring—Always more—Composed of faces—And more—Faceless faces—And more—Facing each other—Without end—In a solid ring—Without beginning—But it will stop—A ring of meaning—Without end—And not go on—Of a series of meanings—It continues—It never goes on—Containing nothing but meaninglessness—On—Since there's nowhere to go—It's a ring—On and on—Nowhere to continue—Both limp and solid—Forever—But the same old place—Meaningful and meaningless—And ever—Again—And every point on it—Without end—And again—Has two faces—Or beginning—And again—Facing each other—Like a circle—Endlessly—It's both good and bad—A sphere—Going nowhere—At every point—A strip—For no reason—Both positive and negative—In motion—Since there's nothing—Pain and ecstasy—

Endlessly—To stop it—And that is the conundrum—It's motion
—So it stops—It's both—Forever—Cold—And neither—And ever
—Since it never started—All at the same time—And ever—But
was always there—Since both and neither—And ever—There—
Are one and the same—Endlessly—Stationary—Both are
essential—Do you hear?—With no sign—To the passage—
Wamblie!—Of motion—To the movement—Wamblie!—Are you
listening?—To the flow—Are you?—And that's how it is—
Wamblie!—It's no other way—Are you?—Not that he can see—
Are you?—Since that's how it is. It's all that, all controlled,
everything is controlled—Controlled!—The forces of opposites
are in control and probably always have been—They
are—That's how balance is maintained—It is—The forces are in
control and the people are robots with no free will of their
own—Do you hear?—These people are robots, but would never
think to know it—Wamblie!—Never think to conceive it—Are
you listening?—It's beyond their capacity—The voices are calling
you—They scurry to work thinking they've made that decision
when, in actual fact, they have nothing to do with it—Calling
you—And that's true of him—Calling you—He has no control—
Yes—He has nothing to say—Do you hear?—He has no free
will—Hear them?—Either does anyone else—Talking—Look at
them pass by—They're talking—Faces coming at him—Talking to
you—From a haze—Of fear—Like shooting stars—Of anxiety—
Burning up—Of dread—From the terrible motion—Of motion—
They rush so fast—Of contact—And comprehend nothing—You
can't attain—Of their predicament—Since you're alone—So he
can't make contact—Completely—Since they're alone—Alone—
As is he—Forever—"Look!"—They call at him—Alone—"At
that man." Since he staggers—Apart—"He staggers"—They
push at him—From them—"Like a drunk." With repugnance—
Who feel—"It's disgusting"—And scowl—No caring—"To
watch"—As they pass—At all—"Him pawing"—As if he's less
—For you—"Along"—Since he's different—Who suffers—"Like

an animal." Well let them!—Alone—Since they don't know—Do you hear?—They're no better—Wamblie?—Since they don't know—Do you?—He's them—Wamblie!—Since they don't know—Wamblie!—They'd do the same—You should listen—After all, he's not hurting them. He's done nothing to any of them. He bears their malice without fighting back—Wamblie!—He walks down the street without a space—You should listen—And doesn't complain—To them—They're squeezing him!—And end it—They want to crush him—To end—And crumble him—Your suffering—And make him disintegrate—Your fear—And disappear—Your anxiety—Their faces—Forever—Are bubbles—And ever—Leaving nothing—Do you hear?—Of space—You should do it—To survive it—Do it now!—He can't—He needs air!—Now!—And why?—They're squeezing!—Now, Wamblie!—He's scared—He must contact—Right now!—And frightened—Make contact—Do it—And terrified—Now—Do it—Can't you see?—Before—Do it now—Can't you?—He disintegrates—Now, Wamblie!—Can't you?—So go home—Wamblie!—Where you belong—Yes—And beg—Or you'll be sorry—Her—So sorry—Plead—Forever—With her—That you didn't—To take you—Didn't do it—Take you back—End it—So do...do...but the divorce! She's got a divorce. She wants nothing but to get away from him and that's his punishment for ever having married her. That's what this is about. It's a punishment for going against the forces, for going against what he was led to do, so, now, he's suffering, suffering for that mistake. That's why he's alone, without friends. That's what he gave up; all his friends for her. And look what he's gotten for it. Nothing! You've gotten nothing, Wamblie. You're being left alone with nothing—Wamblie!—No family and no friends—Listen—Not if I could find them—Listen now—You won't find them—You're talking to yourself—Find those friends—Do you hear?—That's foolish. Why? I could get in touch with them—Do you?—Impossible!—You're talking to yourself—It's been twenty years—

That's why people stare—Don't you think things have changed in that much time?—Stare at you—Don't you think things are completely different?—And think you're crazy—I mean you'd have nothing in common and none of them would remember you—They all think you're crazy—So forget it—And deranged— But I remember them, I remember them clearly, so there's every chance they'd remember me—That's why they sneer—But think of what it would be like to talk to them after so long—And shun you—You were just kids when you split—Because you're so sick—That's why I wonder what they're like and wonder what they're doing—Sick and crazy—I wonder if they're like me and I imagine they've wondered too—Do you hear?—I mean they probably wonder what I'm like—Are you listening?—Yes, but what would you tell them since you couldn't tell them the truth?—You're crazy—I'd have to lie which I could do just for the sake of conversation, just for the sake of a little human companionship—Crazy!—Why not?—Crazy, Wamblie!—It would be good to hear a familiar voice, so I think I'll try after another drink, I think I'll try and see who I can find—Crazy!—There must be some of them still around, some of those I went to school with—Crazy, Wamblie!—There's a phone booth where I can look up some names which I think I'll do, do now before I catch my train, before I lose my nerve and miss the moment, before I miss my chance again—Crazy!—I'll do it now, now after my drink....

That was a mistake since he doesn't need them since he doesn't need friends since he doesn't need anyone since he should never trust anyone. That man didn't care about him, only about himself. "Wamblie, Wamblie!" he said when he said his name, "I don't remember any Wamblie." "From college," he said, "I was your best friend's roommate. You were at my room all the time." "Oh yes," he said, "I remember now. How are you?" he asked. "Fine" he said. "Well, what made you call?" he asked. "Just wanted to talk to an old friend," he answered. "I see, I see," he said, "Well, what can I do for ya? What's been going on?" "Not too much," he replied at first, but, on second thought, he stupidly tried to answer. "Actually, I've fallen on hard times," he said—Wamblie!—"I've had a little trouble in my family"—Wamblie!—"I can't understand you," he said, "your words are garbled"—Don't talk—"Please speak up"—Not to him—"Well, I've had a little to drink," he said—Not ever to him—"To what?"—He can't help you—"To DRINK!"—Not at all—"DRINK?"—Not at all—"Yes" —Not at all—"I've had too much to drink"—Because you're crazy—"Well, look," he said, "I'm just on my way to work"— Very crazy—"I haven't really got time to talk"—And deranged— "But maybe we could"—"Please talk to me now," he pleaded like a fool, "please don't hang up"—So stop—"Why, what's the matter?" he asked—Stop talking—"It's just, I've fallen on hard times, as I said"—Stop now—"I mean I've lost a lot"—Now, Wamblie!—"I'm alone now"—Do you hear?—"My wife has left me and I'm afraid to go to work, afraid I won't be..."—Do you?—"Now, now," he said, "don't go off the deep end. I can only talk a minute, then I have to go. But I wanted to ask if you've considered professional help?"—Say nothing—That made him laugh—Nothing!—But then he started sniveling and whining—Not now—"Yes," he said, "I've been in a mental hospital for over a year"—Not to him—"I just got out Friday" —Do you hear?—"You did?" he said sounding uneasy—Do you? —"Yes," he replied—Wamblie!—"Well, maybe you should talk to them"—He'll give you bad advice—"I really don't have time" —Terrible advice—"But they're all against me!" he blurted out—Since he's one—"Well, I'm sorry, but I have nothing else to suggest and I have to go now"—One of them—"But you don't understand," he told him, "you don't know what they've done to me"—One of those against you—"You don't know the evil that goes on in those places"—Against you!—"Look, buddy," he started in, "I don't know you from a hole in the wall"—Against you!—"Now you call up and lay this thing on me!"—Do you hear?—"What do you expect me to do?"—Do you?—"Cry or something?"—Do you, Wamblie?—"No, I just wanted to talk"—He'll hurt you—"I just wanted someone to listen"—If he can—"But no!"—Can hurt you—"You don't care"—Because he's evil!—"You don't care if I go kill myself!"—Evil!—"That wouldn't bother you a bit"—Evil, Wamblie!—"But think of me when you read it in the papers"—Do you hear?—"Think of how you might have helped, but didn't"—Are you listening?—"Now don't give me that!"—Wamblie!—"I've told you what to do, so do it!"—Wamblie!—"And don't call here again, asshole!"—And with that, he slammed down the phone. But it doesn't matter. He's nobody anyway. Just another face in the mire—A face—He's no different—In the mire—He was stupid to think he'd get anywhere that way—That doesn't care—He was stupid to think anyone would understand—Not about you—He might as well forget it—Wamblie!—Not anymore—But how can he do that?—You should listen—Not since college—He doesn't know a thing anymore—Listen to the voices—Because you're sick—He's a speck in the universe—They're telling you to go—Very sick!—Yet, he still has to decide—Go downstairs—And crazy!—He still has that burden—To the underground train—Very crazy!—Go home and kill himself?—Wamblie!—Or go to work?—And go to the platform—Wamblie!—And deranged—That's the question—Where you should stand—Do you hear?—Very deranged—There's only two choices—Do you?—Waiting for a train—So the time has come—Do you, Wamblie?—He can take the inbound train to work—You're crazy!—To jump in front of—You should end it—And try to make a go of it—Crazy!—Whether it's right—Kill yourself—Or he can take the outbound train home—Do you hear?—Or left—And finish it—And go to the bathroom—Do you?—And fill the tub—Do you?—And slit his wrists—Do you, Wamblie?—You should jump!—Now!—Where Henrietta would find him—Are you listening?—It's coming!—While you can—Wamblie!—Jump!—That would settle everything—Coming!—Do you hear?—Wamblie!—Jump now!—Inbound or outbound?—Wamblie!—Now!—Do you?—Jump, Wamblie, jump—Jump!—Wamblie!—Jump now...

About the Author

Timothy Victor Richardson was born in Edmonton Alberta Canada in 1948 and grew up in the United States. He graduated from Boston University in 1973 where he studied education. In 1975, he received a Master's degree in psychology from that institution. After a decade of working in these fields, he had the background from which his novel, *Ceremony of Innocence*, was derived. The strongly metrical language of this book and his earlier, coming of age short story, "Morning Song" are indications of what became his major focus: poetry. Most of the verse in his intensely visual collection, *Afflicted Love* has been made (or is in the process of being made) into films. *The Force of Poetry* captures a Richardson poetry reading and presentation on the meaning, mechanics and significance of poetry. For many years, Mr. Richardson has been at work on *Mandala*: an epic poem on the inner life of Abraham Lincoln and *The Iniquitous Footstool*: three plays on the destruction of Solomon's temple.

www.authorsden.com/timothyvrichardson
www.authorswriternow.com/09-RichardsonTimothy.htm

also available from *ProseWorks™ Productions*

The Telefax Box (a novel)
Volume, I, The Telefax Trilogy
by Toni Seger
www.CreateSpace.com/3335778

Aurora Rising (a novel)
Volume, II, The Telefax Trilogy
by Toni Seger
www.CreateSpace.com/3364463

Telefax Acclaimed (a novel)
Volume, III, The Telefax Trilogy
by Toni Seger
www.CreateSpace.com/3365423

Ceremony of Innocence (a novel)
by Timothy Victor Richardson
www.CreateSpace.com/3346042

Morning Song (a story)
by Timothy Victor Richardson
illustrated by Patricia Chandler
www.CreateSpace.com/3367084

Morning Song (text) available on Kindle
www.amazon.com/dp/B002NGO38E

Morning Song (a dramatic interpretation on CD)
by Timothy Victor Richardson
interpreted by Jeff Flint
www.CreateSpace.com/1737557

The Force of Poetry (a visual poetry presentation on DVD)
featuring the poetry of Timothy Victor Richardson
produced and directed by Toni Seger
www.CreateSpace.com/260202

Made in the USA
Charleston, SC
27 February 2014